TREADMILL

A NOVEL

TREADMILL

A NOVEL

BY
HIROSHI NAKAMURA

Library and Archives Canada Cataloguing in Publication

Nakamura, Hiroshi, 1915-1973, author
        Treadmill : a novel / Hiroshi Nakamura ; photographs by Ansel Adams.
Previously published: Oakville, Ont.: Mosaic Press, 1996.

Issued in print and electronic formats.
ISBN 978-1-77161-592-1 (paperback).--ISBN 978-1-77161-211-1
(html).--ISBN 978-1-77161-212-8 (pdf)

I. Adams, Ansel, 1902-, photographer
II. Title.
PS3564.A35T742016   813'.54   C2016-904351-7
                                        C2016-904352-5

Published by Mosaic Press, Oakville, Ontario, Canada, 2021. www.mosaic-press.com
MOSAIC PRESS, Publishers

Cover photo and all photos by Ansel Adams Library of Congress, Prints and Photograph Division, reprinted with permission.

We acknowledge Ontario Creates for their support of our publishing Program.
We acknowledge the Ontario Media Development Corporation
for their support of our publishing program.

Funded by the Government of Canada   Financé par le gouvernement du Canada   Canada

MOSAIC PRESS
1252 Speers Road, Units 1 & 2
Oakville, Ontario L6L 5N9
phone: (905) 825-2130
info@mosaic-press.com
www.mosaic-press.com

DEDICATION

Dr. Peter J. Suzuki (1929-2016), retired professor of University Nebraska at Omaha, whose selfless efforts made publication of *Treadmill* possible. His perseverance in finding Hiroshi Nakamura's heirs to obtain agreement to get this novel published and diligence in finding a worthy publisher are unprecedented. The Nakamura and Sato families are so thankful for his bringing *Treadmill* to fruition.

PREFACE

by Hiroshi Nakamura

This is the story of Teru Noguchi, American daughter of Japanese ancestry. This is the record of a people in bewilderment, forsaken by their land of adoption.

We were forced from our homes. We were herded into confinement as a demonstration of loyalty. Yet we were denied the rights of loyal men. Not understanding why nor knowing where, with the whole of our worldly goods clutched tightly in our hands and trying desperately to keep together the ties of blood, we stumbled wearily through shocking heat and stifling dust - without liberty, without home, with uncertain future. We cheered in the darkness on the dregs of disillusionment, of bitterness, of hopelessness; we cheated, we lied, we were honest, we were brave, we stood on the hot burning sands and made our decisions, each according to his conscience. We were different, we were humans. Even as you.

HIROSHI NAKAMURA, 1915-1973

by Mary Sato Nakamura
and Isami Nakamura

By his brother Isami Nakamura

Hiroshi Nakamura was born in Gilroy, California, on March 7, 1915. Interestingly, he was born the third son of a third son of a third son, which, in Japanese lore means great expectations. He was the third child in a family of five brothers and two sisters of parents who had come from the Hiroshima Prefecture, Japan, in 1907. Our Father came in 1907 while our Mother came in 1908. Our parents ran a pool hall in Gilroy just prior to world war II.

Hiroshi was imbued with the three "C"s: courage, conviction, and creativity. Because he was blessed with a near photographic memory, school was easy for him. At age 15, he was graduated from Gilroy High School, where he was the top student with a straight "A" grade-point-average for four years.

Upon graduation, he commuted by train to San Jose State College for a year. He then transferred to the University of California at Berkeley, where he earned his room and board working. Dissatisfied with school, he purchased a bicycle with plans to tour the United States: he wanted to see what the country and the people were like. Heated arguments with his father folllowed because of these plans. A compromise was reached whereby Hiroshi would eventually return to school and get his degree, and his father would no longer stand in the way of his plans.

Because he was a temporary drop-out, Hiroshi did not graduate from UC Berkeley until 1937, with a degree in zoology and a journalism minor. Unable to find work in his field, he went to Los Angeles, where he got a job as a clerk in a Japanese drug store. That was a time when many Nisei college graduates were working in the produce markets.

His first good break came when the English editor of a large Tokyo newspaper offered him a job writing copy translating English to Japanese and Japanese to English. A few months later, he was transferred to the Manchurian branch office where he worked until looming war clouds predicated a sane and prudent return to the States. He was in the photography business until it was cut short by Pearl Harbor.

The Salinas Assembly Center, Salinas, California, was the first of the internment camps where he and his family members were incarcerated. The Poston camp in Arizona then followed. The final camp experience was at Tule Lake, California, where he completed *Treadmill* while working for its Community Analysis Section.

By his wife Mary (Sato) Nakamura

Hiroshi and I were married in Tule Lake on July 29, 1944. I originally was from the Imperial Valley farming community of Brawley, California and had been interned in Poston. Many of the residents in the Imperial Valley were not sent to assembly centers but were sent directly to relocation camps. It was the one good thing that came out of our camp experiences. As his typist for *Treadmill*, I remember using our battered but serviceable old portable nightly to type the manuscript in our camp room ("apartment").

Previous to *Treadmill*, Hiroshi had written several short stories under the pseudonym of Allen Middleton - Middleton being a literal translation of Nakamura. He felt that using a caucasian surname would improve the chances of publisher acceptance. Sadly, none of his stories were published.

After we left camp, we settled in Los Angeles. Our daughter, Dorothy, was born shortly thereafter interestingly enough, on the third day of the third month of 1946. Unable to find employment, we and several of our siblings started a "Pop and Mom" grocery store. Our son Ed was born around this time (1948). Soon after, we opened a slightly larger store.

After the store was sold, Hiroshi decided to try sharecropping for strawberries in Betteravia, California. Three years later, in the early 50s, we moved back to Los Angeles and started another small grocery store. Wanting to try still another type of business, Hiroshi then went into the coin-operated washer/dryer business, placing machines in apartment buildings. In 1972 he contracted stomach cancer and died November 4, 1973, at age 58.

Shortly after the war while in Los Angeles, he sent the *Treadmill* manuscript to several publishers; obviously one copy of the manuscript - whose existence I did not know about - ended up in the National Archives. Unfortunately, he did not get encouraging responses. Several publishers liked *Treadmill* but wrote to him that they could not publish it because they feared publishing it could damage their reputation. They were probably afraid of being considered a pro- Japanese publishing house because of the pervasive anti-Japanese sentiment throughout the nation at that time.

Treadmill, in part, is based on Hiroshi's personal experiences. The novel is also based, to a large extent, on his own observations and what he had heard. As documented in the endnotes provided by the editor, the events described in the novel are historically accurate.

The characters in *Treadmill* are composites of persons he had known, met, or heard about. For example, Teru, the main character, is modeled somewhat on his younger sister. Like Teru in the novel, she was academically the best student in her graduating class but was not recognized by the administrtion of Gilroy High as the class valedictorian because of racial discrimination.

INTRODUCTION TO REVISED SECOND EDITION

by Tara Fickle

Many readers who come across *Treadmill* will already have some knowledge of the historical events which are its focus. They will probably know, for example, that following the Japanese bombing of the Pearl Harbor military base in Hawaii on December 7, 1941, more than 110,000 Japanese civilians living along the West coast (62% of whom were American citizens) were incarcerated in hastily-constfucted, barbed-wire enclosed camps in some of the most barren deserts and harshest climates the United States had to offer. One could know these facts and figures, however, and still have only the barest sense of the human costs of the internment: of the deep and lasting damage inflicted upon the hearts and minds of hundreds of thousands of men, women, children, and old people long after their bodies were released from camp. That humanity is what Hiroshi Nakamura's *Treadmill* restores to those individuals, and to us as readers.

As a historical document, *Treadmill* provides an invaluable insider's account of the internment camps, particularly of the massive bureaucracy that governed internee's daily lives, making even the smallest of tasks – like locating a broom or toilet paper – into a tedious, paperwork-filled nightmare. Yet the book's meticulous depiction of these impersonal institutional mechanisms is softened and enhanced by the equally careful attention it pays to the individual human beings terrorized by them. Exposing the reader to a diverse choir of voices and cast of characters, each with their own unique hopes, fears, and circumstances, *Treadmill* fights back against the stereotypes that were responsible for the internment in the first place: the deeply-held assumption that, in the infamous words of General John DeWitt, the man behind the evacuation plan, "a Jap's a Jap" regardless of age, birthplace, or even citizenship.

Hiroshi Nakamura was born in Gilroy, California in 1915 to immigrant parents from Hiroshima, Japan. A college graduate with a minor in journalism, he was working as a translator for a large Tokyo newspaper when World War II broke out. Upon returning to California, he and his parents and siblings were incarcerated first at Salinas Assembly Center before being moved to internment camps in Poston, Arizona, and eventually Tule Lake, California. After the war, Hiroshi and his wife Mary moved to Los Angeles; he sent the manuscript of *Treadmill* to several publishers, but despite their recognition of its merits, the rampantly anti-Japanese postwar environment led them to decline. After pursuing several different career paths, including running a grocery store, sharecropping, and installing coin-operated washers and dryers, Hiroshi Nakamura passed away of stomach cancer in 1973 at the age of 58.

Although it was never published during Nakamura's lifetime, a copy of the *Treadmill* manuscript found its way to the National Archives in Washington, D.C., where it was discovered in 1974 by anthropologist Peter Suzuki shortly before he became a professor at the University of Nebraska in Omaha. The book, which Suzuki transcribed himself using a microfilm copy of the original (itself typed by Hiroshi's wife Mary), was first published by Mosaic Press in 1996.

As Suzuki rightly notes in his introduction to the inaugural 1996 printing, *Treadmill* is a unique book, being the only known novel to be written during the internment itself. The immediacy of the experience partially accounts for the vivid, detailed descriptions of camp life, which according to Nakamura's widow Mary are based on a combination of first-hand experience and careful observation. Although the book is not a memoir – narrated instead through the perspective of Teru Noguchi, a young *Nisei* (second-generation Japanese American) woman – neither are the characters entirely fictional creations. According to Mary Nakamura, many of them, particularly the members of the Noguchi family, are "composites of persons [Hiroshi] had known, met, or heard about"; it is a testament to what Suzuki calls Nakamura's "keen ethnographic eye" that the author was able to transform even third-hand knowledge into such compelling, lively portraits. We meet the Noguchi family on the eve of internment; the book traces their difficult journey along the same route Nakamura himself took, beginning in Salinas, California and ending, just after the war, in Tule Lake, where Teru, her parents, and younger brother await repatriation to Japan.

The significance of *Treadmill* lies not only in its historical but its literary value, which is evident even from its name. Many readers may find themselves a bit puzzled by the title: what after all, could a fitness machine have in common with one of the greatest civil rights violations in recent American history? To be clear, the treadmill Nakamura is referring to is not exactly the conveyor-belt style exercise device most of us are familiar with, but to a machine invented first to harness the power of humans and animals for agricultural and construction work, and later implemented as a form of prison discipline. Often used interchangeably with the term "treadwheel," the earliest treadmills, which were already in extensive use by the time of the Greeks and Romans, were similar in appearance to water wheels, used mainly for raising water, grinding grain, and powering early earth-moving and lifting machines. In the early 1800s, they were introduced into British prisons by Sir William Cubitt, an English engineer and son of a miller. Inmates were forced to climb the "Everlasting Staircase" for upwards of six hours a day, sometimes as a form of penal labor but also simply as punishment.

Nakamura's choice of title is thus an inspired and grimly appropriate symbol for the exploitative mechanisms of the internment camps, in which inmates were forced to labor endlessly and for the most meager of wages in order to power the very war machine responsible for their incarceration: to, for example, plant and harvest food or weave camouflage nets not meant for their consumption or protection, but the army's. At the same time, the image of the treadmill captures the more subtle psychological anguish of daily life in the internment camps, which the book as a whole takes pains to shed light on. Not only do scorching heat, inadequate shelter, medical care, and rations leave the inmates physically exhausted; in some cases, as with Ayame Noguchi, Teru's mother, the endless struggle simply to survive begins to take its toll on their mental state as well. Faced with the loss of her home, the imprisonment of her family, and the FBI's seizure of her husband, Ayame's mind begins to falter, her slipping grasp of reality linked to the broader incomprehensibility of the U.S. Government's decision to imprison its own citizens. Failing to see the purpose of performing basic chores like cleaning, bathing, or even eating because, as she points out, they will only need to be done again and again, Ayame becomes a tragic testament to the internment's crushing psychological effect, which at its most extreme leads to a grim perspective on life itself as a futile exercise.

The subtitle of the book – "A Documentary Novel" – further attests to Nakamura's aesthetic vision. Like its titular image, the notion of a "documentary novel" might initially seem a strange, if not flatly contradictory, formulation. After all, we tend to think of the two genres as natural opposites: the documentary as a non-biased, informative account of "true" events, the novel as a carefully crafted narrative of fictional ones. Nakamura, however, ambitiously seeks to marry the two. Although much of the book is narrated from Teru's point of view, it frequently switches between various characters and "camera angles," deftly balancing allegiance to an "objective" historical perspective which showed the internment "as it really was" with a literary impulse to turn that body of facts into a coherent and meaningful story.

This novel combination of genres is one innovative strategy Nakamura uses to emphasize that the Japanese American population was not an undifferentiated, homogeneous group but possessed countless internal distinctions and divisions which had a profound impact on internees' daily lives, emotions, and actions. Some of Nakamura's most ambitious literary experiments result from this effort to capture and reconcile individual and collective perspectives. At times, he employs the first-person plural point of view ("we"), a perspective rarely used in either novels or historical non-fiction, in order to communicate common experiences or shared perspectives among internees. At other times, he deftly takes on the perspective of a documentary videographer, switching rapidly between multiple first-person singular ("I") perspectives and omitting the usual formal conventions – like quotation marks or the prefatory "so-and-so said" – to heighten the effect. In the following passages, which take place during the relocation to the camps and a later camp protest, respectively, he powerfully experiments with the potential of a pronoun like "they" to both unite and divide:

> The thermometer at the depot read 122° F. They made them get into the stuffy buses. They made them wait there with the sun burning down on them . . . They waited an hour like that. Hot, tried, and uncomfortable, for something, they didn't know what. The baby started to cry. They avoided looking at him.

> The authorities intend to take them out of camp. They'll never get a fair trial outside. We're supposed to prevent them from taking them outside.

In the first passage, "they" initially refers to the soldiers overseeing the relocation operation, and "them" to the internees. Within a few sentences, however, the line between "they" and "them" begin to blur: at times, "they" refers to the waiting internees; at others, to the soldiers who refuse to look at the wailing infant. In the second passage, a similar merging and blurring takes place, such that it becomes difficult to distinguish between those who are imprisoned and those doing the imprisoning because they are both referred to as "them." Such scenes and experiments reflect Nakamura's novel efforts to capture on the page the cacophony of voices and constant uncertainty and fluctuation that defined the internment experience.

Numerous historical as well as fictional accounts have attested to how the internment camp experience fractured the Japanese American population along generational lines. The older *Issei* (first-generation Japanese immigrants) had long relied on their American-born *Nisei* (second-generation) children to help them navigate American society, whether as informal translators or as legal proxies. *(Issei*, being ineligible for American citizenship because of their race, were unable to own land or enjoy other legal rights, whereas *Nisei*, being born on American soil, were automatically citizens according to the fourteenth amendment). After Pearl Harbor, however, the *Issei*'s closer ties to Japan made them targets of especial government suspicion and, once interned, they found themselves displaced by their *Nisei* children at many levels. Most *Issei* possessed limited English proficiency, having had little free time to study the language, which made it nearly impossible for them to lodge complaints or take any legal or political action against their incarceration. *Treadmill* documents the destructive effects of this "complete reversal in the family order" with poignancy and detail. Rather than simply informing us of the inverted state of affairs, Nakamura demonstrates his literary skill, painting a series of powerful, concise vignettes like this one:

> They [the *Issei*] carried home their eight dollar checks for their "unskilled" labor in mess halls and as janitors and night watchmen. Their sons and daughters grandly exhibited their twelve dollar checks for "skilled" labor.

The generational fracture between *Issei* and *Nisei* often – though not always – corresponded to a division in political beliefs between "pro-Japanese" and "pro-American" factions. Other internment novels – most famously John Okada's *No-No Boy* – tend to emphasize the dualistic nature of this conflict by presenting Japanese American identity as the experience of being pulled in two opposite directions or belonging to two mutually exclusive cultures. The internment brought this dilemma to the fore in painfully clear terms. The Leave Clearance Form, more commonly known as the "loyalty questionnaire," was a document the Army subsequently distributed to all internees over the age of 18; two questions in particular became the source of intense controversy and debate:

27. Are you willing to serve in the armed forces of the United-States on combat duty wherever ordered?

28. Will you swear unqualified allegiance to the United States of America and faithfully defend the United States from any or all attack by foreign or domestic forces, and forswear any form of allegiance or obedience to the Japanese emperor, or any other foreign government, power, or organization?

One's answers determined whether one was labeled "loyal" or "disloyal": and, if one was a male eligible for military service, sent to the front in a segregated combat unit to fight for the very country that imprisoned you, or to jail as a draft dodger for refusing to do so. Like *No-No Boy*, *Treadmill* forcefully reminds readers that this choice between a "life-giving yes" and an "empty no" was not only impossible but profoundly unjust on the part of the government. *Treadmill*, however, seeks to reveal not only the devastating psychological effects of choosing either yes or no, but the complex factors driving the decision-making process in the first place. It offers a particularly rich examination of this issue by using gender, and more specifically the difference between interned men and women, as a vehicle to explore questions of national loyalty and assimilation.

Because women were ineligible to be drafted into the U.S. Army, female internees' decisions to answer "yes" or "no" on the loyalty questionnaire have often been historically eclipsed by men's, or seen in comparison as a largely symbolic political action. "Women don't count so they may as well answer yes-yes," one young man remarks in *Treadmill*, while another suggests that women should simply answer "the same way as their men folk" so as not to be separated. When, after Teru answers yes-yes, her employer gives her an opportunity to leave camp for a secretarial job in Cleveland, she consults her father for permission. Calling together the family, Mr. Noguchi (who has decided to leave America and be repatriated to Japan) informs his three children that, while he and his wife have decided to take their teenage son Tadao back to Japan, Teru and her sister may make their own decisions: not simply because they are of a legal age to do so, but because they are female:

> I regard relocation and marriage in the same light. Your mother and I have known, as all parents now, that we must steel ourselves against an eventual way of parting while at the same time we daily tighten the bonds. It is difficult. In a Japanese family it is considered a disgrace for a married daughter to return home. Her decision is an important one.

Thus, like the main character in *No-No Boy* whose "empty no" constitutes a "total, hateful rejection of self and family and society," Teru's decision to answer "yes" ironically constitutes an analogous abandonment of her parents and her symbolic "motherland" (Japan), but one which, because she is female, is viewed as natural and indeed inevitable.

In having Mr. Noguchi liken a female "yes" on the loyalty questionnaire to an acceptance of a marriage proposal, Nakamura brilliantly brings full circle the metaphorical connections between love and loyalty which are developed throughout the novel. This extended metaphor is introduced first through the developing romantic relationship between Teru and another *Nisei*, George Motoyama, George, whose "white teeth, squarish jaw, [and] clean cut" appearance, like his English first name, clearly make him the "all-American" choice for Teru. When George proposes to Teru just before internment, her indecisiveness rehearses her equally ambivalent feelings towards the nation he represents and anticipates the loyalty oath which it will soon demand. For "Teru had expected [the proposal] but not so abruptly," and she can say no more than "I don't know" in response to George's pleading "Why not? Don't you love me?" Nakamura further nuances this gendered dilemma of marriage and national loyalty by including the perspective of *Issei* women in camp, many of whom were "picture brides" who often first encountered their new husbands and their new country in the same moment. As Teru muses, becoming "American," for her mother and the many women like her, was synonymous with becoming a wife: immigration itself involves the woman's metaphorical consummation with a foreign nation who, like their new husbands, "they'd known of [] only through hearsay," still "strangers when they'd gotten on the train that carried them to . . . a nuptial bed."

For all its literary achievements, however, *Treadmill* remains true to its documentary aspirations. It is resolutely honest. It refuses to downplay or justify the trauma and suffering inflicted upon internees, offering a rare glimpse into the very real fears of internees that the mass evacuation was simply a pretense for something far more sinister: a U.S. counterpart to the European concentration camps which Americans had already begun to receive disturbing reports of – yet which even Teru herself had, before her own internment, simply dismissed as "British propaganda." Nor does Nakamura shy away from exposing the horrific conditions internees were subjected to: in the harrowing scene mentioned earlier, for example, he describes in terrifying detail a day-long dust storm in which numerous internees lose consciousness and an infant nearly dies after armed soldiers force the group to remain trapped in a stalled bus in 120°F temperatures, heedless of their repeated pleas for water and medical care.

To restore humanity and individuality to the internees, however, means showing both the strength as well as frailty that made them human. Indeed, the brutal honesty of scenes like the one above is matched only by Nakamura's equally unflinching commitment to portraying a measured look at the best and worst of the community. Thus, for every open-minded, empathetic character like Teru Noguchi, we are introduced to the repellant egotism of a young woman like Rose Noda, a *Nisei* who takes pains to vocally distance herself from other Japanese, whom she derides as "ill-mannered, nasty, busybodies," declaring that "it curls my hair to be linked with those barbarians." For every honorable gentleman like George Motoyama, there is a Pete Kurusaki, a surly young man who sexually assaults Teru's friend Alice, ultimately leading to her death. Such diverse character portraits emphasize the wide range of characters, good and bad, found in any human community, and hence underscores Nakamura's larger point that there was no such thing as a single, universal portrait of "Japaneseness" that justified the imprisonment of every individual of Japanese ancestry simply because of their race.

Yet even these "negative" portrayals often prove to be less a showcase of individual character flaws and more a testament to the damaging effects of the internment itself, particularly the racial prejudice and xenophobia that helped usher it in. Nakamura places Rose's cruel comments within a larger dialogue among several other *Nisei* about the differences between *Issei*, *Nisei*, and *Kibei* (Japanese born in America but educated in Japan). Ultimately, Rose's outspoken distaste for other Japanese, and her refusal to consider herself one of them, is revealed be the product of displaced self-loathing: a demonstration of the powerful damage wrought by American anti-Japanese sentiment and stereotypes which have been unconsciously internalized even by Japanese Americans themselves. Similarly, the series of violent episodes that later erupt in the novel following the loyalty questionnaire are shown to be the clear result of the impossible choice imposed upon the internees, particularly the *Nisei*, who were forced either to defend a country that imprisoned them (America) or declare their allegiance to one which they had never even seen (Japan).

Treadmill is a remarkable book which deserves far greater attention than it has so far received. Its candid, accessible prose, combined with its historical significance, makes it an especially valuable addition to the high school and college classroom. I have compiled a list of teaching resources and suggestions for further reading (see below) which I hope will assist educators in this endeavor.

Tara Fickle is an Assistant Professor of English at the University of Oregon. More information about Professor Fickle can be found on her website: http://www.ficklet.wordpress.com/.

Teaching Resources & Suggestions for Further Reading

Primary Documents & Archival Sources

Krug, J. A., and D. S. Myer. "WRA: A Story of Human Conservation." United States Department of the Interior. Washington: U.S.G.P.O, 1946.

DeWitt, John L. "Japanese Evacuation from the West Coast, 1942: Final Report." United States War Department. Washington: U.S.G.P.O, 1943.

DENSHO: A rich online repository of original internment documents, oral history interviews, videos, and teaching resources: http://www. densho.org/

Ansel Adams, one of the most well-known American photographers, documented the Manzanar internment camp through a series of photographs; a selection is available for public viewing at the Library of Congress website: http://www.loc.gov/pictures/collection/manz/

The Japanese American National Museum maintains a website containing detailed maps and information on each of the ten camps: http://www.janm.org/projects/clasc/map.htm

The National Park Service (U.S. Department of the Interior) has begun to undertake preservation and education efforts in collaboration with American educators and institutions: https://www.nps.gov/manz/index.htm

Secondary Sources (Literature, History, and Criticism)

Daniels, Roger, ed. *American Concentration Camps*. 9 vols. New York: Garland, 1989.

Houston, Jeanne W, and James D. Houston. Farewell to Manzanar: A *True Story of Japanese American Experience During and After the World War II Internment*. Boston: Houghton Mifflin, 1973. Print.

Okada, John. *No-No Boy.* Seattle: University of Washington Press, 1957, 1981.

Okubo, Miné. *Citizen 13660.* Seattle: University of Washington Press, 1983. Print, Graphic Novel.

Sone, Monica I. *Nisei Daughter.* Seattle: University of Washington Press, 1953, 1979. Print.

Suzuki, Peter. "Treadmill: The premier novel of the wartime camps for Japanese Americans." *Asian Profile* 20.2 (April 1992): 175–180.

Yamamoto, Hisaye. *Seventeen Syllables and Other Stories.* Latham, NY: Kitchen Table, Women of Color Press, 1988. Print.

INTRODUCTION

by Peter Suzuki

readmill is a unique novel. Foremost is the fact that it is the only one which was written about life in the World War II camps for Japanese and Japanese Americans while that singular way of life was being played out. Hiroshi Nakamura, along with his family, spent the war years in Salinas Assembly Center, Salinas, California; Camp II of the Poston Relocation Center, Parker, Arizona; and Tule Lake Segregation Center, Newell, California. It was during this period that he put down on paper what he was observing, experiencing, and hearing, and expressed them in a novel.

Irrespective of the numerous publications presently available on the camps, no other author can claim to have written this form of literature during the camp days. For this reason, *Treadmill* is unique. Considering the fact that there were thousands of others like him in the camps, the irrefutable reality is that only Nakamura had the drive, patience, perseverence, tenacity, and insight to fashion and craft a novel of what life was like in these camps while living out the days in them.

Another noteworthy aspect about this novel is its unblinking look at various aspects of camp life: the good, the bad, and the ugly. It accurately evokes - one might say, to a chilling degree - the fears, anxieties, suspicions, cynicisms, and passions brought out by camp life. Nor are the small joys and pleasant surprises neglected. Therefore, in reading *Treadmill*, one must constantly heed the words in the Prefaceto apprehend fully the reality of the issues and policies in the camps and of the human reactions to them.

> *...We cheated, we lied, we were honest, we were brave, we stood*
> *on the hot burning sands and made our decisions, each according*
> *to his conscience.*

Nakamura captures exquisitely the thinking and mood of the people and the prevailing zeitgeist. An acute ethnographic eye and a keen sense of history with a concomitant respect for historical accuracy (e.g., the "manhandling" in Poston by anti-Japanese American Citizens League forces of "the parents of Masato Shibuya," an incident described in Chapter 11 which I have documented in Note 10) help scaffold this well-told tale.

Nakamura's novel displays considerable courage because most Niseis (second-generation Japanese), especially of that era, were constrained by their own cultural values to mute or temper their deepseated feelings about life in the camps. Indeed, there was an overriding tendency among the vast majority of Niseis to dearly want to be accepted by the larger society and to longingly want to be assimilated as quickly and as unobtrusively as possible, to forget the past, and to get on with the urgent matter of catching up on the lost years. Quite logically, then, it was decades later - when they felt more secure about their position in American society, thanks in large part to the heroic achievements of the all-Nisei 442nd Regimental Combat Team - that those who had been in the camps were able to express even privately, no less publicly, their true feelings about their camp experience.

Treadmill, then, is an honest book. Those who were in the camps must, therefore, be beholden to Hiroshi Nakamura.

The novel centers around the Noguchis of Salinas, California, and their life in the same camps where the author was interned. The events are seen through the eyes of Teru, the Nisei daughter of *Issei* (first-generation) truck farmers.

This work opens in April 1942, when removal to the camps is imminent. On February 19, Roosevelt had signed Executive Order 9066 which ordered the evacuation. FBI agents are at the Noguchis' home to arrest the father, while Mrs. Noguchi, Teru - age 19 or 20 - and "Tad" (Tadao), 14, stand by helplessly. Due to unusual circumstances, Sally, 16, arrives after Mr. Noguchi has been taken away. He ends up in one of the camps for Japanese considered security risks; in his case, it is in America's own Siberia - Bismarck, North Dakota.

The fatherless Noguchis are then moved to the Salinas Assembly Center on the Salinas Rodeo Grounds where a temporary camp has been hastily built for the 3,700 to be interned there through July 4, 1942. They are then transferred to one of the ten more permanent camps ("relocation centers"), Poston in Arizona. There Mr. Noguchi is allowed to join his family.

Mrs. Noguchi, meanwhile, has gone mad. Embittered by the experience, Mr. Noguchi decides to repatriate to Japan after the war. As a dutiful daughter, Teru follows her parents to the segregation camp, Tule Lake, where those opting to go to Japan were located. Tad's youthful age in 1943, when this happens, leaves him little choice but to go with the rest of the family. However, although she is the most embittered of the Noguchis, Sally, 18, decides to move out of Poston ("relocate") to Detroit, to marry her fiancee who will be moving there from another camp in Arizona, Gila.

Treadmill concludes shortly after Japan has surrendered and the *Issei* Noguchis with Teru and Tad are on their way from Tule Lake to Japan. A series of letters from Teru in Tule Lake to Sally in Detroit, which comprise the last of the twenty-two chapters, are highly evocative: anxiety, fear, hope, uncertainty, and optimism intermingle. These feelings and emotions cohere around her concern over such issues as the future of race relations and justice in America.

Despite its obvious somber tone, there are flashes of humor in *Treadmill*.

Nakamura, however, does insistently call the reader's attention to the way certain Niseis arrogated upon themselves leadership roles and the consequences of such actions. In the very first chapter one comes across these words. "She [Teru] wondered who had caused her father's arrest and her thoughts returned bitterly to one thing. Japanese American Citizens League."[1]

The absolute injustice of the evacuation and incarceration is another thread which runs through this novel. So, too, the absurdity of life in the camps and of the camp policies. Another underlying theme is that, despite the seemingly clear-cut nature of many War Relocation Authority (the federal agency that ran the camps) policies, there were always two sides to each of them; that they required great thought and deliberation on the part of the people in deciding which ones to follow, and when, ultimately, choices were made, "each according to his conscience," there were no satisfying solutions as the choices themselves generated unanticipated situations and problems. As a consequence, the incarcerated were forever facing dilemmas.

Participation in relocation-camp councils (from which Isseis were excluded), the loyalty oath (euphemistically termed "Registration"), relocation/indefinite leave (permanent departure from the camps to areas of the United States other than Military Zone 1 (the westernmost strip along the West Coast, part of Arizona, and Alaska)), answering the draft (initially, Niseis had been excluded from the draft because of supposed securi-

---

1 See Deborah Lim's 1990 report on JACL's role during WWII. San Francisco: JACL. Typescript.

ty problems), and volunteering for the all-Nisei regimental combat team were some of the more striking examples of the policies alluded to.

Notwithstanding the gravity of the prospect which the Noguchis face in a war-devastated Japan, Teru voices with poignancy words of hope in her last letter to Sally.

I am certain that the tale of the Noguchi family transcends what happened to a particular Japanese-American family to the extent that it touches on all those who were interned and beyond that, on a contemporary society that is troubled by the injustice which took place in the name of fear and protective custody. Nevertheless, it should be pointed out that a spirit of indomitability pervades the work, and for this, too, the reader must be indebted to Hiroshi Nakmura.[2]

Perhaps the most unusual aspect about this novel is that it has been sitting on the shelf of the National Archives in Record Group 210 for fifty years.

I first came across it when I was visiting the Archives in 1974. My first experience with Record Group 210 had been in the spring of 1952 while doing research as a graduate student. I glanced through the contents and, even then, was impressed by it. Subsequently, I have returned to the Archives numerous times, starting in 1975, to undertake research in Record Group 210 (my most recent work there was for a week, in the summer of 1991). In the 1970s I had a microfilm copy of *Treadmill* made and began typing it in 1985 with an IBM Selectric Typewriter, using the print copy made from the microfilm. Because of the difficulty in reading the print copy, the typing was done only sporadically. The task was finally completed around December 1992, and was greatly facilitated by the use of a PC. In view of the author's forthrightness in *Treadmill*, I mistakenly assumed that "Hiroshi Nakamura" was a nom de plume.

After several unsuccessful attempts in the 1980s to find Hiroshi Nakamura, a paid ad in Pacific Citizen, the official weekly newspaper of the Japanese American Citizens League, which appeared in a January 1993 issue, resulted in a note of February 14, 1993, from his niece, Aletha Watanabe. The note informed me of the sad news that Hiroshi had died, but it did help me get in touch with his widow, Mary Sato Nakamura.

Since then, she, I, Dorothy Watanabe (the Nakamuras' daughter), and

---

2 For more detailed analyses of *Treadmill,* see my articles: "*Treadmill:* The premier novel of the wartime camps for Japanese Americans," *Asian Profile,* 1992, vol. 20 (No. 2, April), pp. 175-180; and "Desertification in Hiroshi Nakamura's *Treadmill,*" Asian Profile, 1993, vol. 21 (No. 6, December), pp. 467-474. (I did not receive galleyproof copies so both articles contain many typos.)

Aletha, have been corresponding about Hiroshi and *Treadmill*.

I have made only minimal changes in typing *Treadmill*. I have substituted "Pop" and "Mom" for "Father" and "Mother"; likewise, I have substituted "Mrs. Noguchi" for the mother's name, Ayame. These substitutions were made at the request of Hiroshi Nakamura's relatives because of their opinion that such changes were more in line with how people spoke.

I am very fortunate in having "discovered" *Treadmill* because it is a real treasure. Correspondingly, it is a distinct honor and privilege
to have my name forever linked with the author and *Treadmill*.

ACKNOWLEDGMENTS

The following members of the Nakamura and Sato families were involved and participated in enabling the publication of and corrections to the manuscript for Treadmill: Aletha Watanabe, Dorothy Watanabe, Susan Lew and Joel Hayashida.

CHAPTER 1

Teru Noguchi noticed the shiny black Ford as soon as she stepped of the junior college bus. She idly wondered whose car it was before she turned to wave a final goodbye to the tousled heads gayly poking through the bus windows. Janet, she would miss especially.

"Don't forget to write," they called, "see you after the war."

"Teroo," Janet called frantically from the retreating bus, "Bye."

Teru let her arm drop wearily when she could no longer make out Janet's face. Strange. Neither her father nor mother was working in the neat rows of vegetables which grew on both sides of the driveway. Must be important, she thought, for both of them to leave the last-minute work which had to be done. She could see they still hadn't bunched enough carrots to bring to the markets in the morning and they had intended to finish hoeing the parsnips, though she had first rebelled at the thought that all that work was going for nothing. Her father and mother, though, had insisted that it was their duty to take care of the vegetables up to the last possible moment. Her wide-spaced eyes were momentarily narrowed in puzzlement but even then it was easy to notice the generous separation of eyebrow from eye which imparted that incredibly soft Oriental look to her inevitably brown eyes. Harder to see was the slight cleft in her chin which was inherited from her father. The photogenic hollows and the olive-smooth freshness of her complexion were from her mother.

The afternoon sun picked out coppery tinges in the dark black hair which curled softly away from her face and ended in glossy curls at the back of her head. Her stride was free and her head was carried with a buoyant lift. Her legs were long for Japanese and she stood a slender five foot three in her stocking feet. It was five months after Pearl Harbor and the army proc-

lamation banning all persons of Japanese ancestry from the coastal areas of California and urging all
Japanese to pull up stakes and relocate in the mountain states and the middle west. That very morning General DeWitt had announced that this voluntary evacuation would end Saturday midnight. It was a period of blackouts, rumors, and uncertainty, especially for persons of Japanese ancestry like Teru. Teru was wondering if the presence of the strange car had anything to do with the sudden family decision that morning to evacuate to Fresno before the Saturday deadline, as she stepped lightly up the porch steps of the red-roofed cottage and pulled the door open.

"Who's a call--", she began cheerily but her voice faltered and was smothered in the strained stillness of the room. The distraught face of her mother looked up from the open suitcase into which she was putting some heavy underwear. Teru remembered washing and packing them away for the summer. The room itself wasn't quite the same. It looked intruded on, somehow. It wasn't exactly in disorder but everything looked like it needed straightening.

"But why?," Teru repeated weakly.

"We have our orders and carry them out," the man said.

"I'm sorry but we haven't much time. Your father tells me your sister is planning to be at a party and that your brother is still at school for a track meet. I would suggest you get in touch with them. We won't stay much longer."

"You mean we won't see our father anymore?"

The man shook his head slowly and glanced quickly at his partner.

"I don't know," he said.

Sally would be at the Motoyamas' until the going-away party that night at seven. It was a little after four o'clock now. The Motoyamas lived on the other side of town and had no phone.

"I'll go get them," Teru said to her father and mother and automatically picked up her purse.

"Just a minute," the shorter man suddenly said, "Let's see that."

Teru looked at him surprised but there was no mistaking what he meant. She hesitated, then silently handed him her purse. He immediately opened it and put a hairy hand inside. Teru watched him, feeling much like a criminal on trial for her life. The man looked up.

"You can go," he said flatly.

Teru walked fast down the steps to the battered pickup they used for hauling vegetables to town. Her father started to follow her outside but the

FBI men shook their heads warningly.

He called to her from the porch, "There are some things I want to talk to you about so hurry back as soon as possible."

"Please wait until I come back," Teru asked the FBI men.

"Better hurry. We can't wait long," they said.

Teru didn't realize she was driving so fast until she nearly overran the car ahead of her. She jammed on her brakes and waited impatiently for an opening so she could pass. She wondered who had caused her father's arrest and her thoughts returned bitterly to one thing. Japanese American Citizens League [JACL]. They must be responsible. Only yesterday, kids who commuted to Salinas Junior College from Monterey had been saying that the Citizens League leaders had been responsible for the arrest of the Monterey Japanese. She hadn't paid much attention because no one volunteered any kind of proof except Yoneo.

Yoneo had sworn that nobody had known of his having kept his rifle and left it with a friend instead of turning it into the police station except for a certain person very active in JACL. Only that person could have reported it and gotten Yoneo into trouble when they questioned and later interned his father....

Mrs. Motoyama came to the door.

"Hello Teru-san," she said cheerfully. "Have you gotten a little ready to go?"

Teru's mind was unprepared to deal with anything else.

"Is Sally here?," she asked abruptly. Mrs. Motoyama sensed something amiss.

"Is something wrong? She just left in the car with Yukiko.They didn't say where they were going."

"They've come to take Father," Teru said.

"They?"

"FBI. They're going to intern him. They're leaving right away, so I came after Sally." The words rushed out jerkily.

"This is terrible," Mrs. Motoyama said. "I don't know where they went. Papa went into town to the WCCA [Wartime Civilian Control Administration] to get the permits to move to Fresno but George is out on the tractor. I'll call him."

They hurried outside. The tractor was coming slowly towards them in front of a cloud of dust, and Teru recognized George in the shapeless felt hat he usually wore when working. Mrs. Motoyama beckoned wildly and George had apparently been looking their way because he immediately unhitched the tractor and came towards them with wide open throttle. He braked the tractor to a stop with a whirling turn and hopped off with eyes only for Teru.

"Hi," he grinned widely, showing even white teeth. "What's doing?"

He was big and looked even bigger in the baggy, dust-covered overalls. His face was caked with dirt and grime but you could still see the clean-boned good looks of him. Teru felt relieved just looking. There was something solid and comforting about him.

"You look like you just decided you'd have to settle for me. Why so sad looking?"

They explained quickly and his boyish grin disappeared.

"Those crazy kids would be out joy riding at a time like this," he said. "I'll take the truck and look around a little. Maybe I'll run into them."

He looked at Teru, "Unless there's something else I can do to help."

Teru shook her head. "Mother is packing. I'd better go back though," she said. "They may leave."

George stepped into the driver's seat of the pickup.

"I'll get off at the WCCA office. Dad has the truck. He should be there yet." He was full of questions on the short ride into town but Teru could only tell him the little she knew.

"I don't know," Teru said. She stared unseeingly at the road ahead. She slumped in her seat. It had been hectic enough without the arrest of her father. This morning they had had a long conference after learning of the unexpected freeze deadline and had decided on moving temporarily to Fresno in Zone #2. George had attached considerable importance to the "probable" in the proclamation which had declared "will probably not be asked to move again." Their families had been doing their planning together in their originally contemplated move to Colorado and had continued to do so in their new decision to move to Fresno to escape the freeze order. Their fathers were from the same obscure ken [prefecture] in Japan and had been quite close friends ever since hearing of each other over twenty-five years ago. Coming from the same part of the home country meant a great deal to the older folks. Even marriages were facilitated or made difficult depending on which ken people came from.

Mr. Motoyama was one of the better-known lettuce growers in Salinas and farmed a large acreage of lettuce and sugar beets while Teru's father was a small-scale truck farmer growing vegetables for the local market. They had nothing definite in mind and it seemed almost foolhardy to pull up stakes and move without more thorough planning, but the freeze order had come as a surprise and they hadn't much alternative. The short three-day notice hadn't given them much time either, especially when Mr. Noguchi decided they would have to meet prior obligations like delivering vegetables to the market up to Friday morning. Teru, Sally, and Tad had made arrangements to quit junior college and high school that very day while Tad was even now at the track meet.

Teru turned and caught George's steady brown eyes on her. He was good looking. Even white teeth, squarish jaw, clean cut. Looking at him now just off a tractor, it was hard to believe that he had gotten his B.S. degree in aeronautical engineering from the University of California just last year. His smooth, unlined face showed no tace of the bitter disappointment of seeing his Hakujin classmates gradually step into the respectable engineering jobs of some sort while he himself had been finally forced to return to the farm helping his father. He'd once shown her a letter from a well-known aeronautical firm that had bluntly stated, "You meet all our qualifications but our company policy does not allow the hiring of persons of Oriental ancestry." After Pearl Harbor, George had simply given up all hope of landing a job.

"Dope," Teru had often thought. He seemed almost happy, sometimes working from dawn to dusk and then dropping in to see her at night. We never mentioned engineering anymore.

"Dope," she said suddenly, "are you driving this car or am I?" George grinned. He took a quick glance up the road and took an arm off the wheel to draw her closer. Teru shook her head. She was still undecided how she wanted her relationship with George. She liked him a lot and she liked his company. Once when she had heard her parents mention George and hint of marriage, she had tried to picture what being married to George would be like but it had all remained a little vague. The GMC truck was still parked in front of the WCCA office. George got off.

"See you before your father leaves," he said and disappeared inside the office. Teru headed the pickup on Central Avenue towards the high school. She hoped that the meet had started early and that Tad would be through with his events. She picked him out immediately near the broad-jump pit watching the officials measure. Apparently he had just made a jump. She called to the nearest track official and pretty soon Tad was standing in front of her. He took after their mother, small boned and slender like herself. He was grinning widely.

"Hi, Sis, I just made 19 feet 6 inches on my second jump," he said, expanding visibly, "first place so far. What's up?" Teru looked at him and hadn't the heart to tell him right there.

"You better come home with me," she said. But Tad had other things on his mind.

"Are you wacky?," he exploded. "What for? Johnson is only a couple inches behind and I still have the hundred to run."

"The FBI are at our home," Teru said reluctantly.

"Holy smoke," then seriously, "After Pop?" Teru nodded her head. Tad was already running for the locker room. "Got to get my clothes," which he flung over his shoulders.... Teru sighed with relief when she saw the black Ford still in front of the house. Mrs. Noguchi looked up when they opened the door.

"Sally *wa?*," she asked. Her eyes were wet and worried. She tried to take hold of herself -- unsuccessfully. Teru wanted to take her slight figure into her arms to give her strength.

"George is looking for her," she said. Only one man was with them in the front room. She could hear the other two poking around in the bed-rooms. One searched right after the other leaving nothing unexamined. Tad looked the man up and down, then found his voice all at once.

"My pop hasn't done anything," he said. His voice was extra loud. The man looked at him curiously.

"Be quiet, Tadao," Mr. Noguchi said sternly. He asked the man if it was all right and then drew Teru aside. He didn't seem to know where to begin.

"I'm sorry I'm causing all this trouble," he began apologetically.

"That's not so," Teru said quickly.

"I may be gone a long time," he continued quietly. "They will say noth-ing definite. It will leave you in charge of the family. I might wish Tadao were older at a time like this but with you I am not worried because I know you have a level head on your shoulders and I have always trusted your judgment. It is a big responsibility but your mother is not very strong and Sally and Tadao are too young."

"Don't worry about us," Teru said. His face was blurring.

"We'll manage. Now what should we do about our plans with Mr. Mo-toyama?"

"I was coming to that," her father said. "We will have to give them up. With only three women and a 14-year old boy, it would be too much to risk to relocate. The only thing to do is to wait here and go into a government camp and wait for a better opportunity. Tell Mr. Motoyama that I am sorry our plans miscarried."

"George will be over with his father pretty soon," Teru said.

"Good, then I can tell him personally." He seemd to want to say something more. He studied her face intently and Teru waited, wondering what else. "George is a nice boy," he said at last. "I always thought that someday --- ," he seemed to have difficulty finding the right words. It had always been like that. There was always the language barrier. Either Japanese or English was adequate for the ordinary things which came up, but when it came to more complicated or delicate matters, Teru could only wish her Japanese were more adequate so she could understand his every word.

"George is nice," she said now before her father could phrase his thoughts. "I suppose we won't see him for a long time now. Sally will miss Yoshiko a lot."

Her father detested this. Teru didn't let herself think too much. She would miss George, she knew. Maybe more than she cared to admit but not so much she couldn't face being separated from him. Other things were more important. Her mother would need her more than ever now. Her father apparently reached a decision.

He gave his nose a twist and said, "There was something else but maybe we had better let things go for the present."

"Yes," Teru agreed, "perhaps we'd better." He looked at her sharply and she stirred uneasily. Perhaps she had said too much. It was done now but she wondered if she had done the right thing.

"I can't help being worried about your mother and Sally," he said, "I'm afraid we've spoiled Sally by giving her too much freedom. I was always intending to have a good talk with her someday. I never did. Tadao, though, is a smart boy."

"Sally is just young," Teru said. "She wants to have a good time."

"Is that all they teach you at school? To have good times, besides bragging about your citizenship," he said with a resigned voice.

Teru looked up surprised. It was the first time her father had mentioned their clouded citizenship. She knew that most Issei were always raking it up these past few weeks.

"We told you your citizenship was only good for fair weather," they said.

But her father said no more about it.

"You can arrange with Mr. Johnson to stay on here until you're moved into camp." He paused and hesitated before beginning again. "About money." The FBI man came over.

"I want to ask you a few questions," he said.

"Yes?" Teru asked surprised.

"Yes," he said and motioned her father over to the other agent who had just come in from the kitchen. Teru faced the man with her heart pounding violently. He was the one who had taken her purse. The one who made them all feel like criminals in their own home. She was suddenly scared. Why, she didn't know. She had nothing to hide. Her father's record was clear. He had come to America as a student and stayed but so had a lot of other people. He had then set himself up as a respected member of the community through hard work and not too much luck. True, he was influential in the Japanese Association but that had come naturally because of his college education and standing in the community. He had contributed to the *heimushakai* (informal groups to support Japanese soldiers) but so had practically all of the Japanese in America. As long as Japan had been at war only with China, they had naturally sympathized with Japan. A few had been against the sending of comfort bags to soldiers in China and the collection of monthly dues, but even fewer had opposed it openly.

The FBI man asked her question after question, often repeating the same question time and again, especially about army and navy training. He asked leading questions, ambiguous questions. He began to fire questions rapidly. Until finally Teru forgot to be scared and turned resentful.

"What are you trying to do?," she asked angrily. "Trying to make me say something that isn't true?" The man immediately changed his attitude.

"We're only trying to protect your father," he said and continued his questions in a milder tone.

Many of the questions about their father's past, Teru didn't know the answer to; and when the man began asking her things about relatives in Japan and her father's activities before and just after coming to America, she said, "Why don't you ask my father? He can tell you much better than I could. After all, I wasn't born until a long time after these things happened."

"He must have told you at one time or other," he insisted.

"I wasn't as prying as some people," Teru said tartly.

"Young lady, that's no attitude to take," the man said.

"I'm sorry," Teru said. "You haven't exactly been acting very pleasantly either." She felt the warm blood mounting in her temples.

"This is war; we can't always be as nice as we want to," he said. "However, we do the best we can."

"The war changes a lot of things, doesn't it?" Teru said.

He didn't answer and went back to the man questioning her father. He shook his head when the other looked in and pretty soon called to her father, "Better say goodbye."

"No," Teru said quickly. "My sister. She hasn't come back.

Can't you wait a little longer?" They looked expectantly at the FBI man for an answer. He seemed to hesitate. He pulled out his watch.

"We'll wait fifteen more minutes."

Teru went out on the porch and looked down the road towards town. Nothing familiar was coming down the road. She went back inside. She couldn't stay still. She went outside again.

Tad said impatiently, "I'll go look for her." Teru shook her head. Where were George and his father? The fifteen minutes passed all too quickly. She begged them to wait a little longer. It was useless. The shiny black Ford was moving away with her father before Teru dully realized that it had actually happened. They were taking him away. She was standing dumbly in the driveway, sharply conscious of her mother standing quietly beside her. Her hand was raised in silent goodbye. What was it she had written in Janet's autograph book? The words ran numbly through her mind. "Parting comes but once forever. If this be it, I shall be sad." The shiny black car disappeared and suddenly Mrs. Noguchi was sobbing softly in her daughter's arms. They tightened protectively. She barely came to Teru's nose. Teru's eyes blindly followed the road. She kept seeing the look in her father's eyes when he had turned for a last farewell. The pleading look in them. Take care of Mother they seemed to say. Be good to her. She needs protection. Tears welled in Teru's eyes but she blinked them angrily out and led her mother into the house.

"He'll be back right away," she said comfortingly. "He hasn't done anything wrong and they can't hold him for nothing." Tad remained outside, hands thrust deep into his pockets, staring at the bits of gravel he kept kicking away. Teru called him but he didn't answer. Teru didn't insist. He had always liked to think things out himself.

When evacuation had first been announced he'd acted the same way, but he had finally pulled himself together and had seemed in good spirits except that he had suddenly quit hinting for a small radio for himself. He'd wanted one badly ever since he'd decided that he was going to take up radio engineering at the University of California.

Teru tried to cheer her mother up but she only smiled briefly each time until Teru said, "I'll cook tonight. You rest." Her mother shook her head no, and they began to get supper ready together. Teru quickly set the table for four, carefully placing the chairs so their father's usual place wouldn't look so vacant. She wouldn't go to the party now, though Sally might since

Yoshiko would still be leaving Saturday. She wondered where Sally had gone. Almost an hour passed before the Motoyama Chrysler turned into the driveway kicking up clouds of dust that had the "Drive Slow" sign posted at the gate.

Sally came up the porch steps closely followed by Yoshiko and Mrs. Motoyama. "Where's Father?" she shouted as soon as she had yanked open the door. She looked around wildly. She stared in disbelief at them. "You didn't let them take him away," she accused. Teru could only nod her head, wondering what turn Sally's unpredictable temper would take. "Why didn't you stop them?," Sally demanded unreasonably.

"At least until I got here." "We tried to get them to wait," Teru replied, "but they wouldn't."

"But they can't take him away," Sally wailed. Tad came in but didn't say anything. He just looked at Sally. Mrs. Motoyama had immediately gone over to Mrs. Noguchi.

"Where are Papa and George?," she asked. The GMC truck rumbled into the driveway a little later.

"A dumb cop hauled us into the police station for questioning," George said after they told him what had happened. "Thought we were violating the travel limit on aliens. We sure are behind the eight ball these days."

Sally threw her hair back in a self-conscious gesture. "Yoshiko and I were scared for a minute today when a motor cop stopped us. He didn't seem to know the difference between an alien and a citizen and told us he was going to lock us up."

Mrs. Motoyama turned to Yoshiko. "Baka," she scolded, "I've told you not to ride around so much. Suppose you got into trouble? It would spoil our plans to move Saturday."

Teru said, "Motoyama-san, we're not going to move with you after all. Father thought it best that we didn't go."

"What?" George was the first to find his voice after the abrupt silence. "You can't do that. What would you do?"

"I never heard of such a baka thing," Mrs. Motoyama said.

"Father wanted to explain further when you came so all he told me was that it would be better if we went into the government camp for the present."

"Those Places are no good. You'll be locked up for the duration of the war," George said emphatically. "You'll never get out of them once you get in. Didn't you see the sentry towers they're putting up at the rodeo grounds?"

"Yes, you'll have to come with us," Mrs. Motoyama said definitely. "We've gone over this so many times before."

Teru's mother spoke up quietly. "We'd only be a bother now. We better do as my husband says and wait for him in a government camp. Perhaps after they release him...."

"But Teru and I could work," Sally interrupted. I'm practically through school now. She tossed her hair back defiantly when they all looked at her.

"That's the spirit," George said approvingly. "You see, she wants to go."

"Yes, we can still work something out together," Mrs. Motoyama said. "They may release your father before you know it and it wouldn't be so good if you were all stuck away in a camp. Mrs. Shibata was telling us she heard from a *Hakujin* friend that you can't get out of them once they get you inside."

Even Yoshiko had an argument. "We could all live together."

"Why not?," George said, looking at Teru.

Mrs. Motoyama turned to Mrs. Noguchi. "They were saying at the Oriental Market last night that they were going to separate all the young people into different camps and make labor crews. The boys would build roads and dig ditches and the girls would have to work on the farms and in canneries." In the end, the Motoyamas prevailed and Mrs. Noguchi gave in hesitantly. Tad said he didn't care either way though Teru knew he had never wanted to move at all.

"They can't do this kind of thing," he commented, and added, "why don't we just stay and the heck with DeWitt and Roosevelt."

Teru had some misgivings but she finally said, "If the rest of you want to go, it's not for me to say no."

"Atta girl," George said. "You're doing the right thing."

"I don't know," Teru said doubtfully. She still felt weak and undecided.

CHAPTER 2

In a way, Teru was almost glad they were leaving. Sentiment was beginning to run high in Salinas. Perhaps it was because Japanese had so much power. People like Mr. Motoyama practically controlled the lettuce market

George observed, "They figure this is their best chance to kick us out and take over our property. One fellow came over the other day and offered us $5,000 for all our holdings. He knows darn well our equipment alone is worth $20,000 cold cash. Said we wouldn't be allowed to keep them much longer anyway. Gosh, he sure made me mad. I told him to go jump in the lake and offered to kick him off the place for nothing."

Early the next morning Teru was only half awake as she and Tad loaded the vegetables into the back of the pickup, thinking for some reason that it was Saturday and she wouldn't have to hurry back to school. Fool! She woke up fiercely and shoved the carrots hard into place. There was no more school for her. As soon as she crossed the bend in the road she could see the kids waiting for her at the arterial stop on the main highway. She rolled up the window of the cab. It was cracked where a rock had hit it on Wednesday. They were standing right by the road today. Five of them. Usually they stood a little back. She hadn't told her father about the kids and explained the cracked window as a rock kicked up by a passing car. He had enough worries already. She hopefully looked up the highway but it was no use. There were too many cars coming and she had to stop. She grit her teeth and grasped the wheel tightly as they advanced on the pickup with cries of "Get the Jap." The rocks landed on the cab with loud thumps but fortunately none hit a window. She heard glass breaking in back, but a quick glance showed the rear window intact. Must be something else, she thought, as she let the clutch out desperately and jerked out on the highway in front of a truck which slowed with a squeal of brakes. Her heart was still pounding violently when she pulled up at the supermarket. The manager came out to the pickup and poked his head over the side.

"What's this?," he asked and picked the broken neck of a bottle out of the bunched carrots. Teru looked too. The strong smell of kerosene made her nostrils flare. She suddenly wanted to hide and cry, or run away, but could do nothing. So that was what had made the crashing noise in back. There was kerosene and broken glass all over the back of the pickup. "Looks like these vegetables aren't much good anymore," the manager said, "I'm afraid we can't use them." "Too bad," he added as an afterthought. "How did it happen?"

Teru didn't feel like explaining. "This is my last trip like I told you Monday,"she said. "Thank you very much for your business all these years. My father was going to come with me this morning to thank you, too, but he couldn't make it."

"Heard he was picked up by the FBI," the fat manager mouthed. "Didn't know he was mixed up with them Japs. He seemed like a nice guy."

"He still is a nice guy," answered Teru vehemently. "He hasn't done anything wrong."

"He must have done something to get picked up."

"He hasn't," Teru gritted out.

"Sorry," the manager retreated, "but war is war, you know. We've got to protect ourselves." Teru turned around and climbed quickly into the pickup. She stepped on the starter viciously. There was no use going to the other places now except to say goodbye. The vegetables were a complete loss. Perhaps if she did sell some and a customer found a bit of glass in a bunch of carrots, he would begin saying that she had tried to kill him by purposely placing the glass there.

People were too ready to believe anything these days. Like the rumor of the discharged houseboy who had vengefully threatened the understanding employer who had just promised him his job back after the war, "After the war is over, you work for me."

She had heard the same story three times already, and always about a different person who had told it to a cousin related to the person who had told it to her.

After what the man at the supermarket had said, she didn't feel like finishing her route but she found her car automatically headed towards the next place on her usual route and she dutifully went to each market in turn. She was glad she did because the rest of the people went out of their way to be nice. She felt a little better going home, although the back of the pickup was still filled with the unsalable vegetables.

She recognized the Pontiac parked by the cottage as belonging to Mr. Yamada, who had been one of the fifteen men taken away for internment yesterday. It was terrible not knowing what was being done to the men. Hideo had told her that her brother-in-law in Monterey had been given nothing to eat for a day and a half. Things like that were very real now. It brought everything very close to home. Mrs. Yamada had come over to see if Mrs. Noguchi had had any word.

Teru had never seen Mrs. Yamada drive a car before and wondered how she had managed. She asked Mrs. Yamada and after piecing together her description decided that she had driven all the way in low gear and had stopped the car by stepping on the brakes.

"The car jumped up and down when I stepped on the brakes," she ended happily, "but I kept pressing harder until the engine stopped."

They had apparently been discussing the latest freeze order because Teru's mother said almost immediately, "Mrs. Yamada was just saying it wouldn't be so good if we left now without knowing where Father is being taken. We won't know where he is and he wouldn't know where we went. We'd be so uncertain about everything and we wouldn't know for how long."

"Our case is a little different," Mrs. Yamada said. "Bill hasn't come back from Colorado and I can't move out of Zone I by myself. But even if he were home, I don't think it would be safe for us to move."

Teru had graduated from high school with Bill and had gone to parties with him several times. He had been helping his father the past two years and was now in Colorado looking for a place to farm. It seemed Mrs. Yamada had wired him to come home immediately as soon as she learned voluntary evacuation would be prohibited after Saturday, but so far received no answer. She wasn't even sure that the telegram had been delivered and was worried he wouldn't get back into California before Saturday and be stuck in Colorado. Bill had phoned last week that he hadn't been able to find a room in town and was staying with a group who had evacuated from Chualar, near Salinas, two weeks before.

"If I can't find anything better than what these people are going through, we definitely won't come out here," he had phoned.

"They're living in a barn ten miles from nowhere. They have to lug their drinking and cooking water from a ditch a mile away. They have to worry about water rights for the land they intend to farm. They're afraid to come into town unless they absolutely have to. I was threatened by a drunk myself after dinner but don't worry, I'll be back in one piece to give you the details."

"The more I think it over, the more I'm convinced Mrs. Yamada is right," Mrs. Noguchi mused. "Teru, what do you think?"

Teru didn't answer her mother right away. She was seeing the look in her father's eyes when he had asked her to take care of her mother. It had been such a pleading look. Naked and unashamedly pleading. She hadn't wanted to go against her father's request in the first place but everybody had been so insistent and her mother and especially Sally, had seemed so eager to go with the Motoyamas that she hadn't been able to refuse since she wasn't sure herself which was the right thing to do. Either way left the future pretty much in the air. With voluntary evacuation you at least had the feeling that you were doing something. As long as you were doing something you felt that you were shaping your own destiny. Once you gave in to the impulse to sit back and wait for the government to take care of you, you would no longer have control of your life. You would be penned up with 100,000 other people and when they let you out, if they ever did, you would come out with nothing and have to start all over again with even less than you had when you went into the government camp. And then where would you be?, so George argued. Voluntary evacuation was a gamble but if you had the ability you would come out on top with a few breaks. At least, whether you succeeded or failed you would have had your chance. The ones who evacuated ahead of the rest would also be in on the ground floor and grab all the good opportunities.

Teru had gone over this many times wIth George, with friends, with her father and mother. But she'd never been sure. Personally, she sometimes agreed secretly with Tad that it would be a good idea to refuse to obey the evacuation order. After all, that was what this war was being fought for. Rule by force. Oppressed minorities. America always cried out so much about democracy, Christian principles, the Four Freedoms. But a clean boxer stayed a clean boxer only as long as he didn't use dirty tactics. He had to win by using only those clean tactics. Anything less made him no better than the foul. This was war, total war, but the stakes were the same. She could understand the first January 29 order prohibiting enemy aliens from certain strategic areas like Monterey, but the March 3 order had been different. Citizens had been included. Citizens who had Japanese fathers or mothers. But citizens of German and Italian extraction had not been touched. Race -- determined at the time of conception -- was the dividing line. Justice, humanity, human progress had been shrugged off in a second like an ill-fitting mantle. Even John whose father was Greek, and Salvador whose mother was Mexican, were to be incarcerated along with the rest. It was hard to understand. Something she'd never dreamed would happen and had been unprepared for. The Issei had been right after all. Their American citizenship meant nothing. Their color gave them away. How hard she had argued against it long before the war started!

Especially with Hiroshi just back from Manchuria, who had heard over there of U.S. Army plans drafted in 1937 for evacuation of all Japanese from the Pacific Coast regardless of citizenship. Of how they were ready to evacuate them all in 48 hours, if necessary, or over a period of several months if there was no threat of invasion. How she had poohpoohed the idea as something dreamed up by the Japanese war lords to keep all Japanese looking to Japan for their final security. She remembered all too well those days how Hiroshi had told of a growing desperation in a Japan faced with national disaster for lack of oil and industrial resources. Of eyes turned resolutely towards the Netherlands East Indies because there was "no other way out." The world had known but the world had thought she wouldn't dare!

Then, Teru hadn't answered right away. Mrs. Yamada had mentioned the camp being constructed on the rodeo grounds just outside town. People generally thought Japanese were to be put in there but nobody was sure. All they heard were rumors with nobody to deny or corroborate them. The WCCA people said nothing helpful and the army remained silent. Like the big camp that was supposed to be nearly completed in Manzanar. Nobody knew for sure just what was going on down there. The other day one of the market people had told her how wonderfully the Government was intending to take care of them with nice prefabricated houses and all the facilities of an average home.

"Of course, it won't be quite as good as you have now but you'll have everything. Movies, stores, beauty shops. You're pretty lucky this is America." Maybe life in a concentration camp, American style, would not be so bad since it would be only for a while anyway.

CHAPTER 3

Just four months ago, concentration camp to Teru had meant those horrible places where the Germans were said to have tortured and mistreated people who refused to conform to the New Order or were simply of Jewish ancestry. She hadn't paid much attention, however, and had passed much of it off as British propaganda. Was it only four months ago she had been wondering if they could invite George and his family over for Thanksgiving? She remembered how Sally had immediately seized on the idea.

"It would be fun," she'd said and it had been practically settled right then. Once Sally went to work on anything, it was a foregone conclusion that she would get her way in the Noguchi family. None could resist the wide pleading eyes and the bubbling enthusiasm. It had been fun. It had rained hard all day Tuesday and Wednesday and the ground had been too wet to work. The rain had seemed to rid the atmosphere of all work and pretense of work, and the unexpected rest had put everyone in good spirits. It would be at least a week before the fields would be dry enough to work.

"Mother can just sit and watch," Sally said; and so Teru did the shopping and got the turkey ready to roast while Sally helped fix the salad, dessert, and all the fixings. She had made a special point of getting George's favorite maplenut ice cream, and a whole gallon was in the refrigerator.

Mr. Motoyama came over early to play 'go' (a Japanese strategy board game) with Mr. Noguchi and the two sat in the living room oblivious of the rest of the household until Yoshiko, George, and Mrs. Motoyama had come.

Sally and Yoshiko immediately made so much noise that Mr. Motoyama looked up at them disapprovingly, "Too noisy. Why don't you go outside?"

"Ha ha, Motoyama-san, you must be losing," Sally taunted impishly, then, "that's an idea. Let's go for a ride." She turned her eyes on Teru. "The turkey won't be ready for another couple of hours will it? Let's all go."

Teru demurred but George said, "Mom, you watch the turkey."

Mr. Noguchi beamed approval. "Yes, why don't you young people leave us in quiet for an hour or so?"

Teru sat in front with George. Sally, Yoshiko, and Tad were in back but Sally was practically in the front seat with them, especially until they'd agreed to drive out towards Monterey. The air was still a little damp from the rain and it felt cool and refreshing against their faces. They drove along the coast and they pointed out to each other the spots along the beach where they had picnicked, where they'd spent a Fourth of July, the likely spots where they'd come next time. Teru felt George's eyes on her when they passed the lighthouse and felt the color rising in her cheeks. That was where he'd parked the car last Saturday night. It was the first time they'd ever been really alone together and Teru remembered how gruff and surprisingly shy George had been.

She looked out the window and put her face against the cooling breeze sweeping in from the ocean. He'd kissed her for the first time that night and Teru had only to close her eyes to bring it all back.

"Nice spot," George said.

"I liked it," Teru murmured but only the wind carrying her voice away could have heard. They drove through the streets of crazy Carmel and headed for home. They were hungry and their appetites were enormous. Still, they couldn't finish the two turkeys, and when the ice cream and cake came around even Tad didn't ask for more.

"I ate too much," he groaned but he was the first to suggest taking in the show at the Fox. George's hand quickly found hers in the semi-gloom of the theatre and Teru felt warm and relaxed. It was pleasant sitting there. It was good to be alive. After the show she and George might be able to sneak off again. The skies were clear and the moon would be coming out tonight....

Teru had just come home from her Sunday school class and had switched on the radio for some music when H.V. Kaltenborn's voice suddenly cut in with the electrifying news that enemy planes were bombing Pearl Harbor. Teru listened stunned. She hoped desperately that the black planes were really sent by reactionary admirals acting without orders from Tokyo.

War between Japan and America would be a catastrophe. America was the only country she knew and could call her own but Japan was the place where people like her mother and father came from. Ever since the war in Europe had started she had hoped that neither Japan nor America would be embroiled and had viewed with dread each country's preparation for war. With her father and with George she had tried to figure out power politics that would put Japan and America on the same side. It had all been wishful thinking, Teru knew. It was so evident now. She could hear someone banging away in the tool shed.

"Father." Her father looked up and waited for her to get control of her breathing. "Some planes just bombed Pearl Harbor," she said. "They think they're Japanese planes."

"What?" her father stared at her. "Are you sure?" He put away his tools and carefully locked the box. George came over right after lunch.

"I think we're in for a tough time," he said. "I get those dirty looks already. They probably thought I was piloting one of those planes." Bill Yamada came almost right away.

"Hi," he said to George. "I saw your car outside and thought I'd step in for a while, I suppose you've heard." George nodded.

"I was just telling Teru it looks like pretty tough sledding for us."

"What do you mean?" Bill demanded. "I know what you're thinking, but you're wrong. Not us. We're citizens. The same as everybody else."

"Yeah, up to a certain point," George said cynically. "Remember what happened in the last war. They can't single us out as long as we live up to our citizenship. We'll have our rights as citizens, of course, but I'm thinking of the people around here. People get pretty hysterical in war time."

"Maybe our parents, but not us," Bill insisted.

"I'm not so sure, George," Teru said. "I think people have learned a lesson from the last war. After it was all over they cooled down pretty quick and were sorry they'd treated the Germans here like they did." Teru's father looked up from his paper.

"You won't like this, but hate and war go together. People must be taught to hate and fear before they can be persuaded to kill, and there will be a tremendous effort to mobilize that hate and fear because the leaders will be a little hesitant at first to rely too much on making this another war of ideals. They have too clear a picture of the disillusionment which followed the last war." He sighed with resignation and continued, "Later on, perhaps, the same minds will prevail but I am afraid that we will be under severe pressure at first. People are not going to stop and ask if you have United States citizenship...."

Teru felt a little strange going to school at first. Her *Hakujin* friends went out of their way to make her feel that the war would make no difference in their relationship, but sometimes when she came unexpectedly on a group, conversation would stop suddenly and an awkward pause would follow.

They seldom discussed the war when she was around, and Teru lay awake at night wondering just where she stood. Whenever her close friends avoided mentioning the war in her presence she knew it was because of an unconscious coupling of her with Japan and a desire not to hurt her. Outside of school though, Teru immediately felt the thinly veiled hostility in the numerous glances that were thrown at her too often to overlook. The middle-aged women were the worst. The venomous looks they gave her dripped with stark, staring hate. It was ugly and repulsive. She tried hard not to pay attention. I believe in America. I must be an American, she cried herself to sleep. Her father and mother must feel the same way. They must have come to America as a land of promise and must have decided to make this their permanent home. Otherwise, why hadn't they gone back before this? They never even mentioned going back in their old age as some Issei did. Why had they placed their children's American schooling before everything? Why had they made Sally quit her Japanese language school when she'd gotten poor grades in her first year in high school? They'd been so proud, too, when Teru had given the valedictory address. And why their purchase of educational endowments to ensure sending Tad through college? Why their purchase of the land they farmed and the house they lived in? Why should they be sending their roots down so deep?

Teru remembered a story in which a mother told her adopted child, "You weren't forced upon us by circumstance like most babies. We chose you because you were the nicest child we could find." Her father and mother too had come of their own free choice to make America their home.

Teru began to feel more and more helpless against the inevitable tide of events. Increasing acts of violence were reported. Display windows in the Japanese stores, whether owned by citizens or not, were broken in the middle of the night. In Gilroy, a Japanese girl was shot in the leg and her sister abducted by Filipinos. In Mt. Eden a woman was shot and killed. Others were wakened in the middle of the night by the crashing of lead slugs through the walls of their homes. A young boy was seriously wounded.

Chinese took to wearing their "I am a Chinese" buttons.

A Chinese-American friend told Teru, "We know what the score is but what can we do? The older folks feel we have to protect ourselves. We can easily picture ourselves in your shoes, don't worry." Filipinos began strutting up and down Main Street in increasing numbers, although *Hakujin* seemed to be eyeing them a little askance. She noticed an increasing friendliness on the part of Germans, Negroes, Italians, and Mexicans.

An Italian neighbor said in a confidential tone, "The only reason I live in this country is because I can have a car, a radio, a refrigerator, and a good house. In Italy, I couldn't have those things."

A German-American told George, "This time we'll do it. They've been hanging on to the best things in the world long enough."

Mexicans said, "Hope Japan wins. We don't like Americans. They treat us like dirt."

Negroes patronized Japanese stores more and more. "You people are all right," they said, "you don't go high hat like Chinese. When they have businesses in the poor part of town they give us the glad hand, but when they move downtown to the ritzy joints, they turn us away."

A pretty, blond-haired Portuguese-American girl said, "When I say American, I mean them. I don't think of myself as American." Teru felt confused. What did all this mean? Janet Martin was the only *Hakujin* Teru drew closer to in those tangled months. Her father and mother were French. Was there something to the racist theory after all? The French were supposed to be the most tolerant of all white races....

CHAPTER 4

Teru became aware again of her mother and Mrs. Yamada, quietly discussing the possibility of ever returning to their homes.

"Our places will have been taken over by *Hakujin* and they won't want us back," Mrs. Yamada was saying, "because they would be afraid we would provide too much economic competition and push them back to where they were before they forced us out." Mrs. Yamada wasn't saying so, but Teru knew that she was thinking Mrs. Noguchi was in worse straits than herself. The Noguchis had their whole future tied up in their home and their plot of land while the Yamadas leased their land from year to year and had most of their assets in cash. When they left their home behind them the Noguchis would have practically nothing. Without their father they would be very dependent on the Motoyamas if they moved to Fresno. It was the same story all over again when they drove over to the Motoyamas' that night. George and his parents were insistent.

"We could wait until Saturday night. Maybe your father will wire by then," George remarked, and looked at his father who nodded assent.

But Mrs. Noguchi was firm this time. "I was wrong to have given in before. He told us we should give up our plans and that is what we must do. It wouldn't be fair to him. We wouldn't be carrying out our trust."

"I don't want to go into those shacks they're building at the rodeo grounds," Sally shouted. "What will my friends think?" But it did no good. George caught Teru's eyes. She looked around at the others. They were still earnestly trying to change her mother's mind.

Sally looked up quickly when George and Teru rose to leave but averted her eyes. It was dark outside. Teru shivered a little when the cold air hit her face. George didn't say anything until they were driving slowly along the dirt road leading deeper into the countryside. Lights from farmhouses twinkled only in the distance. Teru twisted the knob on the radio and left the volume low. George watched her hands for a while then paid close attention to the road ahead.

"It's going to be tough," he noted.

"I guess so."

He turned quickly to look at her. "I mean leaving you."

"Oh." Teru's voice was barely audible. The trees lining Gabilan Creek loomed ahead. George's hands tightened whitely on the wheel but he said nothing until he turned the car off the road following the creek. He switched off the ignition and turned to face her. He looked at her steadily.

"Will you marry me?" Teru had expected it but not so abruptly. She'd expected him to try at first to urge her to go with them to Fresno. She knew she'd have to give him the answer tonight. He'd asked her before but always with an undertone of kidding as if to say, time to get more serious later, and she'd always laughed it off. She drew in her breath sharply, afraid to trust her voice. She shook her head. He stared at her unbelievingly a long minute. He pulled her head against his chest and his face was against her hair.

"Why not? Don't you love me?"

"I don't know." Her voice turned low and husky.

"No?"

Teru shook her head dumbly. Her mind was whirling dizzily. He'd never made her feel like this before.

"I always thought you did."

"Maybe," then quickly, "Oh, I don't know, George."

"You must when you hold me tight like this." Teru pulled away. She looked at him pleadingly.

"With Dad gone, they need me at home."

"You want to though," he insisted. Teru shook her head slowly.

"I'm sorry, George. I can't now." She raised her head.

"Then this is goodbye."

"For a while anyway."

"It may be forever. This is a tough war and it's going to last a long time. This will have to last, too." He bent suddenly and his lips were hard against hers. His arms tightened. It was a long time before he raised his head. Teru sat up straight. She was trembling.

"I didn't know you cared so," she gasped, flustered, and tryed to inject some laughter into her voice.

"Now you know. Marry me?"

Teru shook her head. "Let's go back." George reluctantly reached for the switch....

The Motoyamas left Saturday just before noon. Saturday night Mrs. Yamada came over again, this time in second gear. Her eyes were dull from lack of sleep and worry. Bill hadn't come back. They tried to comfort her but there wasn't much to be said.

"Why don't you stay here with us?," Teru's mother suggested.

"It must be lonely way out there all alone."

"Yes." Teru said. "When curfew and five-mile limit go into effect tonight, you won't even be able to come into town to shop." Mrs. Yamada said no again, but it grew late and she decided to stay overnight anyway. She was afraid to drive home in the dark. The next morning they learned that the freeze deadline had been extended until that night. Bill came back on the 6 p.m. train. He had a lot to tell. He'd located one fairly promising farm with guaranteed water rights, but his mother's telegram hadn't given him any time to look further into it. However, he wasn't too enthusiastic about moving out there.

"I wouldn't mind going by myself," he said, "but it's no life for a family, and I didn't hear too many good stories about the reaction of the Hakujins out there. Most people I met were nice but there were some really bad ones. In New Mexico they slapped some families passing through into jail and told them to keep moving the next morning. And I heard of several cases of overturned trucks and manhandling. Not only that, the Japanese aren't too receptive either. They say our moving out there is making it bad for them. It seems we'll contaminate them. They call us California Japs. In a way I can't blame them. The newcomers usually have a lot of ready cash and are throwing it around and making it felt. They're probably afraid we'll take over the country and leave them holding the bag. Kind of sad, though."

Teru felt really lonely for the first time after Bill and Mrs. Yamada left. Sally and Tad had gone right after supper to visit the Sakaguchis.

"They live way over the five-mile limit from here and we won't get to see them after tonight," they said. It was too quiet without the usual Sunday night music from the radio. She had turned in their radio and Tad's 22-calibre rifle sometime before in compliance with the order prohibiting all Japanese aliens from possessing radios, firearms, cameras, and maps.

"It's my rifle." Tad had complained, but Teru had turned it in anyway and had been very glad when she heard that Satoru's father had been arrested when they found Satoru's target pistol in a routine search. It seemed Mr. Matsuda hadn't been on the original list of men scheduled to be picked up, but the FBI had walked into their home by mistake and had decided to search. The target pistol had been found and Mr. Matsuda was taken away despite Satoru's protests. They hadn't found anything at the Noguchi home except a Japanese dictionary with a few random check marks and ink spots which the agents said might be some sort of secret code markings, and they had still taken her father into custody so it wouldn't have made any difference, but Teru was glad anyway. This way she had no guilty feelings. She tried to read but she kept thinking it was the first Sunday George hadn't been over in a long time. At first it was only on Sundays, though lately he had been over more often.

She looked at the mantle clock. It read eight o'clock. It must be closer to nine, she thought. It must have run down. She stood looking at the motionless black hands. Then the significance of it hit her all at once. Her father had always wound that clock himself. It was the kind of clock that needed winding every three days; and after they let it run down a few times, he took over and boasted that it had never once run\ out of wind ever since. Teru lay still, her mind a dumping ground for bitter thoughts.

Why was all this necessary? Her father was innocent, she ought to know. And yet they had just barged into their home and locked him up without even a by-your-leave. They had shown no proof at all. That old Japanese dictionary had been no more a secret code book than her Delineator cook book. Probably all they had was the suspicion of some snooper, possibly some JACL leader who might not have liked the way Teru's group was so outspoken about their having nothing to do with JACL. Funny, all the people picked up had no connection with JACL. Probably just coincidence but she didn't like it. Some people were already saying that the JACL leaders were seen cashing suspicious looking government checks. That sounded like a vicious rumor but there still might be some basis for it. Perhaps she shouldn't be so harsh, but she hated people like that. She wondered why the authorities trusted them. They were so obviously misfits in their own society if they would squeal on it falsely and without good cause. Were the FBI so ignorant for all their excellent record as G-men, or were they scared, or did they just feel they had to do something to keep up appearances? She'd be willing to swear that the people picked up the other day were innocent of any kind of subversive activity. She knew them. Mr. Yamada, Mr. Matsuda, and Mr. Kataoka, she'd known as long as she could remember. In Watsonville, a man had been picked up for having 70,000 rounds of ammunition and several rifles in his possession ready to be used to aid a Japanese landing force, so the local headlines screamed. Teru knew better. The man's son came to junior college and according to him his father had received permission from the local police to keep them as long as they were under lock and key. But when the FBI came, the home town police had disclaimed any knowledge of such an agreement. The papers had also failed to mention that the rifles and ammunition were part of the man's hardware store stock.

She heard the pickup rattling into the driveway and got up to wind the clock. She half moved towards where the radio had been to switch it on and get the correct time before she remembered there was no radio.

The next day there were all sorts of rumors about what was happening to the people who had left Salinas over the weekend. Armed men with rifles and shotguns were turning them back at the outskirts of Fresno and the backroads. Several people had already returned because of the hostile reaction of the local people. Several others had been set upon in the middle of the night and clubbed rather badly. Notices to get out were found pinned on tents and cars. Teru wondered if anything had happened to George and if he would come back too. But he couldn't now, with the curfew in effect, or could he? She asked the person who had told her about the families returning and he guessed they had returned sometime Sunday night, ahead of the deadline. He didn't know who they were. He'd just heard. A letter came from George on Saturday and he said nothing about having had any trouble or of any other people having had trouble, except in finding a place to stay. Some local Japanese were refusing to let the newcomers even camp on their land, much less move into unoccupied barns and buildings. George had felt like turning back when he couldn't locate a decent house to stay in but had finally found a cabin at an auto camp just outside Sanger. The owner was very unfriendly, but George had seen about a dozen other Japanese families already there and had moved in. The second day they'd been offered jobs doing something to the grape vines and Teru gathered that it was back-breaking work. Stoop labor, George called it.

He wrote nothing about Friday night but he closed, "Always with love."

Mrs. Yamada came over the following Monday with Bill, and asked

Teru if she would do some shopping for her. It was about six miles from the Yamadas' to the Noguchis' and another two miles into town.

Bill shushed his mother, "What do they expect us to do, starve? If they want to stop me, let them. I'm not committing any crime."

"Of course not," Mrs. Yamada replied. "But other people are obeying the order. Look at Mr. Koike."

Teru had heard of the Koikes from Sally. They had been living on a little rice and hot water ever since the curfew started until yesterday, when a gas company checker had found out and brought them a huge load of groceries. The oldest of the four children was only nine and the alien father hadn't dared drive the ten miles into town. Teru suspected too that Mr. Koike was low on funds since he'd lost his job right after the five-mile travel restriction on aliens had gone into effect. There was a movement now to use Japanese Association funds to take care of people like Mr. Koike whose income had been shut off. The question was how to distribute the money without hurting the people involved. It was suggested that they reimburse the *Hakujin* who had brought the groceries for Mr. Koike, but people who knew the man told them they were crazy to think he would accept it.

George wrote again, the following week. They'd been asked by the auto-camp owner to put in 40 acres of tomatoes for him. They'd told him the land was unsuitable for tomatoes, but the owner had been insistent and they had consented to do so on a share basis. According to George the owner had changed his attitude towards the Japanese families living in his auto-camp after they began buying all their gasoline at his pump and practically bought out his whole stock of groceries the first week. He was all smiles now. George had also talked to an oldtime resident of Sanger and had been told that much of the antagonism towards the newcomers arose from the fact that they flashed their cash around and stripped the stores of goods they wanted themselves. They also looked askance, or perhaps enviously, at the high-powered cars driven by the newcomers. The store owners were happy at first about doing more business in two weeks than they had done the first three months of the year, but they were beginning to feel the pinch of having to turn away old customers after being sold out. George asked her what she thought of the news Bill had brought back from Colorado. Bill had written him but hadn't been too enthusiastic or definite about anything. That was why they had taken the auto-camp owner's offer to grow tomatoes. They'd stay where they were for a season anyway and see how things turned out. He missed her and hoped that things were more settled and they could plan something for the future. On Bill's advice Teru drove the family into town for typhoid shots after hearing water in the camps might be contaminated. The shots cost twenty dollars. Teru felt sick because she hadn't asked what they would cost beforehand. They couldn't afford it.

The next day their arms were swollen and feverish and neither Teru nor her mother felt like working. But when Mr. Johnson came over he begged so hard that her mother agreed to do what work they could. Mr. Johnson was the one who had taken over the Noguchi farm. Teru rebelled but there was nothing she could do even though it seemed the height of something or other to be working for wages by the hour to harvest crops that would ordinarily have been their own. She could cry when she thought of all the money somebody else was making from their hard work. Money that would certainly come in handy. She was glad Sally and Tad had gone back to school. It would at least keep their minds off things.

Mr. Noguchi wired from the internment camp exactly two weeks from the day they had taken him away. He was all right and he arranged to give Teru power of attorney so she could draw on his slender bank account. There was less then $200 left and Teru felt hesitant about drawing out even the $50 per month allowed under the Alien Property Control Act. However, in spite of her careful shopping she had to make two full months' withdrawals before the army finally posted the one week notice requesting them to get ready to move into the rodeo grounds. They had so many things to buy and their former income was now going to Mr. Johnson.

Everything had to be bought now. Especially clothing that would stand heavy wear, blankets for each person in case they were separated into labor camps as rumored, heavy shoes, suitcases, straw hats, and all sorts of odds and ends. They couldn't sell their furniture as so many people were doing because Mr. Johnson would be moving in and\ wanted the house furnished. However, after hearing of the ridiculously low prices being paid evacuees for refrigerators, stoves, and household furniture, Teru wondered whether she would have sold anything anyway. They were requested to assemble at the armory on Tuesday at 2 p.m. It didn't say how they were to get there. Teru went to the post office for more details but they did little more than show her the army order. They would be allowed to bring only what they could carry. There, a man said, "Oh, I imagine you should take enough things, for say, a weekend trip into the mountains."

Sally was dismayed, then mad. "I can't carry anything at all."

She wailed, "I won't do it!"

"I'll carry the two big suitcases," Tad volunteered.

It was a problem deciding what to bring and what to leave behind. Sally wanted to bring all her clothes, but Teru thought it best to bring only clothes that would stand hard wear and things like sheets and blankets.

Teru noticed on her trips into town that even the town fellows were wearing shiny new leather boots, blue jeans, and heavy-duty shirts. The girls weren't wearing them yet but she saw them buying slacks and rough shirts of cotton and denim. The movement into the rodeo grounds was a mad topsy-turvy affair. Bill's landowner who had bought the Yamada's Chrysler drove them to the armory. It looked impossible at first, but they finally squeezed in by strapping luggage to the fenders and running board. They saw Janet moving towards them in the crowd.

"How did you get here?" Teru shouted and barely heard herself.

People were calling to friends and trying to keep together with their families while they milled around the armory waiting their turn to register.

"Ditched school." Janet said.

They moved a little away from the crowd. But neither could think of much to say and pretty soon it was time for Teru to go.

"Be sure to let me know how I can reach you first thing," Janet said. She was smiling but through tears. Teru knew her own eyes were wet. A curious passer-by remarked, "I didn't know there were so many Japs in town." Janet gave him a dirty look. A tiny five-year old raised his piping voice above the noise.

"Mommy, am I a Jap too?"

Teru knew the mother slightly. She was the Mrs. Sato who'd been a senior when she and Janet had just gone into high school. She'd married a dentist. "Hush, Junior," Mrs. Sato said. "You're an American." But she was smiling uncomfortably and her chic, smartly tailored suit and white gloves suddenly seemed out of place.

CHAPTER 5

Buses carried them to the rodeo grounds. The younger ones joshed each other as they passed through the guarded gates under the tall sentry towers. *Hakujin* craned their necks from cars rolling by on the highway to San Francisco. "So this is our duration home," someone sighed facetiously, but no one answered.

"Wonder if we'll be home by Christmas?" Sally asked of no one in particular.

"Christmas?," Fay Omada echoed. "Quit your kidding. We'll be home by the Fourth of July. Good old Independence Day. They won't keep us locked up then."

Itchy Nakata said dolefully, "We ain't got no more home, we sold out. This is all the home we got now."

Several older folks sadly looked their way. For the most part they eyed their surroundings with set, worried faces. They filed out of the buses and looked about them seriously. They looked at the strange uniformity of the barren barracks with a feeling of wonder. Was this where they were going to live, even temporarily? The long lines of empty windows and closed doors stared vacantly back at them row after row, leering at them, waiting to engulf them. They were immediately herded into long, shuffling lines by people like Bill Yamada who had gone the day before. For typhoid inoculations and small pox vaccinations. For three blankets apiece. For assignment to one of the barracks. For a mimeographed sheet of instructions.

A guide led them to 80-C, one of five "apartments" comprising barrack 80. Teru wondered why they called them apartments. Compartment or just plain box would have better described the 20 feet by 20 feet of space allotted them for living quarters. "For a minimum of five persons," the instructions read. An electric light globe dangled from the raftered ceiling. The three windows let in a garish light that picked up the wide cracks in the wall and floor. They could see the green grass growing under the barracks. A cold wind was sweeping up through the cracks.

"Hell's bells. Do they expect us to live here?"

Teru recognized Itchy Nakata's scratchy, indignant voice next door.

"I want my congressman! Gangaway!" They could hear the sound of running feet, then, "Oh, I forgot. He's the guy who put me here." Sally snickered and they could almost see the look of mock bewilderment on Itchy's homely face.

"Hey, Sally,I thought that horse laugh couldn't belong to anybody else."

They looked around in surprise. The voice was coming from the wall. "Yoo hoo!"

Sally suddenly threw her handbag at a knot hole. The eye disappeared and a voice came back, "I'll be seeing more of you, ta ta."

"Ichiro, hurry and unpack the suitcases." Mrs. Nakata's scolding voice could be heard plainly through the thin wall.

Sally looked at Teru. "I can't stay here," she said but she immediately set to work covering the cracks and holes with handkerchiefs, newspapers, wrappings -- anything she could lay her hands on.

Ken Kimura poked his head in the door. "Tad, let's go get some of those empty cardboard cartons to lay on the floor. Pop says it will help keep the cold out." Ken was the oldest of the Kimuras in 80- B. Matsuo was 11, Bett was 9, and the baby was just beginning to sit up. Teru nodded and Tad went with Ken. So that was why so many people had been carrying those empty cartons. Teru had noticed them but hadn't known what one wanted them for. The floor was dirty but there was neither broom nor mop to be seen. They set to work unpacking, looking for sheets and curtains. Teru and Sally brought in the army cots which had been stacked outside and struggled to set them up. They weren't getting far with the stubborn cots when Itchy popped in the door.

"Mom said to help you," he said, and put his young muscles to work. He was big and he was bony and when he flopped back on a finished cot, he sat up immediately, rubbing a shoulder. "And to think, I volunteered to sleep in a hammock," he said in grieved tones. "Am I glad they turned me down."

Janet's brother had volunteered at the same time as Itchy just after Pearl Harbor and according to him, the navy recruiting officer had told Itchy crisply and to the point, "Get the hell out of here," and Itchy had, "got" his mouth twisting wryly.

Tad came back empty handed but with the information that a line was already forming for supper. They hurriedly dug out towels and soap and went to the wash trough. There was just one for the whole camp and it was outside. They couldn't miss it with the hundreds of others hurrying there with the same idea. They had to wait their turn while the early ones splashed in what Sally immediately labelled "the horse trough," and when they reached the mess hall, a long line was ahead of them. The doors didn't open right away and a good half hour passed before they stepped up for their serving of a spoon of spaghetti and a small helping of rice. They carried their food to the third and last row of tables. Their plates were of tin and their thick cups were heavy and chipped. Sally had a huge oversize "spear" and Tad a battered salad fork. They changed. Teru's was rusty and looked like it had been salvaged from a junk yard. Teru immediately lost all appetite. She felt overwhelmed by the noise and clatter of several hundred people of all ages and sizes packed shoulder to shoulder in the dim mess hall, groaning over the unappetizing food or talking loud and fast to cover their confusion and bewilderment.

Tad was the only one who ate his rice. The others were satisfied with one mouthful. Sally didn't even taste hers. It looked and smelled as uncooked, burnt, and unpalatable as it was.

"I'm hungry," Tad complained and went after a second helping of spaghetti. There were no seconds. Teru wondered in a moment of panic, are they going to use the same method of slow starvation that Germany was said to be using in the occupied countries? Are they going to keep us so undernourished there will be no energy for unrest within the camps? Her dissatisfied stomach said, yes, but her mind said no, this is America.

They stopped in to say hello to the Nakata family and were still there when Mr. Nakata came stomping in. He'd owned the American Cafe outside and was already working as one of the cooks.

"*Baka Hakujin*," he moaned. "They don't know the first thing about cooking rice but they make us cook it their way."

"I felt ashamed," his wife said. She was bigger than he. Her face was broad and flat.

"We had to use garbage pails to cook in so it was rather hard but even then it should have come out eatable," he said indignantly, "but not the way they made us do it. Dump in the rice and lots of water and crazily stir it up while trying to bring it to a boil. They wouldn't listen to us."

"Is that all we're going to get to eat?" Itchy wanted to know. "My stomach is peko-peko, empty."

"That made me mad too," Mr. Nakata said. "The *Hakujin* insisted that one sack of rice was enough to feed one thousand persons. He told me I was wasteful when I told him that in my restaurant I used one sack for about 200 servings."

They left him still fuming and sputtering and went back to their own compartment to put up curtains and get ready for the dark. There was no place to put anything so they stuffed as much as possible back into the suitcases. Bill came over and offered to put up shelves for them. He would be busy with registration tomorrow but maybe he would have time the next day. He was in 84-A together with newly married Mr. and Mrs. Jack Yatabe.

"One of those evacuation marriages," Bill said. Quite a few young people had hurried into marriage before evacuation. "We've pulled a drape across the room but it doesn't give much privacy." Teru looked around their own compartment. The four camp cots were lined up against one paper-patched wall. Their clothing was hanging from nails Tad had dug up and pounded into the walls with his shoes. Half their baggage was stacked against the far wall. The other half, they were sitting on for lack of chairs. It looked pretty junky.

Sally said to Teru, "Can we get some drapes too?"

"We'll order some tomorrow," Teru replied, thinking they ought to make things as livable as possible.

"There's a place in camp where you can order things from outside," Bill offered.

"We need a broom too. This floor is filthy."

"There's supposed to be one for each barrack," Bill said, "but we're going to get one anyway. I don't feel like waiting in line to use a broom too."

"I wonder who's using ours now. I'm going to look it up," Sally said and went to search for it.

Bill looked at his watch.

"About time for me to be heading back for roll call."

"Roll call?"

"Don't you know? You're supposed to be in your apartment every night from seven to seven-twenty. Somebody will come around to check."

"Oh."

"Haven't you read that paper they gave you this afternoon?"

"I had too many things on my mind to read it all. I hope Tad knows."

Bill rose to go. "I almost forgot to tell you. They're looking for a steno at the Administration Building. You might look into it tomorrow," he added, and left. Of course, she'd have to find work right away. They needed more money for all sorts of things they hadn't counted on. Drapes, a mop, a bucket, a face pan. And food, if they could. They couldn't live on meals like the one they had just been served. She wondered if she would get 12 dollars a month or just 8. She remembered the talk that had gone the rounds just after evacuation had been announced. They were going to be paid as high as ninety dollars a month for working in the camps.

"Not bad," George had said. But Tom Yamada, who was a foreman on the Hunter ranch, had sniffed, "It's little enough. I'm getting over three hundred a month this year. And look at yourself. With that stand of beets and the price of sugar where it's going, you ought to have cleaned up plenty. Probably would have made my three hundred look like chicken feed." And then later on there had been the announcement that they would be paid the same as an army private. The loud and vociferous protests from an outraged population had reached the authorities and the final decision to pay 16, 12, and 8 dollars a month for evacuee labor had quickly followed.

"That's only 21 cents a day, 3-1/2 cents an hour, for guys like me," Bill had protested, but he seemed to have landed some kind of an administrative job that paid 16 dollars, which meant six cents an hour.

Tad came running back with Ken a minute before seven. They'd been playing softball. Teru looked out the window after the noise of people hurrying back into their compartments had quieted down. The barrack alleys were deserted. A high fog had rolled in during the afternoon with the five o'clock wind from the west, and it was gloomy outside. Across the way, so alone she could almost reach her with a whisper, a girl of about fifteen was looking out an uncurtained window of the next barrack. A black, desolate look pinched weary hollows into her young face. She was staring in the direction of town where the room lights could be faintly seen. Teru turned away.

The quiet outside and the four walls crowding in so closely turned their room into a prison. Only the bars were lacking. They sat on their cots waiting. They looked at each other now and then, but even Sally said nothing. She reached up to turn on the light but the feeble, yellowish glow from the tiny globe only accentuated the feeling of murky gloom.

Their mother's voice broke into the depressing silence. "Father must be going through something like this too." Her voice was barely above a whisper and invited no comment but it brought a picture of their father huddled despondently in some prison cell. Sally immediately got up and went to her. She smiled encouragingly. Two letters had come from the North Dakota internment camp. Meager, one-page letters written in pencil on a piece of blue-lined, tablet paper. He was well and that was all he seemed able to say. At one place a whole passage had been partly cut.

There was a loud peremptory knocking at the door. Teru got up but Henry Tanaka poked his head into the room before she could move. Henry was in 80-A. "Everybody here?" he asked in a loud, authoritative voice.

"Sure, big shot," Sally said. Henry looked down at his chart and carefully checked them off. "Ayame Noguchi. Teru Noguchi. Sally Noguchi. Tadao Noguchi." He turned to go, paused, and said, "All settled?"

His voice was so irritatingly bossy and smug that Teru felt a childish urge to say, who're you? But she said nothing.

"Gaze silently upon the evidence before your eyes. But Silently."

Sally said from her perch on a half-empty duffle bag. She wrinkled her nose in disgust when he had gone. "When I went after the broom he tried to make me think he was doing me a favor lending it to me. The goon." She added, "he told me to bring it right back."

"Did you?"

"No. I passed it on to Mrs. Nakata."

"Good." Teru wished someone else had moved into the end apartment. She preferred having nothing to do with their recent visitor. During registration she'd seen Henry walking back and forth trying to look so important and she'd thought fleetingly that he could very well have been the one who had turned in their father's name to the FBI. He was one of the half dozen Nisei who had gotten together and set themselves up as spokesmen for the Valley Japanese -- without consulting anyone but themselves. They'd been cordially disliked not only for their high-handed assumption of authority but for their policy of directing the finger of suspicion away from themselves by letting it rest on the Issei through default. The Issei had fumed but they could say nothing. Henry's group had also tried to draw a hard and fast line between Issei and Nisei. Teru suspected that they had distributed the "I am an American Citizen" signs that a few Nisei had posted in their display windows. The signs were all right but Teru didn't like the way they were used. It was wrong to try to separate arbitrarily

Issei from Nisei. They were flesh and blood. Maybe it was all right for people like Henry who had no Issei parents or had "risen above them" in the process of setting themselves up in their businesses and professions. Maybe -- but not for Teru. She looked out the window again. People were gradually trickling out of their compartments. A girl was standing by the window, alone. Teru tapped on the window and she looked up, instantly startled into recognition.

"Teru, wait," she called and disappeared. A moment later Teru was opening the door for the dark-eyed girl. "I was so glad when I saw you," the girl sobbed in relief. She had been one of Teru's Sunday School students before the curfew. "I feel terrible. None of my friends are here. They're all coming in tomorrow." "The Nakatas are next door."

"Itchy?" Teru nodded.

"I saw June Katai going into Barrrack 75," Sally said.

"Let's go see her."

"I can't. Mom said I can't go anywhere tonight, except here. She said to hurry back because you would be busy." She noticed the patches on the wall. "I better get back and fill the cracks too. You can see right into the next room through one of our walls. They're all bachelors."

Sally was looking at her in surprise. "Gee, curtains too? We didn't bring any." When she'd gone Sally looked at Teru with a flabbergasted look.

"Did you notice?" Teru nodded smiling, "She did talk more than usual didn't she."

"More than usual?," Sally echoed, "that's the first time I ever heard her put two sentences together."

"It must have been pretty lonely out there in the country" Teru said. But even with the patches and the curtains Sally refused to undress for bed without turning out the light. Teru could hear her fumbling in the darkness. Sally's cot was next to Teru's. Then Tad's. Then "Ayame's." It was a pretty name, Ayame. Teru had felt a little strange hearing it spoken out loud. She couldn't remember ever hearing their father call her that. She wondered why. He didn't use endearing terms either. Sometimes his language sounded rude when she translated it into English and yes, she knew that it was never meant or taken as being rude. Language could cause some misunderstanding. She remembered her first impression of Japan-educated Saburo Naito. She'd thought him such a sissy after hearing his half-lisping speech at a Young People's conference last year. He'd slicked back his hair every half minute and kept wiggling his body in an effeminate way. Then later she heard him speaking in Japanese and was amazed at the transformation. He'd stood straight and composed and his voice was warm and strong. There were other things. "Anata" was often translated into English as Honorable Sir. It sounded silly calling a person that; but it was really one of the most beautiful words in the Japanese language when said with the right inflection. It was dearest, darling, and sweetheart -- all in one. Was it language or was it color? Why were they here now, sleeping under the occasional prying sweep of searchlights that flashed into their compartments? Being protected from their fellow citizens like they were told? No, being watched. The machine guns pointed in at them. They didn't point outward at a threatening populace. A fine kind of protection! Sally was still awake. Teru knew when she saw a wet glitter in the darkness. She reached out and held the hand that lay whitely on top of the blanket. She pressed it comfortingly. Sally held her hand hard.

"It'll be all right," Teru whispered. She could feel the tensing in Sally's slim body.

"Oh, Teru."

"Get a good sleep and it won't be so bad in the morning." She could feel more than see Tad turning over and peering their way.

"Let's make the best of what they give us. Show them we can take it."

Sally pulled Teru's hand against her cheek. It was moist. She went to sleep like that. Teru's arm was cramped and cold when the chill wind sweeping up from the cracks finally forced her to pull away from the trusting grasp. She lay awake wondering what was in store for them. She could hear Mrs. Kimura talking softly to the baby. She could hear a girl saying good night in the next barrack. A truck rumbled by on the highway. She dozed off. She was at the end of a long line of people that kept growing longer and longer. The unfortunate people at the head of the line were getting only a half slice of bread but nobody dropped out. Itchy was there staring at her with a woebegone expression on his hollow, starved face. Tad was sitting down to conserve energy. It got colder and colder and she woke with a start to find her mother bending over her with another blanket. It was rough to her touch and it took a moment for her to realize that she wasn't in her own bed back home. Her shoulders were cold and her neck was stiff from sleeping without a pillow. They'd packed them into a cardboard carton but no one had been able to carry it. She fell into a cold restless sleep.

CHAPTER 6

A baby was crying. Baby? Teru sleepily tried to orient herself. She opened her eyes. To bare rafters and a cavernous roof. She must be in a barn. She was instantly awake -- painfully. It was cold and foggy and still dark outside but her mother was already dressed and poking in one of the suitcases. She immediately hopped out of bed. There was no comfort in the cold, soggy blankets. She dressed quickly, her teeth chattering, and went outside to wash. A dozen people were ahead of her, splashing in the open air "horse trough." Teru waited behind a tiny girl who was barely able to thrust her head over the side. Her checkered red pinafore was sopping wet with water splashing up from the trough.

"Phooey," she grinned up at Teru, "I'm all wet."

Teru got wet from another direction. She bent over to wash, and a big drop of icy water descended down her neck. She gasped and jerked around, but the middle-aged lady behind her couldn't possibly have done it. She looked up. Big shivery drops were running together and dripping all along the eaves of the roof which extended just far enough to make it miserable for the washers. The fog was turning into a heavy mist almost like rain. There was no escaping the dirty drippings. They slid off the eaves into her hair, down her neck, on her back. Teru only half brushed her teeth and washed as fast as she could. More and more sleepy-eyed people were disgorged from the boxlike barracks. She'd never seen so many people with hair uncombed and faces swollen and unwashed.

She passed Mrs. Goto carrying towel, toothbrush, and soap. Sanae was only a couple years older than Teru, but right after high school she'd married an Issei ten years older than herself and seemed to have taken on some of his years. They'd called her "Sunshine" in school but calling her that now would be making fun of the straggly bun in back of her head and the heavy hips that had borne two bouncing baby boys.

"Good morning, Sanae," Teru greeted. Sanae stopped surprised.

"Teru, I haven't seen you in ages. Where are you?"

"80-C. And you?"

"84-B. Terrible isn't it?" Teru wiggled assent. There was a coldly wet reminder right at the small of her back where her dress felt uncomfortably dirty.

"I look a sight," Sanae said. "How do you manage to look so pretty as soon as you get up?" Teru wrinkled her nose.

Sanae sighed, "Lucky girl. A lot of men are going to be awfully disappointed when they see how the rest of us females look at six o'clock in the morning." Then abruptly, "Are you married yet?" Teru shook her head quickly and thought of George. His last letter hadn't said much. Only that he wished they could get settled permanently some place so they could think in terms of the future again.

Sanae looked at her wonderingly. "It doesn't seem possible nobody has grabbed you yet. I'll have to speak to my husband about it."

"Don't you dare," Teru said.

Sanae laughed. "I'd better hurry. I have the toothpaste. See you at breakfast."

Sally and Tad were still curled up in their cots. "Time to get up."

Sally opened her eyes and closed them again. "It's dark yet," she protested.

"No breakfasts in bed here. Better get up or you'll go hungry."

"Oh." Sally sat up and shivered. "It's cold."

"Tad." She reached over and yanked at his blankets. They ran to wash and Teru helped her mother make the beds. Itchy caught up to them on their way to the mess hall. He walked with an exaggerated limp favoring his left arm.

"What's the matter?," Sally asked.

"Those typhoid shots," Itchy indicated his left side. "Boy, I was cooking with fever last night. How's yours?"

"Mine? It's perfectly normal," Sally hesitated. She winked at Teru. They hadn't had to take the typhoid shots. Dr. Kato had remembered giving them before evacuation.

"You say you had a fever? And your arm is sore?" Itchy nodded.

"It's red and all swollen up."

"Your father and mother and the rest of the family too?"

"Not so much," Itchy admitted, "but none of us could sleep much last night."

Sally shook her head doubtfully. "Must be something wrong with you. Maybe you're not normal."

"What do you mean? Maybe YOU'RE not normal -- for not showing a reaction."

Sally turned to Teru, then Tad. "Did you have a fever last night?" They shook their heads. She asked "Ayame" who said, no, while she wondered what it was all about. She hadn't been paying much attention. She was wishing her husband was there to put up some kind of closet and make a few chairs. She felt so lost and bewildered without him. Sally clucked her tongue sympathetically, "You see,it's YOU who's not normal."

Itchy felt his arm carefully. He winced and a worried frown stayed on his face.

"Hey, Doc!" He suddenly spied Dr. Kato on the other side of the barrack and went running that way. Sally snickered, grossly satisfied with herself.

Itchy rejoined them a few barracks down. "Hey, YOU'RE the one who's not normal," he said. "Doc says it's natural to have a little fever and soreness." But he kept asking everyone he knew, "How's your arm?" Most answered with a groan and a commiserating look and Itchy seemed satisfied though he kept looking at Sally doubtfully.

They took their places at the end of the long, bleary-eyed line in front of the mess hall. Breakfast consisted of "dishwater" coffee, cold cereal, and two pieces of soggy toast. They shivered in the cold hall. They sat down on the hard benches lining the tables and gulped their food down. There was no relish in the eating. It was just food to give them energy to carry on the day's work. When they'd finished, it lay heavy and cold in their stomachs. They were outside again less than five minutes after they'd reached the head of the line. Only a few lingered in the cold and fog. Most immediately disappeared into their compartments.

Sally poked here and there without results and finally asked, "Where's that map they gave us yesterday?" Teru found it in an overcoat pocket. "That must be it." Sally pointed to a small isolated building labeled "latrine" on the map. Neither knew what the word meant but the location and the absence of anything else faintly resembling what they wanted made it appear the only possibility.

Tad enlightened them when they paused indecisively "We had those things at our scout camp." A girl of about Teru's age came out of the latrine as they rushed in. She smiled weakly and gave them an embarrassed look. Teru opened the door and her nose flared in distaste at the sudden stench. Her eyes took in the long, benchlike affair with the square holes in them, and she stopped in consternation. She looked at Sally and saw her own dismay mirrored in Sally's face.

Immediately after cleaning up their room Sally left to see June Katai, and Teru walked to the administration building. Bill wasn't there but good-looking Setsuko Sato was the receptionist and showed Teru to the camp director's office. Mr. Budd was in his early forties, with premature grey hair and a slow smile that put her at ease right away. He looked at her with interest while he asked her about her experience, then turned to consult a sheet of paper when she told him she had still been going to J.C. His voice held a trace of a Texas drawl.

"Your school recommends you very highly. You can start today if you wish." Teru was willing since there was nothing else to do.

"We're all new at this so we'll have to go slow at first. The girls will tell you more what is expected of you." The "girls" were all from the Salinas area. Kay Hori and Rose Noda she knew quite well. They'd been working as secretaries in the junior college and high school offices before evacuation. Masako Shiba and Florence Koyuma she'd seen only now and then when they made infrequent visits home from their civil service jobs in Sacramento. Yaeko Ito had had a job with the Mitsui firm in San Francisco. Their names had all been handed down for their excellent scholastic records in school, and there were few people in Salinas who hadn't at least heard of them. They were the envied few who had actually made use of their school training. Teru's group had always looked upon them with a tinge of awe. They were doing what they themselves hoped to do when they finished school. It was so much better than helping on the farm developing "daikon" legs and a hard, calloused body, or clerking in some store at pittance wages.

Teru felt young and inadequate at first but quickly found after a fumbling start that she could take dictation and type almost as well as Kay, who had the reputation of having been the fastest typist to have graduated from Salinas Junior College. But it was some time before she could shake off the feeling of incompetence that came when she saw the other girls carrying out their work with their "professional" efficiency. The rest of the

Japanese from the Salinas area came into the center that afternoon. Then the influx started from the surrounding districts. Watsonville. Monterey. Hollister. Gilroy. San Martin. San Juan. Gonzales. San Felipe. San Ysidro.

Teru had never seen so many Japanese faces before. It was odd at first seeing only Japanese wherever she went -- to wash, to eat, to mail her letters.

Kay Mori said, "It must be like being in Japan."

Florence, who had spent two years in Japan, answered, "In a way, yes. But something is missing. It seems the same and yet it's different somehow."

"How?," Kay wanted to know.

"I can't put my finger on it," Florence said doubtfully, "but it might be the people. They're not the same."

"I'm glad to hear that," Rose said from her desk by the window. "It curls my hair to be linked with those barbarians over there."

"I didn't mean it that way," Florence said defiantly. "Those 'barbarians' were nice. I won't say they were any better, though I might, but they were more courteous and polite. More polished, you might say. No, maybe that's not the right word. More old, more settled, more traditional, I don't know. They're different. Even the lower-class people. I remember the motor bus girls. A lump used to come to my throat watching them working so hard and so cheerfully for so little pay. They take so much pleasure in the little things. Maybe because they have to. You'd think that with the low standard of living they'd be unhappy all the time but it's not so. Sometimes I used to think they squeezed more pleasure out of life than we did in spite of our cars and our radios."

"You sound like you like Japan," Rose said.

"I do," Florence said cooly. "What wouldn't I give to be there now."

"Not me," Rose declined emphatically and continued, "all these Japanese are getting in my hair. I never saw such ill-mannered, nasty, busybodies."

Yaeko Ito stopped typing. "Most of us in here are farmers," she interrupted, her face flushing slightly. "That may be why we seem so crude to you city people. And maybe we can't help ourselves with the kind of living quarters they've given us."

"I have it," Florence said triumphantly. "It's because we're so Americanized. That's the difference. In here would be little different if all of Salinas Valley instead of just Japanese had been evacuated. Look, we talk American. We act American. We are Americans. It'd be strange if we weren't, after being exposed to it all these years in school and at work. They'd call it indoctrination or the making of an American, you are just as surely molded into a good German, a good American or what have you."

Teru listened carefully without venturing any comment. If they had asked her if she wished she were in Japan, too, her answer would have been a definite no. Japan was simply outside her ken. She knew no life but America and Japan was still a foreign country. And yet, the thought of the last few months intruded a doubting whisper into her mind. Everything America did was making it clear they weren't wanted, and the thought of living where they weren't wanted wasn't an inviting one. It was all too believable now that they had been merely tolerated because of their economic usefulness. They hadn't been really accepted for better and for worse. The first days were fun in one way. It was almost like homecoming week. All her classmates from Monterey and Watsonville came stepping curiously off the buses the first week. Teru watched their reactions to their surroundings with mixed feelings of amusement and sympathy. She tried to steer them gently over the first shock of looking into the barren, barnlike compartments that would be their home. She went with them to their first showers. She made a point of going with tiny Esther Mitsuda because she knew Esther would never be able to reach the faucets to turn on the water. The showers apparently had been built for six-footers and Teru herself could barely turn on the water by getting on the tips of her toes. She was much in demand whenever she was in the shower room.

Especially from some of the older women so stooped over from hard work they could no longer straighten their backs. Teru found herself looking at their crooked bodies wondering what life had held for them. She'd gotten only the barest glimpse through her mother of the kind of life they'd led. They'd probably come to America when quite young. Sometimes they'd known the men they were marrying. Sometimes they'd even been intimate with them before they'd left for America. But often they'd known of their husbands only through hearsay and they'd been strangers when they'd gotten on the train that carried them to some rented plot of land, an un-painted farmhouse, and a nuptial bed. There had probably been a flurry of shopping for strange looking clothing and tearful laying away of their kimono and dreams. And all too quickly they'd probably found themselves rising before the sun to cook and wash and then take their places in the fields beside men they gradually grew to accept as their husbands. It was life and it was living and they accepted their lot with patience for soon there were children for whom the future must be made secure. The sore and aching backs, the blistered and calloused hands, the patched and ugly clothes their own children were ashamed to be seen with. What a small price to pay when they were seeing their sons and their daughters going on -- to high school -- to college. What matters if Sunday was just another day of backbreaking toil? They were getting an education. Someday he would get a fine job and take care of their parents in their old age.

And suddenly. Why was Taro working in the produce shed?

Why wasn't he sitting behind a nice shiny desk in his new suit? Why was he here now, confined with them behind barbed wire? He'd always explained so carefully to them that in America everyone was free and equal. They'd fought a bloody war to prove that point. Innocent until proven guilty, was one way he'd put it....

Teru wrote George. The lack of privacy is what we miss the most. We eat together, we walk together, we even think together. We're always at each other's elbows. If a door is left open or a curtain is lacking or isn't drawn, every passerby invades your privacy. You don't try to look but everything is so cramped and close, it's unavoidable. You can't go walking down the barrack alleys staring straight ahead. People would think you're awfully stuck up for you don't know who you're going to run into next. We can not only hear every word our neighbors say but at night we can even hear conversations in the next barrack. Mrs. Kimura was over this morning apologizing for her baby's crying so early in the morning but what is there to do? The baby is probably cold and miserable and can't rationalize like we do. At first, I told Sally to picture herself as roughing it in the mountains somewhere, but it doesn't work. This kind of life may be all right for a weekend of fishing but when we don't know how long it is going to last, the thought of having to endure more is almost unbearable. And I don't like those people who say, think of the poor soldiers in the front lines. We're not soldiers, and we're not in the front lines. If I were a man and free, I'd willingly take my place in defense of my country, but I'm not a man and I'm not free and I'm not willingly submitting to this evacuation because I know that it's not right and is falsely described when it's called a patriotic duty. It's all very primitive and not near anything we had pictured. We didn't dream we'd be treated like this. They must regard us as an inferior people or something. As though we have no feelings. Certainly, I could never wish this kind of a humiliating life on anyone. Tad brought home this box I'm using as a table to write on and he's put up a shelf and a length of rope to hang our clothes from but some people have nothing while others have already made chairs and tables from scraps of lumber they manage to pick up somehow....

Teru was typing out the next day's menu when she heard her name called over the loudspeaker system. "Teru Noguchi. Visitor." She banged the keys hard on the final, maddening entry and hurried to the reception hall, thinking it must be Janet. It was Janet. She jumped up excitedly when Teru walked into the long room where several other *Hakujin* were talking to camp inmates. It was like the reception room for a penitentiary.

"Your letter came this morning," Janet said. Her eyes were wide with wonder. "I never thought it was anything like this. They just told me the only visiting we could do was right here. I can't go inside."

"There isn't much to see."

Teru had felt her heart start beating happily inside, but suddenly she felt uncomfortable when she thought of the ugly quarters they lived in. She wouldn't have wanted Janet to see their compartment for anything. Their morning wash was spread all over the room. It would have been too degrading. She saw it all again through Janet's eyes -- as she herself had seen it her first day in camp.

"At least you have good meals," Janet said, smiling brightly, as she seemed to sense Teru's discomfiture. "I was in the school library this morning and read an article in the Watsonville paper how wonderful the meals were. It sounded pretty appetizing."

Teru averted her eyes. She didn't know what to say. The whole camp had been in an angry uproar over Henry Tanaka's letter to the Watonsville paper. Teru had been mad, too. That was why she had been seething when she typed out the menu. Creamed cod and potatoes a l'Orchiodoise. Which actually would bring on their plates a stinking chunk of dried cod and half a tasteless potato. She still couldn't understand what had prompted Henry to perpetuate such a falsehood. Maybe he thought he was being patriotic. The food had been terrible. Some meals had been even worse than the first one. Last night her whole meal consisted of a paper-thin slice of spam, six peas, a spoon of rice, and tea. The night before, one canned sardine three inches long and rice and tea. The only ones who had enough to eat were those fortunate enough to have electric hot plates and friends on the outside to bring in food. The rest were lining up in front of the mess halls as much as an hour and a half before mealtime because those first served seemed to get a little more to eat. There were those few, too, who went to two and three different mess halls each meal.

"But it's not true," Teru finally said.

"No?" Janet seemed surprised and a little taken aback.

"Henry Tanaka is the most hated man in this camp for what he wrote. They give us terrifically fancy menus and the meals sound good until they're dished out on your plate and you have to eat it."

"Oh." Janet looked at her strangely. "If you say so."

Teru knew that Janet believed her and yet from that moment she felt unwillingly that their friendship would never be the same again. They were being exposed to such totally different environments and interpretations and as time passed they would inevitably grow away from each other. It hurt to see the future so starkly and when it was time for Janet to go, Teru could barely speak for the lump in her throat.

"I'll be back again," Janet said, and Teru was sure she would be. But next time she would find it harder to understand the unwanted influences that were changing Teru as slowly and as surely as the winds bend the oaks. "Bye."

Teru watched her go, then walked slowly back through the door with the neat lettered sign. "No visitors allowed beyond this door."

CHAPTER 7

A cold drizzling rain started to fall the week following Janet's visit. By the second day it turned the black adobe underfoot into a soggy quagmire that threatened to suck off oxfords and saddle shoes at every careless step. The more hardy scoffed at pneumonia and took off their shoes and rolled up their trousers while the more fortunate ventured forth in all manner of boots. The short walk to the mess hall became a slipping, sliding, shoulder-grabbing affair. The lone laundry at the south end of the camp was inaccessible to twenty-nine hundred of the three thousand evacuees. Mr. Yabe's laundry agency did a flourishing business. Yaeko wished she lived nearer the laundry. Florence disagreed. "You people can let your wash pile up for a while. I have to walk out here twice a day. Look." She exhibited mudsplattered stockings above a neatly turned ankle that had been protected by galoshes.

"They ought to at least lay some boards or something." Masako Shiba joined them. "I wish they'd do something about the wash trough, too," she said petulantly. "I couldn't get near the thing this morning. It's impossible to hold an umbrella and wash your face at the same time."

Rose said smugly, "We go after our water with a bucket and wash at home."

"No bucket," Masako said succinctly.

"This sounds like a pet gripe session so I'll put in a bid for a good tub bath," Yaeko remarked. The only time she'd been away from her steaming, country-style baths had been her past year in San Francisco where she never got accustomed to the lukewarm porcelain tubs. "These showers leave me cold, especially when the hot water runs out. Which is often by the time I get there."

"What I dread is next week," Florence said, "with nature due for a visit. There's no place to *nani* (no privacy for personal hygiene). My brothers are always running in and out of our two by four room, and in the latrine, well, you know how it is in that place."

"Uh huh," Yaeko embarrassedly nodded assent. "Those times are the worst. I don't think the army took account of us. This is a man's world."

"Yeah," Masako added cynically, "poor Michiko."

Teru felt her ears grow warm. She'd known Michiko ever since she started to go to church.

"Who was it?" Yaeko asked. No one knew.

The night watchman who flashed his light in on the oblivious pair in a corner of the mess hall described him as being kind of hefty and wearing a bright plaid shirt. "But no pants," he said subsquently. He seemed to have looked longer at the girl from his more detailed description. "She had an upswept hairdo, big sparkly eyes, and a nice chassis."

The story had spread fast and everyone who had ever noticed trim, sparkle-eyed Michiko and the practically non-existence of upswept hairdos among Nisei girls focused no further than 79-C where Michiko lived right across from the Noguchis. To be on the safe side Rose put her hair in bangs.

Teru stared curiously at Michiko after she heard the story at the office. It was right after supper and Bill had walked home with her. Bill often came looking for his mother around meal time and always stayed even when his mother wasn't there. Tonight she was going with him to the graduation dance. She didn't especially want to go but wasn't able to think of any good reason not to. Bill stared covertly, too. Michiko squirmed under their innocently searching eyes. She thought in panic, God, even Teru knows. Why didn't I stop him?

"Hello, Teru, Bill," she said and encouraged by the firmness of her voice, continued, "having to walk all the way to the wash trough to do dishes is the worst part of eating at home."

"Isn't it though?" Teru was surprised that there should be nothing different about Michiko.

"She's a cool cucumber," Bill said admiringly and looked at Teru to see if she knew what he was thinking about.

Music throbbed from deep throated radios set up at opposite ends of the mess hall. Gay crepe-paper streamers and soft-colored lights made them forget the drab mess hall lines, almost. Bill remarked that they should have worked for the atmosphere of a barn dance which would have been easy to do.

"But we wanted it as much as possible like it would have been outside," Sally said. "One doesn't graduate every day."

Teru looked at her and thought, it would have been such a big event. Both of us graduating at the same time. I hope you like the charm bracelet we got for your graduation present. It's nothing like what you would have gotten if Father were here, but please don't be too disappointed. Bill danced smoothly. Teru's friends were all there. It was almost like home. Missing were the newly bought graduation suits and the flowing formals all neatly packed away in moth balls at home. Slacks, sweaters, saddle shoes, and bobby socks were most in evidence. Present were too many strangers who had "crashed." They cut in on Teru every time she danced with anyone but Bill. He glared belligerently when they came near, and they steered sheepishly away from his football shoulders. He'd been regular guard on the high school varsity and looked as tough as his all-conference selection indicated. Two years of successfully taking his ailing father's place and shouldering the family decisions had made him, at twenty, aggressive and self-reliant, more mature than George who was his senior by three years.

He held her warmly close. "You're easily the best looking girl here to-night."

"Ah, and you're the best looking man," Teru smiled demurely up at the hard jaw and the dark eyes set deep in a sternly angled face.

"I'm not kidding," Bill answered, and his heart was in his eyes to prove it. Teru shook her head....

Dances and parties crowded the weekends and continued into the work days. The routine of dawn breakfasts followed by day-long toil, or early morning work before school then school and more work, no longer limited them to Saturday nights three or four times a year. Buddhist groups, Christian groups, clubs, newly formed center groups scheduled their dances in rapid succession. The "country" boys crowded the mess halls, trying hard to make up for lost time and opportunity. The Issei looked on in bewilderment, not knowing whether to approve or disapprove. There were always the four or more unfortunate "incidents." Mr. Nakata, who had no daughters, said, "If we don't let them have healthy fun, they'll turn to worse things." Mr. Nakaguchi imposed a seven o'clock curfew on Alice. She wasn't to go out after roll call. Mr. Omada crowed, "I'm lucky. My daughter doesn't know how to dance." Which was strange because Fay was the leading exponent of jump and jive among the high school set. For the most part, they finally ignored the matter uneasily and retired into their rooms to discuss the war and take comfort in the steady progress of the Japanese army. The rationing, the high cost of living passed them by. The seeing off of friends and relatives with every induction call had ended with Pearl Harbor. They had fallen off the pace.

The sewage overflowed from the girls' latrine. It came up through the floor and formed puddles in front of both doors. To those who had to teeter across them, the lack of wider planks to lay across the puddles of sewage was more important than the lack of rubber on tires. The inefficiency of the local administration and the self-interest and petty bickering of the Evacuee Council were of paramount concern. Masako summed up the attitude towards the *Hakujin* personnel with the unkindly, all-encompassing, "What can you expect of a bunch of Okies and Arkies?"

Fay said, "Oh, Mr. Rudd is not bad even if he doesn't seem to know what it's all about. The rest of them may mean well, but...."

The Evacuee Council was a sore point with the Issei. It was composed of practically the same group who before evacuation set themselves up as spokesmen for all Japanese in the Valley.

"If we oppose them they'll tell the administration that we're radicals," Mr. Tanaka complained. Only those who spoke good English and were citizens had any chance of getting the ear of the Administration and the Issei got nowhere. Loud-voiced, pro-Japanese "Cooky" Pete threatened to beat up every member of the Council once he got them "outside." It was funny because before the evacuation "Cooky" had threatened to beat up the same individuals once he got them "inside."

Teru went to one council meeting to take notes when Kay broke her glasses and had trouble getting new lenses. The whole meeting revolved around the necessity of curbing private enterprise in the center. Some thought it was necessary to stop Goro Ikuta from distributing newspapers in the camp. Dentist Dr. Sato exclaimed angrily, "We've got to stop private enterprise in here. We're got to stop that paper peddling."

Teru took it carefully down, thinking bitterly, why pick on the paper selling? Just because you don't get along with Goro? What about your friend Mr. Yaka's agency for the Consolidated Laundry, and your pal Jimmy's trinket selling? Why don't you bring those up? They're making real profits. So far, Ken and Tad who sold papers for Goro had not yet made enough to buy the baseball gloves they were saving for. They made a cent a paper and Goro a half cent.

Henry Tanaka stooged for Dr. Sato. "Doc's right. We've got to pass an ordinance." The ordinance was passed, and Tad and Ken had to pool their money to buy a "partnership" glove.

Pay day brought a flurry of excitement. People who had been so angry when they first saw the wage scale announced in the papers lined up early for their month's pay. Teru wanted to frame her twelve dollar check but she used it to buy overshoes for her mother, some canned food, and a five dollar book of script.

Later, she heard that the books of script were to have been distributed free; but nothing was said about it and the Issei found what satisfaction they could in labeling the Council a spineless bunch of stooges for doing nothing. They carried home their eight dollar checks for their "unskilled" labor in mess halls and as janitors and night watchmen. Their sons and daughters grandly exhibited their twelve dollar checks for "skilled" labor. They were perturbed and upset by this visible evidence of complete reversal in the family order. Those still in the prime of their life and earning power accepted with qualms the virtual retirement into which the older ones immediately settled upon entering camp. Accepted because of a resignation to their lot as enemy aliens. They were reminded of the stigma of their status at every turn. When they asked for representation on the Council. When they complained of being ignored. For bitter comfort they turned to talk of their experiences before evacuation. They compared the losses they incurred in selling out and the money they would have made if they could only have harvested the present crop. Now for the past several years they had sunk all their profits into machinery and improvements and were just beginning to visualize good years for their old age. How Mr. Kimura borrowed and scraped together twenty thousand dollars as down payment on 100 acres of land with the expectation of paying the balance through farming operations in the following years. He was defaulting on the rest of the payment since he could find no one to buy his equity. The one who had sold him the land scared off interested farmers.

When they plumbed the depths of self-pity they found solace in telling each other of the short-wave broadcast of their Emperor expressing his great sorrow that the war would inevitably cause hardships to Japanese subjects abroad. It was so thoughtful of their Emperor to take special notice of them in such a time of crisis. With tears in their eyes, all gratefully acknowledged the promised protection of the Japanese government. There was nowhere else to turn. Pro-American sentiment was rare. Anyone who bitterly laid the Pearl Harboring of his life to a dastardly and treacherous Japan quickly found himself persona nongrata.

Sometimes to his intense surprise, because officially almost all were friendly to the cause of the United States, Mr. Kimura refused to accept the offer of the American government to place his family on the Gripsholm for return to Japan. So did Fumi's father. Only in their homes did they give as their reason the fear that the repatriation offer was simply a trick of the American government to secure what amounted to an outright expression of loyalty to Japan and thus lay open the road to prosecution.

Mr. Terada had only daughters and feared the going might be economically difficult in wartime Japan. Mr. Morita refused to go on the Gripsholm because of the money he had tied up in California. Both vehemently that they intended to return to Japan as soon as the war ended.

Nisei were less concerned with the war than with their future. Among her own group, Teru noted increasing distrust of the evacuation order. The growing agitation to keep them locked up for the duration seemed suspiciously part of a larger scheme to force them completely out of California. It fell into too neat a pattern. In the forefront of public attention was the Growers-Shippers Combine, bitter rivals of Japanese lettuce growing interests. They indiscriminately hurled charges of dishonesty, disloyalty, and undesirability. They hired a propagandist at 10,000 dollars a year to lobby in Washington for banishment of Japanese. A Chamber of Commerce representative was sent to the Middle West to warn against allowing any Japanese to settle in their midst. Nisei listened hopefully for word from their friends and former associates. There was only silence or condemnation. A district representative to Congress who had formerly posed as their best friend became violently abusive on the floor of Congress. A farmer who had been a constant visitor to the Motoyama home to ask, What kind of seed is best? When do you think I should plant? Do you think it's time to irrigate? Will you come to look at my lettuce? Could I borrow your cultivator for a few days? A few days more? Could I use your boys to harvest? I don't have a place to house them, wrote a letter and sent copies to all the local newspapers. "We don't want Japs in California. They're no good. I ought to know. I had to live next to one for five years."

They waited in vain for answers to their letters, even from those they had left property with to be disposed of in a better market. Nowhere in the Valley was a public voice raised to protest the removal or their continued incarceration. It was a cold, friendless countryside they left behind when they packed their belongings a second time and boarded the train that would bundle them away to the Colorado River Relocation Project in Arizona, to Poston.

Questions thickened on every tongue with the spreading of rumors of their coming transfer. Young and old pored eagerly over the rare, contraband maps that unexpectedly turned up. A few heard an on-the-scene broadcast from Poston but they could pass on only a smattering of information. It was located near a town called Parker on the Colorado River Indian reservation and that was as close as they could place it on the map. The whole region was dotted to indicate desert topography. The Colorado River flowed somewhere nearby and there was a lot of mesquite, whatever that was. Some said a shrub, some a tree.

Everyone under forty suddenly wanted a pair of sun glasses; straw hats were in demand; orders were placed for coolers and electric fans.

Teru, Sally, and Tad bought dark glasses but when it came to a cooler which cost anywhere from thirty-five to sixty dollars, they hesitated. Ayame first mentioned it, and Sally looked questioningly at Teru. "Do we have enough money?," she asked cautiously.

Teru nodded, "Just about enough. Bill says he'll order one for us together with his, but I don't know whether we should."

"Let's save it for something else," Sally said.

"We don't know how long we will be in Arizona," Ayame said, "so it is hard to say."

"We'll be needing other things too, won't we?," Tad asked.

"Clothes, hats, and things to eat."

"We have to keep sending some to Dad too," Teru said. She'd learned from Bill that internees at North Dakota got no money at all.

When Teru told Bill, he exploded, "You're crazy, it's hot as Hades down there. You can't live without a cooler."

"The Kimuras aren't getting one and if their baby can stand it, we certainly should be able to."

"They're different. They probably can't...." He looked at Teru with sudden understanding. Teru squirmed under his gaze.

"We'll get one later if it's really too hot,"she defended herself lamely.

"They may not be so easy to get later. I'll order two just in case."

"No," she protested quickly.

"Someone else may want it," he said, and she was confused into silence.

The week before they were scheduled to leave, Ayame began to feel severe pains in her stomach. Teru took her to see Dr. Kato at the clinic when she was told he wouldn't make a house call. At the clinic he looked at Ayame perfunctorily and said, "It's nothing much.

Probably something she ate."

"She's been in pain since the day before yesterday," Teru said.

"Come back next week if it still hurts," Dr. Kato said in dismissal.

"But we leave for Arizona in four days."

"There will be doctors down there," Dr. Kato said coldly.

"Couldn't you give her something to ease the pain? She couldn't sleep much last night."

"If I babied along every little stomach ache I'd never get anything done."

"I'll be all right," Ayame said wanly.

"Of course, goodbye."

Ayame turned to go but Teru furiously stood her ground. "It's true then," she said seethingly. "You WON'T give more than sixteen dollars worth of service."

"Teru!," Ayame said alarmed. Teru glared defiantly at Dr. Kato daring him to deny the charge. He shrugged his shoulders and turned his back to them. Teru stared at the back of his head, a long bitter minute. She led her mother back to their barrack.

It WAS true then. Mrs. Kimura had told her how indifferent and unsympathetic Dr. Kato was when her baby had the colic, but Teru had laid it to a misinterpretation of his habitual gruffness.

It was foggy when they left Salinas. The kind of cool weather that made the firm heads of lettuce Salinas was famous for. "See you in a couple of days," they told each other, but they said their goodbyes with the lingering sorrow of a last farewell, weighted down with an unamiable fear of what lay ahead of them. "I told you we'd be out of there by Independence Day," Fay Ikeda announced bitterly in the bus that carried them away from the rodeo grounds. They looked back at the cramped huddle of barracks that had been their home for almost three months. They looked back and hated to leave, even though it had held so much misery. It was their last hold on the homes that had taken a lifetime to build.

CHAPTER 8

The Fourth of July found their train rattling through desert country. The windows were pushed up as far as their rusty grooves would permit. The hot, dry air fanned through their crowded coach. They sprawled and shifted uncomfortably on the lumpy seats. They looked at the soldiers guarding the exits. They eyed the barren, forbidding desert and felt the growing hotness. The vague uneasiness looked out of their eyes and at each other. Teru anxiously kept an eye on her mother. All night, she jerked sleeplessly to the steady clanking of the rails and twice heard a suppressed gasp from where her mother curled restlessly on the seat they shared. Her eyes were closed and sunk deep in their sockets. "Is there something I can do?" Teru asked when she opened lusterless eyes to stare out the window.

"I'll be all right as soon as we get there and I can get a little rest," Ayame said.

"It's hot," Itchy protested.

"It's too hot for me." Patsy said, plaintively, "Mommy, let's go home."

Mrs. Kimura patted her head and clucked anxiously at her baby, who began to whimper. His face was red and blotchy. It was hottest when they dragged their luggage off the train at Parker. The thermometer at the depot read 122OF. They made them get into the stuffy buses. They made them wait there with the sun burning down on them. On the sunny side, they shrank away from the hot metal and found what comfort they could against the luggage piled high in the aisle. They waited an hour like that. Hot, tired, and uncomfortable, for something, they didn't know what. The baby started to cry. They avoided looking at him. His face was bloated and his ears were swollen to twice normal size. Sally was afraid he was going to die.

Teru tried to get the doctor. He was busy with prostration cases. A whistle blew somewhere and the first buses slowly began to move. They clattered out on a bumpy, dirt road that seemed to lead to nowhere. The long cloud of dust burrowed deeper into the desert. Inside the moving dust, hidden from the buses ahead and behind by twenty yards of swirling sand, they huddled forlornly in their straightbacked seats. The windows were closed in a futile gesture against the choking dust. Handkerchiefs, neckerchiefs, sleeve ends were held tightly against their noses to filter out the clogging dirt.

Mrs. Kimura bundled her baby in a blanket. She blew air from her own lungs into an open space near the baby's head until the heat became worse than the dust. The sweat stood out on their noses; the grime seeped into their sticky clothes; and they said nothing. How much longer was the only question in their minds and it was no use asking. God, the heat and dust, won't you do anything about it?

The buses stopped. The dust thinned and they could see. Ugly machine gun snouts leered at them from the side of the road. They waited for the stragglers to catch up. They moved slowly past the sentry house.

They saw the endless rows of black, tar-papered barracks. They saw the heat was distorting their squat ugliness with shimmering lines. They felt the tires squishing to a stop in the powder like dust. They looked at the dust piled on the window sills. They strained their eyes to peer into the barracks. They saw nothing. Only rough-boards walling in each apartment. The doors were sections out of the wall with the tar paper left off. There was no mistaking the end of their trip. This was what had been planned especially for them. This was to be their home, like it or not. Prefabricated houses. Modern styling. All the comforts. Where were they? They wept silently inside. They pulled themselves together. Those barracks had to be cleaned. They had to sleep in them that night. They stepped cautiously off the buses and sank up to their ankles in the fine silt-like sand. "You eat in that mess hall over there."

The words ran up and down the line. They weren't hungry but their stomachs were empty. They were immediately ordered back into their buses. Why? We're here. It's hot and stuffy inside those buses. At least let us get into the shade. Some of us have heat stroke. Dust storm coming up. See. Over there. They looked and saw a solid wall of dust headed out of the east. All down the line of barracks they could see people scurrying madly from mess halls. Teru looked at her watch. It was six o'clock. Suddenly the barrack alleys were clear. Only lone figures could be seen running here and there.

The dark cloud reached the edge of camp and the far barracks disappeared from sight. They quickly rolled up the squeaky windows. The wind turned gusty, kicking up little flurries of dust. It began to howl and whoosh through the barracks. The crude doors rattled on their hinges. The dust came. Ten yards away, the barracks disappeared. The bus in front, bumper length away, vanished completely. It grew dim inside the bus. The dust puffed up into their noses. Fay Omada's younger brother began to yell and cry. He was suffering. He wanted to get out. Mr. Omada slapped him hard, and he subsided into a convulsive sobbing. Claustrophobia. I must have a touch of it too, Teru thought. I'd scream myself if I had the energy. I'm too hot and I'm too tired. Ayame was mumbling something. Teru bent closer to hear and for the first time noticed how alarmingly red her mother's face had become. "Mother, are you all right?" There was no response from the limply slumped figure. The mumbling continued.

"Father, *Anata*, why aren't you here?" Her eyes opened wide and she stared wildly at Teru. "Where is Father?"

Teru was frightened. She looked at Sally and Ted but they both had their faces buried in kerchiefs. Across the aisle half hidden by the luggage, Mrs. Kimura was wiping her baby's red, swollen face. Ken peered curiously back at her through the dusky gloom. Mr. Kimura looked up. She beckoned desperately. He squeezed across the aisle. He took one look at Ayame and shook his head. "It's heat stroke."

"Should I call a doctor?" Mr. Kimura glanced significantly out. They could see nothing but the dust beating against the windows.

"No use in that. I would go but I'd get lost."

"Isn't there something we can do?"

"Not in here. Mrs. Umeda and May and the youngest Nakata boy are almost as bad. Our baby seems to be getting worse. He had slight convulsions just now." He went back to his seat and Teru sat alone by her mother. Her incoherent mumbling had stopped and she was breathing rapidly. Teru felt her forehead and it was turning hot with fever. She began to feel a clammy sweat breaking out on her own face. She suddenly felt dizzy and leaned back but the straight-backed seat gave no support. She slid against her mother. She woke up with a splitting headache and a loud ringing in her ear. She didn't know how long she had been unconscious. The dust was thicker inside the bus but it was clearing a little outside. They could make out the nearest barracks. The wind died down and pretty soon they could see people leaving the nearest mess hall. Teru called Sally to watch Ayame and stepped off the bus into the ankle deep silt. Mr. Kimura followed. They looked in vain for someone to turn to. They didn't know which way to go. An ambulance drove up to the first bus. Teru stumbled to it. The driver and doctor were both *Nisei*.

"Can you come look at my mother?"

"Is she very bad?" the young doctor asked.

"I think so."

"Is she conscious?"

"Yes, but she seems to be delirious."

"There are others, too. I'm sorry. There are five people in this first bus who've already passed out. We'll have to bring them to the hospital first. Bathe their faces with water till we get back."

"Our baby, too. He's pretty bad," Mr. Kimura said. The young doctor explained again in Japanese. They found a faucet at the end of the nearest barrack. Teru unknotted the kerchief tied over her head and washed out the dust.

"Running water in every apartment. The comforts of an average home."

Mr. Kimura wet his handkerchief and filled his hat with water, and they went back to the bus to wait. Teru placed the wet kerchief on her mother's face. She told the others what to do and went back to her mother. Ayame stared strangely at them. She held her face in her hands and started to cry -- softly, sadly. It was the first time they'd seen their mother cry. Sally and Tad looked on silently. They groped for Teru's hand for comfort. They strained their eyes for a glimpse of the ambulance. The ambulance came and went three times before it stopped in front of their bus. Teru wanted to go along but there wasn't room. "Better get something to eat instead," the doctor advised her. "There's nothing you can do."

There was no waiting in line. They straggled into the mess hall and looked about in wonder. It was practically the same as in the Salinas Assembly Center. Ceilingless, framework uncovered, seats for three hundred. Plates of stew were laid out on the long tables. Mutton from the smell and on closer inspection carrots, horseradish --dusted with sand. Waitresses were clearing away the tables. They picked up the plates, the spoons, and the forks, and the thick outlines stayed on the tables. They brought out hastily made sandwiches of melted oleo and jam, and the newcomers chewed grittily under their sympathetic eyes. A waitress whispered, "I don't feel so good watching these people. Masami says some are almost dying at the hospital."

Teru looked up wildly. She couldn't tell which one had spoken.

"I'm going to the hospital," she told Tad and Sally, "you stay with Kimura-san." They pointed out the hospital but they stopped her from going.

"You've got to be processed first." They slumped on their baggage and waited in line again, too tired to stand. A printed sheet of paper was thrust in front of them and they were told to sign it. Tom

Yamada refused.

"You can't get a room unless you sign."

"I'm not going to sign anything I haven't read."

"Read it then."

He peered dopily at the writing. "I'm too tired to read anything."

"Orders are that no room can be assigned unless this is signed." He stepped wearily out of the line to sit on his luggage with the paper.

He brought it back. "I can't make sense out of it now. I'll sign it tomorrow after I've read it carefully."

"I'm sorry, you have to sign it before we can assign you a room." He was beaten when he looked back at his wife and two kids slumped on their suitcases. He scrawled his name with a few angry slashes. Teru didn't have the slightest idea what she was signing but she was too tired to protest. She wanted to get it over with so she could go to the hospital. A canvas-topped truck carried them deeper into the regularly spaced maze of tar-papered barracks. They were unloaded in front of the last barrack in Block Sixteen, right on the edge of camp. The Noguchis, the Kimuras, the Nakatas, and the Sakaguchis. They looked briefly out at the desert. At the low craggy hills in the distance. At the scrubby mesquite trees dotting the land. It wasn't the treeless, flat, sandy waste they'd pictured, but it was unmistakably desert.

It was eight o'clock and the sun was still an hour from setting, but the habits of a lifetime made them hurry to get ready for bed. They gingerly pulled open the doors to their future homes. Four doors, four rooms to each barrack. Twenty feet wide by twenty-five feet long. Larger than the rooms at the Salinas Assembly Center but for a maximum of seven persons, not five.

The eight Nakatas peered into Apartment A. The six Sakaguchis peered into Apartment B. The three Noguchis minus their father and mother into Apartment C. The six Kimuras into Apartment D. They saw the same ceilingless roof. They saw the dust covering everything. Everything consisting of the floor, the window sills, the naked framework. A half inch of dust everywhere, except over the abundant knotholes and the cracks in the floor where it had sifted through. They left their luggage in the "cleaner" dust outside.

Teru, Itchy, and Mr. Kimura set out to find whoever was in charge. The others waited wearily on their luggage. They met people coming back, loaded down with blankets and cots. "We got them over there. The barrack with the 'Block Manager' sign."

They were issued three blankets apiece, a cotton bag, and an army cot. "The straw to stuff your mattress is piled on the other side of the ironing room," the young man grinned smirkingly at Teru. He stepped outside to point out the ironing room. "That's the laundry next to it, then the combined women's latrine and shower room, then the men's. The two barracks together on the other side of the ironing room is the mess hall. Breakfast is at seven. My name is Yoshitaka Kai, your block manager."

Teru ignored the questioning look in his eyes and pointed at several brooms stacked in the corner. "Can we get one of those?"

She was too tired to talk and she wanted to get things over with so she could go to her mother. Yoshitaka Kai brought her one of the brooms and picked up a notebook . "What's your name and apartment number?"

"Noguchi, 16-7-C."

"No first name?" The grin on his face was asinine.

"Teru."

He wrote it down. He said, "You'll have to return it here as soon as you're finished. You see, we don't have enough to go around yet." Teru wished he would wipe the silly grin off his face. She dared not try to carry more than a couple of blankets and the broom. Itchy and Mr. Kimura loaded themselves down and they plodded back through the sand where the others waited. Mrs. Sakaguchi and Alice were gone. Sally said to Teru in a low voice,

"Mrs. Sakaguchi started to cry and they're on the other side of the barrack."

Mrs. Sakaguchi told Emily, "Hurry and get your mother and sister. I have to go after the blankets and cots." They pushed out the dust and carried in their luggage. Teru waited only until the cots were set up and Sally was wrapped in wet towels. She gave one last look at the dust that refused to settle and went to see if Mr. Kimura was ready.

She was counting each exhausted step halfway to the hospital.

Only the sight of Mr. Kimura slogging steadily ahead beside her kept her going. At the hospital they found Ayame sitting on a bench holding the

Kimura baby in her arms.

"What's wrong?" Teru asked.

"I've been waitng here for you," Ayame said meekly.

"Here? How long?"

"About a half hour. I didn't know where you had gone so the ambulance driver couldn't take me."

"What did the doctor say?"

"Nothing special. He told me I was ready to go and to wait outside because more patients were waiting."

"What did he do for you?"

"The nurse put wet towels on my face and neck."

"That's all?" Ayame nodded. "I'm all right now," she said.

But she'd been so deathly sick such a short time ago. Teru went to look for a doctor. He told her they didn't have room for all the heat prostration cases and they were releasing those who responded to treatment the quickest. "What if my mother gets worse?"

"We're still getting relapsed cases but that can't be helped."

"Can't I leave her here overnight? Our barrack is so hot and dusty and so far away."

"Where do you live?"

She told him.

"I'll have the ambulance take you back." Bouncing back on the ambulance, the seemingly endless walk up was reduced to three blocks and two firebreaks. Each block about two hundred fifty feet square, containing twelve barracks housing anywhere from two hundred and sixty to three hundred people. Four blocks in each quad, the quads separated by three hundred feet firebreaks. Mr. Omada hailed the ambulance at the entrance to the block. "I was just going to the hospital to call you," he said to the ambulance driver, "My wife is pretty sick again." He climbed into the front seat. He turned to Mr. Kimura, "I don't know what to do. Something is wrong with everyone in the family." The suddenly hated sun faded redly, splashing the western sky with stupendous color, as though in repentence. They noticed but they didn't stop to admire. They slipped out of their sweat caked clothes and crawled wearily into their cots, too tired to take a shower. Something was wrong with the heating equipment and there was no hot water anyway. It was too hot and they flung off their blankets. The straw poked through the cotton bags and they folded their blankets and placed them underneath. It was too hot for sleep until past midnight. They heard the coyotes' faraway yelp. The desert shushed and they felt alone and forsaken.

Sally woke up with the sniffles. She'd finally taken off her pajamas too. They were too sticky, she said. After breakfast, they were told that they wouldn't be permitted to eat in the mess hall unless at least one member of the family worked as a cook, dishwasher, or waitress. They walked back to their barrack wondering what to do. None of them felt able to work. The stupor and exhaustion of yesterday was too recent in their bodies. At eleven, Teru reported for duty as a waitress. Alice Sakaguchi went with her and they stopped in for Fay Omada on the way. The other waitresses were strangers though they remembered seeing some of them in Salinas. "Are you well enough to work?" Teru asked Fay.

"Somebody had to," Fay said. She wiped the sweat from her flushed forehead. They sat down with the rest of the kitchen crew to eat the steaming soup and wished it was cool lemonade instead. It was like sitting in a hot oven. The sweat dripped off their faces into their bowls. It oozed from their pores so continuously, they gave up trying to keep their faces dry while eating. The rice and the omelette they washed down with long drafts of water, surreptitiously letting it run down dresses and shirts which were sticky on their bodies. They stood up and the sweat had seeped through to leave dark wet spots on the bench.

They told Fay who left her food untouched, "You'd better eat or you'll get sick."

"I can't." She blinked the sweat and the tears from her eyes.

"You should. We don't feel like eating either." Fay turned away. They immediately set to work. They made trip after trip with the bowls of soup, the plates of omlette, the rice, and the pitchers of water. They paused to run damp sleeves over their flushed faces. They blew the sweat off their noses when their arms were full. The walls echoed and throbbed with the clatter of dishes, the wail of babies, the chatter of children, the loudness of youth, the scolding hurt of their elders trying to quiet them. Teru was dead tired when the last table had been cleared and wiped. She walked home with Alice. Her feet dragged and her shoes filled with sand.

"I"m going to lie down and sleep as soon as I get home."

"Me too, I'm tired."

Sally was sitting on the doorstep. She jumped up and came running towards them. "Mother's sick again." Teru was reassured when Ayame smiled up at her.

"Don't look so alarmed. It isn't much. I just need some rest."

Questioning revealed that the stomach pains had come back again. "I'll get a doctor."

"No, not now. You're tired. I'll be all right."

Sally and Tad offered to go, but Teru felt she should go herself. Before she left, she wrapped wet towels around Ayame. The hot sun beat into her brain. The sand dragged at her feet. She had to stop to empty her shoes. The tiredness came back and her heart was pounding violently. She would never forget that grueling walk through the sand.

Never. Dear God, what have I ever done to deserve all this? This dust, this heat, these dirty barracks, this futureless life! What did I do? What have I done?

They told her to bring her mother the next morning to the regular clinic, since it wasn't an emergency. She didn't even get to see a doctor.

CHAPTER 9

Teru unwillingly opened sleepy eyes to her second morning in Poston. She was getting ready to dip her spoon into a crushed raspberry sundae. She groped blindly for the clock on the floor. She knocked it over and the dinging alarm shocked her awake. It was dark and she didn't want to tum on the lights hanging from the central rafter. Still she was sure she had set the alarm for five-thirty, so she pulled on her clothes and went to the latrine to wash. The wash trough, shower, and watercloshets were in one building in the center of the block. Six pairs of faucets lining the tin wash trough, six shower heads, and ten waterclosets. Alice hurriedly got up when Teru walked in the door. "My poor insides," she said, "I've been wearing a path to this place all night long. Me and ten dozen others. Must be something we 'et'." Erni Koda said, no, it was due to the mineral salts in the water. She had come into Poston a month earlier from Los Angeles.

"The way I heard it, there's lots of oil in the water pipes," Itchy said. He was a dishwasher. Mr. Nakata had enough of cooking under center conditions. Too much trouble, he said. "The Brawley people never had it. They thought it was a great joke," Erni pointed out.

"The ground is higher out there but whatever it is, excuse me kindly," Itchy said and started to walk away. Half way to the door he broke into a hasty run. They laughed.

"Chew your water and it won't bother you," an Issei cook advised them.

"What earthly good can that do?" Fay asked, but more than a few people carefully "chewed" their water before drinking it down .. ..

The clinic was hot and stuffy. The early arrivals slumped on the backless benches. The late comers stood listlessly against the wall or waited patiently in the line leading to the registration desk. The Nisei receptionists concentrated desperately on grasping the patients' descriptions of their aches and pains. Sometimes they put their heads together but often they looked at the long line and put down "internal" or "general malaise" and let it go at that. Some older people crouched despondently on the floor, sick and tired and not shamed into caring about appearances. More sick people came, until there was no standing space left and the line dribbled out into the corridor. No one talked much. The faces gradually changed. The room slowly emptied.

"Noguchi-san," the nurse's aide finally called. The doctor was the same one who had been in the ambulance that first day.

"Didn't you come in from Salinas?" he asked. He looked even younger than she remembered. Teru said yes.

"Do you know George Motoyama?" he asked. The nurse was asking Ayame a few routine questions.

Teru nodded. "Quite well."

"We used to room together at the Japanese students club at U. C." The nurse handed him the file card. He studied it with professional deliberation. He pulled the stethoscope out of his jacket pocket and adjusted it around his neck. "You aren't Teru by any chance?"

"How did you know?" Teru was surprised.

"Oh, George still writes me now and then. I didn't think there were too many Noguchis in Salinas." He seemed slightly flustered and made a visible effort to retain his professional composure. He paid complete attention to Ayame for the next few minutes.

"It looks very much like stomach ulcers," he said at last, "probably aggravated by camp food and worry."

"Can you do anything for it?"

Dr. Katayama concentrated. ''I'll prescribe some medicine to ease the pain but proper diet is what is really necessary."

"In here?"

"Eventually, we expect to have a separate table in each mess hall to take care of people like your mother who need a special diet." he said. "We have a great thing planned for Poston." Ayame said not to worry about it anymore.

Teru was writing to George the night of the famous July 22nd storm. She had the fibreboard suitcase pulled against the bed. It had the smoothest top. She wrote, I didn't know God's world held such a place. This is Hell. Even the wind has a hellish howl tonight. I started to write a few nights ago but I only got as far as those first two sentences. It was too hot and I didn't have the energy to go on. Sim Ogawa was over from Camp 2 today with Bill and claimed he lost thirty pounds already. His baggy clothes certainly showed it. He sweated that much. Those of us who work in the kitchen have to take showers three times a day and change our clothing each time if we want to feel at all fresh. People don't know how to take care of themselves in this awful heat. Mrs. Kimura' s baby was pretty bad when we came in but she kept him in a tub of water practically all day long and he recovered pretty quick. Serao Goto, though, was told by someone that water should be kept from babies at first and her baby dried out and almost died. A friend of yours is here. Dr. John Katayama. I met him the first day here and a couple of times since then. I've heard good things about him. He's reputed to have turned down an offer to work in a hospital outside with the statement, "These people in here are my people and I intend to stay here and take care of them. He impressed me as being quite capable of that.

He's quite young though, isn't he? To have roomed with you. He seemed shy though he did uncover our both knowing you. He examined Mother and it seems she has stomach ulcers. He says it's nothing too serious but I'm worried about something else. Mother isn't quite the same. She's been acting a little differently lately. She does things I've never seen her do before. Maybe camp life is changing her. Mrs. Omada was sent to an asylum in Los Angeles yesterday. A few days ago, she took to running around in her underclothes and they had to have her locked up. It was terrible hearing her screams at night. As if that weren't too much for Mr. Omada, Fay broke down completely from the strain of wonying about her mother plus working in the sweltering kitchen and was hospitalized this morning. Dr. Katayama doesn't hold out much hope of her pulling through. We went to see her this afternoon, but she barely noticed us while we were there. Remember James Kido? He died two days ago. He was in the next barrack from us. Having to take care of everything during evacuation and moving out here, his old ailment got the better of him. Saburo Miyake, two barracks down, died of the measles last week. Measles! I didn't think people died of that anymore. People are afraid to get sick. You may think I'm painting an over-gloomy picture, but you should have seen our faces when the older residents told us what the Indians told them. They said that when this Indian reservation was first filled, over half of the total number of Indians who were earmarked for this reservation died either on the march here or within the first months after arriving. They are surprised that we don't die off like they did. However, if they had been in camp when we Salinas people pulled in from our cool lettuce bowl, they might have been less surprised after seeing the people collapsing right and left and keeping the ambulances running all night. No one can say that the heat is killing these people, but our hygiene teacher at J.C. told us that the death rate definitely rises during a heat wave, and so, I myself believe that those people would be living today if they hadn't been forced to come to this awful place. The wind is getting worse. The whole barrack is shaking and rattling like it's going to fall apart. It's scary.

Poston is really three camps. We're in Camp 1, capacity 10,000. Most Salinas people, however, are in Camp 2, capacity 5,000, about three miles from here. Camp 3 capacity 5,000, is about three more miles down, empty as yet. We call them Poston, Roaston, and Toaston. Those of us who wish to move to Roaston with the rest of the Salinas people were asked to sign up yesterday. About half of the Salinas people are staying here. Mostly because they're tired of moving.

Bill is head of housing in Camp 2 and has arranged for us to move into Block 213 where he lives. It's on the edge of camp and not half as dusty as the other blocks. You have to be in one of our dust storms to appreciate what they're like. Today, I was washing -we have to wash every day to keep up with our change of clothing -and was stranded for an hour in the laundry. None of us even considering trying to reach our barracks. After it was over, we drained the water and washed all over again. Even inside the barracks, it grows dim and dusty and everything comes to stop until it blows over and it's time to wait for your tum to use the hose and wash out the dust which gets into everything. We have two lengths of hose for each block and it takes a little over a half day for each family to use it once, because the water pressure is so low and only a thin stream comes from the nozzle. Washing out floors is a daily routine with the dust storms calling for another session with the hose.

There was a big crash just now somewhere on the other side of the block. Tad wanted to go see what it was but Mother said no, so we're sitting here wondering what it was. Maybe a barrack blew over. Ours feels ready to go any minute. Have to start packing now because the trucks will call for us first thing in the morning to avoid the midday heat; I 00 degrees when you place the thermometer a foot off the ground. Other thermometers read 120 to 130 degrees in the shade. I think the hottest Salinas ever got was I 08. Remember how we suffered that day? That was nothing ..."

Tero dismantled her "table" to pack it with clothes. A loud rending crash split their eardrums. They jumped. They looked up and saw a comer of their roof bend away from the wall and crash back on itself The wind howled through the jagged opening and the stinging dust swirled into the room. ''Get outside quick. '' Mr. Kimura's hoarse shouts and Mrs. Kimura's shrill cries came from Apartment D. They rushed outside, the Kimuras tumbled out, wildeyed, excited. "Our roof blew off," Ken cried. With one accord, they bent their heads against the wind and reached the Sakaguchi apartment just as the door opened to reveal a cautiously peering face.

"Was it here?" Mr. Sakaguchi asked.

"Our roof blew off," Ken repeated. Mr. Sakaguchi instantly came out. All the Kimuras were huddled outside in their bedclothes. One whole side of the roof over the Kimura and Sakaguchi apartments was gone and careening away across the desert. The other half of the roof was flapping dangerously and threatening to break loose at any moment. ''Have to get some clothes.'' Mr. Kimura started to go back in. Mr. Sakaguchi stopped him.

"Too dangerous," he said. He told the children to go to his apartment and went to bang on the nearest barrack doors for help. A dozen men joined them. They brought a ladder and an ax from the block manager's. Mr. Sakaguchi crawled up and expertly chopped away the last supporting timbers.

The damaged roof crashed down and Mr. Nakata said to no one in particular, "He was a fireman in Japan so no wonder."

A few drops of rain beat wetly against their faces. They carried cots into the Nakata and Sakaguchi apartments. There wasn't room for them all. Teru, Sally, and Ayame moved their cots into the Omada apartment, Ted and Ken into the Kidos'. The rain started to come down in earnest. Huge pelting drops. They went after the rest of the luggage and got wet to the skin. They crawled into their cots and waited for the morning to come. The next morning they climbed into the truck with the Sakaguchis and the Nakatas. The ground was muddy and slippery from the night's rain. People stood in doorways and poked their heads out of windows with bantering comments on the ' 'sad case'' of the poor people moving into the ''sticks.'' ''Camp 2 is waste time,'' they said. That was easy to counter but Teru didn't know what to say to the Kimuras standing to one side in the rain. They smiled and waved now and then. She wished the truck would start moving. Mrs. Kimura held up the baby. How often she'd played with him when shy little Betty carried him over -- which was whenever she was left alone to watch over the baby. Betty who seldom spoke a word but smiled all the time.

She wondered what Ken and Tad had done with their "partnership" glove and the live rattlesnake they'd captured two days ago and made a cage for. Whether Ken would eat with his own family or join the other boys of his age who ate separately from their families. At Salinas and until today, he'd never missed a meal with the Noguchis. The Kimura family ate in shifts because of the baby and Ken was always playing with Tad.

Matsuo jumped on the tailgate and pushed Shiro Nakata. His eyes stopped briefly on Tero. Matsuo never failed to bring her every new species of bug he caught, after she found him playing with a scorpion and told him how deadly its sting was. Mrs. Kimura thought it was a baby shrimp and asked him to get some more. They all wanted to move, too, but Mr. Kimura heard there would be no hospital in Camp 2 and thought it better for the children and baby if they stayed nearer medical facilities. The truck began to move. They looked back at the Kimuras. They saw the damaged barrack in the background. They passed other barracks with their roofs partly tom off They bumped out on the dirt road leading deeper into the desert. They saw the dust hills and the tar-papered barracks, no different from those they had just left.

213-5-C was the same as 16-7-c had been. There were the same cracks in the wall, and along the eaves, and in the floor. There was the dust, even though someone had moved out less than a week ago. They washed out the floor, set up the cots, hung the curtains, pulled the drape across half the room, and they were as ready as they could be to carry on again. The next day, Tero went to the Administration Building at the camp entrance for more information about the teachers' training courses that were soon to be started. When she returned, Bill was there with some lumber and was knocking together a table with Tad's help.

"Where did you get the wood?" Tero asked. Tad and Ken had been unable to find any at all in Camp 1.

''Scrap piles here and there,'' Bill answered, but a few pieces looked too long to have come from a scrap pile. Tero noticed, because while she waited in the Administration Building a *Hakujin* joshed Tom Hamada about the mysterious shrinking of the lumber pile.

Tom said only, "What do you expect? You don't let us bring in more than the clothes we wear and you don't even give us boxes to sit on. We're family people, not bachelors, remember that."

Bill was in one of the pint-size apartments in Barrack 13 set aside for couples and families of three. They were twelve feet wide by twenty feet long. He came over again on Saturday to make three stools and the framework of a closet. He handed her a letter he'd gotten at the office that morning. She started to read.

Mr. Housing Head. I am living in 215-A with 3 person, but one have piles and one has asthma and they have to fart every night as like the skunk, of course they are ignorance -- I am a man of great knowledge, as I don't like live with them and I wish to move small room only me if you can please."

The signature was unfamiliar. Teru looked up and Bill's chuckle touched off a peal of laughter that brought Ayame over. Teru showed her the letter. Ayame spoke bitterly, unexpectedly, "This is no laughing matter. It's only natural, throwing us in a place like this."

Teru listened uncomfortably, taken aback by the invective in her mother's voice. Her mother had never used that tone of voice before. Ayame left the room abruptly and in a little while the dinner bell clanged. They waited but Ayame didn't come back. Teru went to look for her. She wasn't with Mrs. Yamada.

Alice said, ''Looking for your mother? I saw her taking a shower just now." The last of the people were disappearing into the mess hall. Teru hurried to the latrine. Ayame looked up surprised.

"What is the matter?"

"The bell has rung already."

"Oh."She made no move to come out.

"We're all waiting for you."

She stepped reluctantly from the shower. Teru had to go in and shut off the water. It was cold. Ayame waited helplessly. "I have no towel." Teru ran directly back to their barrack. She felt sick inside. There was no escape from it. There were other things. Back home Ayame had done most of the laundering and in the Salinas camp she had reluctantly let Teru and Sally do the lion's share. But now she made no attempt to do any washing or housework at all saying it would get dirty again right away. She continually complained about the pain in her stomach and querulously asked Teru to do something about it. She told Bill and Tad and Sally not to wait.

''Is something wrong?" Bill asked.

"No, we'll go later." She flung the towel over her shoulder and raced back. Bill was still waiting when they came back. They hurried to the mess hall. People were already straggling out. They sat down to an unappetizing mixture of mustard greens, pigweed, and parsnip flavored with dried shrimp.

"I'm not hungry." Ayame said and left the table. Teru couldn't very well stop her. She carried home the food, but Ayame said it was grass and refused to touch it. Bill came and started to pound together the framework for the closet. Ayame said, "It's hot. My stomach hurts. Finish it some other time."

Teru walked outside with him. "I'm sorry Mother is acting like this"

Bill looked at her strangely. "How long had this been going on?" Teru hesitated, wondering what to tell him. "About two weeks, I guess. I don't know just when it started. Today's the first time it's been really noticeable.' "'Hadn't you better call a doctor?"

"No," Teru said quickly. She didn't want her mother sent away to a crazy house. "She isn't that bad."

"Does anyone else know?"

"I don't think so."

"Sally or Tad"

"I'm not sure. They're not home very much and Mother doesn't act like this very often."

Mrs. Yamada agreed with Teru that they shouldn't call a doctor yet. ''All the times I have seen her the past few days, I haven't noticed anything unusual. Anyway, our Camp 2 doctor is a quack. We intend to circulate a petition to get him out of here. His license was taken away for malpractice and he may even have to go to the penitentiary yet."

He comforted Teru. "It's probably a result of the heat stroke she suffered when we first came in. She'll get over it."

"Is the Hidaka girl the same thing?" Bill asked.

"No, her case is different, I think. It runs in the family."

''Last night, she propped a stick against the door and kept everyone out of the latrine while she took her shower," Bill said.

Teru told Sally, "Mother is not quite herself so you'll have to stay here and kind of keep an eye on her." She went on quickly,

"She' ll be all right as soon as she gets adjusted to this heat." She wanted to stay home herself but they needed the money she would get for working. Twelve dollars a month while going to summer session and sixteen or possibly nineteen for teaching later on. There was such a demand for teachers that college and J.C. graduates would be assigned at least as assistant teachers, according to Mr. McBain, the school superintendent. Kay was working in the administration office again and told Teru a position would be opening when she transferred to the high school. Teru asked why she was transferring and she talked vaguely of internal jealousies and bickering.

"Dr. Sato, Henry Tanaka, and the J.A.C.L. big shot in 212 are trying to gain control of the camp but they're running into stiff opposition," she said, "on top of that, the city slickers from L.A. in Camp 1 are trying to run Camp 2 and complaining of noncoooperation while our end complains of too much bossing. It looks to me like we're headed for trouble all around."

Teru wondered briefly if she should work in the administration office for the extra four dollars and discarded the thought. She remembered how enthusiastic Mr. McBain was about the educational system planned for Poston. "You young people are entering upon an exciting career. .. to mold character ... to build healthy minds ... to build a better future ...."

Teachers would attend summer sessions and receive credits towards an eventual B.S. degree. She was excited when she woke up Monday morning. Over the weekend, people from the Fresno area had moved into Camp 3 and the remainder of the blocks at the south end of Camp 2. No letter had come from George since she'd written that they were leaving Salinas for Poston and could give him no address. Almost three weeks had passed since she mailed her letter from Camp 1 but everyone was complaining that mail was slow in reaching them.

"They probably censor our mail, too, after they started to inspect our packages," was Bill's explanation.

Sunday, she waited half-expectantly for George to put in an appearance until she learned that most of the former Salinas people had moved into Camp 3. There was no way of traveling between the two camps that she knew of She was excited, too, because it was the first day of the teaching classes. At six-thirty, she was sitting in the front of the bus with Kate Tani. A stranger poked his head through the door. "Is this the bus that's going to the Indian school?" He saw Kate. ''Hello, Kate.''

"Hello, Jiro," Kate answered.

"You didn't say anything about teaching, Saturday night." Jiro was looking at Teru. "It's not definite yet. Gary Harada asked me yesterday so I thought I'd look into it. Where is he?" He searched the twenty-odd faces scattered through the bus.

"He went ahead with Mr. McBain in a car."

"Oh." His eyes returned and stopped overlong on Teru. She unconsciously stared back. He was darkly tanned and that was all she noticed outside of his smiling, friendly eyes.

"Let's go sit in back," Kate suggested, and they did. "Teru has been asking me all sorts of questions after I told her I met you."

"Is he the one who just came from Fresno?" Teru asked Kate. Kate introduced him.

"Jiro Nishikawa. Gilroy born but you'd never know it from living there. I don't think he's been home since high school. U.C., '38, architecture. And what was the name of that place you worked for in San Francisco?"

"Goodson and Smith."

"As an architect?" Teru asked.

"I just did routine drafting. Going to be a teacher?"

"If they'll let me."

"No question of that. Question is, will the students learn anything? ",

"Why, what do you mean?" Teru asked surprised.

"They'll spend so much time looking at you." There was a chuckle in his voice. He smiled easily and his eyes crinkled.

"Jiro is a wolf"

"Cousin Kate, you know that's a deliberate lie."

"He usually plays hard to get. You know, the strong silent type." Kate said to Teru.

"What makes you so mean this morning, Cousin Kate?"

"I think Teru is turning to ask you some questions." Jiro look questioningly at Teru.

She flushed slightly. "It's just about a family who went to Fresno from Salinas."

"She means one certain member of the family," Kate teased.

"What's his name?" The smile on his face was a shade disappointed.

"Motoyama."

"George?"

"You know him?"

"He was in an auto camp a couple miles down from the one we moved into. I worked for him planting his tomatoes. I hadn't seen him since our U. C. days."

"Are they here?"

"No. They were on the other side of the line and they' re slated to go to Gila. ''

"Oh."

"Is it that bad?"

"Oh no. It's just that they're such old friends and we hoped they had come here.' '

"Tell her about some of the other people."

He paused before answering. ''The worst were the people living on opposite sides of L Street. It was the dividing line and those on the north side had to go to Gila and those on the south side had to come here. Some of the newcomers slipped across the street with their baggage during the middle of the night but the old residents couldn't do that. It was a rotten setup. We were separated from some old Gilroy friends, too."

The bus stopped at Camp 1 and filled with more prospective teachers. Kate counted eighty. The Indian school was built of adobe but it was hot. They were told that they would be privileged to work with a new method of teaching. Their main purpose would be to make the individual ready for society. Reading, writing, arithmetic, geography would not be stressed -- only brought in as they came up in relation to familiar things real to the individual. The students would be taught writing by writing their own stories, reading by reading what they wrote, spelling by the words in the stories. In high school, English, civics, history would be learned as they came up in daily discussion during a special "core" class.

Teru was rather doubtful but Jiro was frankly skeptical. "Might be all right for little kids but I hate to see the mess in the higher grades," he said. "I don't think I care much for this 'activities' program." He walked home with Kate and Teru. "Going tomorrow?"

Kate asked when they said goodbye to her at Block 216.

"I don't think so." Jiro said. He walked to 213 with Teru.

They talked about camp life. The lack of privacy. The absence of facil-ities.

" Why hasn't something been done about it?" he asked. "We can't live like this."

"You were never in an assembly center," Teru pointed out.

"You haven't been moved around at the point of a gun. We' re pretty helpless in here."

"Not that helpless. We have some rights. After yesterday afternoon, I'm ready to go see somebody about it. ' '

"You mean about the water being turned off'

"Yes. Does it happen often?"

"Every now and then." "Flush toilets aren't much good without water are they?' '

"Worse than assembly center," Teru admitted.

"They ought to at least give us enough water in a place like

this" Sally came back with the wash, her hair in curlers and a kerchief tied over her head. "This is my sister, Sally."

"Big sister?" Jiro asked. Sally giggled. "I must be wrong." He looked from Sally to Teru and back to Sally. Teru followed his appreciative look and thought, no wonder she'd gotten so choosey about the style of her clothes and spends so much time with her hair. She's growing up. He talked in Japanese when he met Ayame. Teru forgot to be uneasy. He didn't know enough about them to notice anything odd about Ayame's conversation.

"He is a very nice young man," Ayame said after he left.

"Who is he?" The next morning, they recognized his erect figure coming from the direction of 227. Teru breathed in the crisp desert air and noticed how well he carried himself Her pulse quickened.

"Good morning, teacher," they greeted him. His eyes crinkled and focused on Teru.

"This school business seems to have gotten into my blood." His mouth twisted in a wry smile as at some shared secret. The breath caught sharply in her throat.

She said, "Aha, you see its good points now."

He chuckled. "No, Gary tells me I'm to teach straight physics and with no monkey business."

Classes lasted from eight to three-thirty. After the first day, they were separated into elementary and high school sections. They went to demonstration classes, orientation classes, lectures.

Teru emphasized, ''All they teach the demonstration classes is about Indians and the surrounding country."

"Maybe they're trying to make Indians out of us," Kate said.

A visiting dignitary told them: "High officials in Washington think this war will last seven to ten years .... You people are lucky to be in here. The cost of living is going up outside and it gets tougher each day. You are to be envied. At the end of the war, you will be better off then those outside."

''Bushwha!'' Jiro exploded under his breath. He walked home with them every afternoon. Gary Hamada and his sister Lana joined them from the second day. They lived in the end apartment of Teru's barrack. Lana was a State Teachers' college graduate and an accredited teacher in adult education. Gary had been a U. C. Army Air Force cadet until Pearl Harbor.

CHAPTER 10

Teru glanced quickly through George's neatly lettered writing with a feeling of guilt. The Army order forbidding us to leave California came as a surprise because our land owner kept assuring us up to the last minute that he had the word of high authorities that we wouldn't be evacuated. I'm frankly disappointed in America. Chasing us out of this interior part of California was adding insult to injury. This totally unnecessary ouster after we were practically promised that we wouldn't be asked to move again convinces me that even the first mass evacuation can be laid to political demagoguery of the worst kind. I wouldn't be surprised now if the next move was the imprisonment of all Japanese in America. We left the tomato crop as is. The only thing we lost is our labor, but I'm a little peeved because I told the owner to dig the vines under several times as not worth taking care of He said that the prices of tomatoes was going up so fast that even a small crop would pay. Shucks, prices would have to double before he makes anything, so before we left I told him to forget about paying us our share of the crop returns. I doubt very much if he can even find a crew to contract for the picking.

"I've been to the Leave Office twice now trying to get permission to go to Poston but so far no soap. Will keep trying, though they don't hold out much encouragement."

She tore up four sheets of paper before she was half satisfied with her answer. She wrote: "So many things have happened since I last saw you. So many changes. New surroundings, new interests, new faces, new friends. Especially since coming to camp. This is a smaller camp and the people are more friendly than in Camp 1, possibly because we're mostly country people. In Camp 1, you walk about without paying any attention to people passing you on the road and they don't pay any attention to you. Here it's different. People think you're awfully stuck up if you don't say hello to everybody. Before evacuation seems such a long time ago. The assembly center and the first two months in Poston have made those days seem like part of another existence. We haven't forgotten you but we seem to have put too many happenings between us. Happenings which no doubt have changed you as much as they have changed me. We seem to have gone through a lifetime of change and emotion during the past several months. Even assembly center seems like a small lifetime in itself Poston seems slated to be our duration home, much as I hate the prospect. We're getting accustomed to the heat slowly but not well. Gila seems to be much cooler than here. You' re lucky you didn't have to come to Poston, though it would be nice for our families to be together again.

She read it over and wondered if she should have mentioned Jiro. She wished she could write, I like you, George, an awful lot, but it was never the real thing. I know that now. I felt flattered and loved when you looked at me, but you never made my heart sing -- never made my blood surge and pulse go swiftly, my face feels hot and cold. This is different. I wait so eagerly to see his face each morning.

Sunday seems an empty day for he doesn't come to church. I suspect he is a Buddhist though not a very devout one. Monday, the sight of him is even better than I'd pictured over the weekend .. ..

On Wednesday, a telegram came. Mr. Yamada was en route to Poston with seven others and would arrive around Saturday. Mrs. Yamada brought it over for Sally to translate. Ayame was sitting on her cot knitting the sweater for Tad she'd started at the Salinas Assembly Center. It seemed a good sign and Sally watched her hopefully while she ironed. She appeared to be paying no attention to Sally and Mrs. Yamada until she said abruptly, ''Is that why I haven't seen Yamada-san lately?''

Sally looked at Mrs. Yamada. Should they try to straighten Ayame out? Explain carefully once more in the hope that she would snap back to her senses? Mrs. Yamada shook her head. No one came on the early morning train, so Bill, Tero, John Mochizuki, and Ema Hiraga stayed up Saturday night playing bridge. Bill to wait for his father, Tero hoping against hope that her own father might be one of the seven others, and John and Ema because they liked bridge.

It was close to midnight and they had just bid a vulnerable small slam in spades when the *Hakujin* escort brought Mr. Yamada home.

Mrs. Yamada let him in. "You have come home. It is good," she said simply.

He cleared his throat. Until he smiled broadly at them, he looked older and more sickly then they remembered. ''I have word from your father, Tero," he said. "Is your mother still awake?"

"Papa, it's late. Why don't you do that tomorrow?" Mrs. Yamada said and called him aside. She lowered her voice. Ema picked up the score pad and started to add up the points. Mr. Yamada looked oddly at Tero. "Your father asked me to tell you he is in the best of health and not to worry. His hearing is finished and we were expecting his release before mine."

The following week, Mr. Matsuda came back from internment. He raved and ranted about the terrible camp conditions. They couldn't treat his wife and children like that. Something had to be done about it. He sizzled and sputtered out after a week. A few days after, two more Salinas people returned. They dribbled back by one's and two's through September and October. Then they stopped coming. Something was holding up Mr. Noguchi's release. Nobody knew what it was. School opened in October. Tero was assigned to teach one of the fourth grades. A Miss Emily Hansen taught the other. All the grades were divided like that. A *Hakujin* taught one class and an evacuee taught the other.

Jiro had one class in physics and three math classes. Kate taught typing and shorthand. James taught the seventh grade and Lana the first grade - at nineteen dollars a month. "It's a shame," Kate said after their first faculty meeting and their first look at the regular

Hakujin teachers. "Lana is so much more qualified to teach and she gets only nineteen. Look at them." Two of the white-haired *Hakujin* carefully eased their rheumatic legs off the foot-high stoop ahead of them. "These aren't as bad as the one who was sitting on the other side of me. She has St. Vitus Dance or the seven year itch."

"If they paid Lana what she's worth, they'd have to make a lot more adjustments," Gary said. "Think of all the doctors, nurses, accountants, engineers in here."

"To make it fair, include the janitors, garbage collectors, farmers and all the rest," Jiro said. "I've often wondered why a premium is placed on brains over brawn. I mean specialized usages of brains -- like the ability to accumulate money through fair means or foul. How one gets it doesn't seem to matter after a few years. A Jewish classmate once told us in a bull session how his father had outsmarted his own company out of fifty-thousand dollars and scrammed to Florida before they could check up on him. He wasn't ashamed or anything close to it. He thought it was a neat deal. I guess he wasn't brought up to have scruples."

"After going through evacuation, I wonder if any Jews have scruples when it comes to making money," Mike Tanaka said.

"No," Mike was emphatic.

"You' re crazy," Jim said. "You beef about being put in here. You say it's discrimination; and yet you tum right around and do the same thing yourself."

"A Jewish salesman told me all those Jews who came to buy things just before evacuation were New York Jews," Gary spoke out.

"One of them offered Mochizuki fifty dollars for five hundred dollars' worth of cameras in his store and when Mochizuki told him nothing doing, he told Mochizuki, 'The Government will confiscate them pretty soon anyway'. He didn't sell, though," Mike said.

"At Dad's grocery they took a careful inventory and offered him fifteen hundred dollars. Dad sold because evacuation was only three weeks away. Our own inventory was eight thousand dollars without counting fixtures which cost us about three thousand more," Kate said.

"Terminal Island was worse. Though I don't know if the buyers were Jews," Lana said.

"They must have been. Five dollars for Norge refrigerators,"
Mike snorted.

"You don't like Jews?" Jim asked. "Right after evacuation, I listened to an open radio forum and the only one who stood up on two feet and denounced the whole evacuation was a Jew." "They make a fetish of education and brains. Our parents tell us we have to be lots better than *Hakujin* before we can get an even break. Their parents tell them they have to be two hundred percent better before they can get anywhere. They're plenty smart." "Not the head doctor at the hospital. Dr. Katayama says he doesn't stack up very high compared to the evacuee doctors. His eyes bugged at Dr. Watanabe's surgical technique. He didn't think Japanese doctors were good for more than sloppy tonsillectomies. According to Dr. Katayama though, what makes them madder than having to work under someone less competent than themselves is his continual talking about how he did it this way with the Indians and how he did it that way with the Indians. He's an old Indian Service doctor."

"Maybe because we look so much like Indians."

"There's someone in charge of the school adobe project who thinks the same way. Tom Hamada was a foreman there and he thought up a way to make four bricks where they're making one now. He demonstrated to the *Hakujin* in charge and the *Hakujin* told him, 'The Indians have been making their adobe bricks this way for centuries and their buildings are still standing. You do it the way they did it.' Tom got disgusted and quit.••

School had barely opened when the Western Defense Command gave permission to evacuees to enter certain parts of Arizona to help harvest the cotton crop . Classes were dismissed for three weeks. Teru went out with the others to pick cotton. What little wages they earned were turned into school and community funding.

Teru thought, no wonder the negroes can't get ahead. At this rate they can't put anything aside to build a future on.

For some reason the army rescinded its previous order and the cotton picking ended.

The Matsuda' s moved out of the block. The return of Mr. Matsuda made eight in the family and they were allowed to move into two apartments in 215.

The Kais moved into the vacated apartment from camp 1. Yoshitaka met Teru coming out of the latrine and followed her home. He kept her outside talking-- about the weather which was hot and did she know Charlie Colo. You know, the famous halfback at Stanford. He was a year ahead of me at Hollister High. We were great pals. Then did she know Sam Ishida, he worked in the lettuce sheds last season. He's in the next block. He's a nice kid. You ought to get to know him. I'll bring him over sometime. Then, did she know Sam Ogawa. You ought to know him. He's in this block, isn't he? He moved to Salinas five years ago from Hollister.

Teru finally said, "I have to correct some papers. If you'll excuse me."

"I've always wanted to see how teachers corrected papers. Do you give a break to your teacher's pet?"

He followed her inside. His eyes stared covertly at everything.

Teru was glad the drapes were drawn across the room. She tried to think of some way to get rid of him.

It took two weeks of being practically rude before Yoshitaka quit tagging after her. Then he transferred his unwelcome attentions to Sally.

Teru became disturbed when she saw him parked on their doorstep every afternoon when she came home from school. It was hard on Sally having to stay home so much but she wished someone else was keeping her company.

She was a little relieved when Sally said, "He's a goon. He's twenty-six and he's still a sissy."

"Doesn't he know when he's not wanted?"

"Not him, he's always asking me to go someplace and I turn him down every time. What more can I do? I can't sock him on the nose."

"I wish we could leave this place." Sally said. She was thinking of the new WRA regulations in effect since the first of October. They could leave for temporary or permanent residence provided they had definite jobs or means of support; were not disloyal; submitted evidence that they were acceptable in the community they intended entering; satisfied authorities whenever they moved.

It replaced the two-month old ruling that any American born who had never visited Japan could leave for private employment provided he was cleared by the FBI. The clearance had been hard to get.

"Work."

"Doing what? maid? laundress? Father would have a fit if he heard we were working as domestics. We couldn't leave mother and Tad here. And if we rented a house big enough for the four of us, we'd have to buy all sorts of things. Pots, pans, dishes--.' '

"Oh, I didn't tell you? There's a letter in my suitcase from Mr. Otis of the real estate office. I was going to show you."

''What does he say?''

"Mr. Johnson finished harvesting the crops and moved to San Jose. He took all the new furniture, the silverware, the dinner set, the electric mixer, and a few other things."

"He can't do that. Those things belong to us."

"I know, but Mr. Otis says the only way we can get them back is for us to go back to California and identify each piece."

"He must be in cahoots with Johnson. They know we can't go back to California"

"I don't think so. He sounded pretty sorry in his letter and he's already found another tenant to take care of the place in return for paying the taxes."

"With rents going up so high, we should be able to lease the place for more than taxes."

"We can't rent to just anybody. We wouldn't have a house left when we went back."

"So we pick and choose someone like Mr. Johnson."

"I know we need the money but father arranged it that way with Mr. Otis."

"Has anyone come back recently?"

"Not for almost two weeks."

Teru was worried about Yoshitaka until the day she discovered that Bill was dropping in to see Sally and not herself After that she wrote off Yoshitaka as a nuisance who would be taken care of in due time ....

The class was drawing, and Teru was correcting papers when Sally burst into her roomful of fourth graders.

"Teru," she excitedly waved a telegram, "Look, Father's coming home."

"When? Let me see." Teru found herself trying to grab the telegram while holding the sheet of uncorrected papers in one hand and red pencil in the other.

Helen, Jimmy, and Itsuko left their seats and stood on their tiptoes to see. "Is your father really coming home?"

Jimmy Morita said, "Maybe my daddy is coming home, too."

He scooted for the door. He turned and asked, "Can I go, teacher?"

"Of course," Teru said.

"Me too, teacher?"Little Nancy Ota asked timidly.

" Yes, you may go too."

"Me too?" Goro Minato asked eagerly.

"Goro, your father isn't in an internment camp."

"Yes but he's a bad Jap, too."

"Why do you say that?"

"He listens to the Japan radio."

Sally grinned. She said, ''I have to hurry back.''

"Does mother know?"

''I told her and she said she wondered why he was taking so long.''

Teru picked up Jimmy's drawing from his vacated desk. Five crudely drawn battleships filled the page, in what was evidently a tremendous sea battle. Three of the ships were upended to indicate a sinking condition. All three had the American flags. The other two with guns booming were Japanese. In the background was the inevitable flaming red sun with spreading rays which could be easily taken for a Japanese battle flag.

She'd asked the class not to draw war pictures but when she gathered up the rest of the drawings, she found two more epic sea battles and a preponderance of brilliant red sunsets with their suggestive rays. All were labeled, Sunset. She thought, oh well, Arizona does have colorful sunsets.

In the next apartment, she could hear Miss Hansen say to her class, ''All together now. One, two, three.''

Forty pairs of shoes began to pound rhythmically on the floor. The whole barrack shook and echoed to the deafening racket.

It wasn't time for recess, but Teru led her pupils outside. The stomping would continue for some time until Miss Hansen decided her poor chil-dren's feet were sufficiently warmed. The promised stoves would arrive any time now." She watched their play at recess and knew that most of them were little changed from their attitudes outside. In their mock war, few wanted to be 'the Jap.'

"If l be the Jap, I have to die all the time." Goro explained. She wished Jimmy's father would come home from internment. His mother worked in the kitchen and had little time for more than keeping their clothing mend-ed and washed. The youngest was the same age as the Kimura baby and needed suckling and diaper care.

Jimmy was beginning to run with the gang which was under suspicion of stealing from the clothes of people taking showers. They stole to satis-fy their ''outside'' wants for things their parents could no longer buy for them. Ice cream when it came to the canteen once a week. Soda pop. A pair of basketball shoes.

The first week of school she scolded Jimmy for refusing to take off his hat in class. For answer, he released a series of foul invective which left her helpless. When he finished, he looked at her uncertainly. She told him to go home until he learned to behave himself.

The next day, she sent him home once more when he again refused to take off his hat. The third day, he left the room but stayed on the school grounds. Teru saw him watching from the edge of the grounds each recess.

The fourth day, he embarrassedly took off his hat. Henry turned to look at him and immediately punched him. Teru didn't make an issue of the punching.

Two weeks later, Mrs. Morita came with Jimmy before class opened. She thanked Teru profusely for the change that had taken place in Jimmy since school had started.

Teru stood embarrassed, unable to answer in Japanese.

Jimmy spoke up, ''My old woman means well, even though she can't speak a God damn word of English, I mean any damn word of English.'' ...

The night they expected their father, they all sat up to wait. Teru sat by the door, correcting papers and nervously listening for the first sound of a car stopping on the road. She wanted to prepare her father before he talked to Ayame.

By midnight, Sally and Tad were yawning sleepily and Teru sent them to bed. It was hard for them to stay up with nothing to do. No radio to listen to. No books to read.

Ayame seemed to realize he was coming home from internment during the early hours but when he unexpectedly knocked on the door at three o'clock in the morning, she said, "Father, where have you been?"

Mr. Noguchi frowned fleetingly, "Our train was three hours behind schedule."

He handed Teru his suitcase and looked around at the dingy room in the feeble glow of the unshaded light. He looked tired and thinner than when they'd taken him away.

"It's not good for the children to stay up so late waiting for you."

"What?"

"You should come home earlier."

He stared at Ayame. "That's a strange way to greet a person."

"Father, why don't you wash up first. I'll show you where the washroom is."

Teru quickly grabbed towel and soap from the rack by the door. He looked back at Ayame but good naturedly allowed himself to be pulled outside.

Teru explained hastily. "Mrs. Yamada thought it might have been caused by the heat stroke she suffered our first day here. It's not very bad. She just can't remember anything."

He stopped abruptly. "Why didn't you let me know?" His face started to grow stem.

"We thought you'd worry too much, being helpless to do anything."

''What does the doctor say?''

"Mrs. Yamada said these things cured themselves better at home. They would have taken mother away. Mrs. Umeda is still in the crazy house in Los Angeles."

"We will discuss this later." He said wearily. He walked thoughtfully into the latrine.

Teru woke Sally and Tad. They went to meet him.

"Hi, pop." Tad went into the latrine and Sally met them coming out. They joyfully escorted him home arms linked tightly with his.

They looked nervously at Teru when he told them all to go to bed. He wanted to talk to Ayame alone. They crawled into their cots. They heard his lowered voice. They heard a sob and wondered what had caused it.

They watched in the gloom while he slowly undressed. He stopped to survey once more the row of cots and the darkened room before getting into the cot. The last thing they heard was his restless turning on the straw mattress.

Monument in cemetery
Manzanar Relocation Center, California

Original neg. no.: LC-A351-3-M-13

Manzanar street scene, spring
Manzanar Relocation Center, California

Original neg. no.: LC-A351-3-M-27

Manzanar Relocation Center from tower
Manzanar Relocation Center, California

Original neg. no.: LC-A351-3-M-4-Ax

Entrance to Manzanar
Manzanar Relocation Center, California

Original neg. no.: LC-A351-3-M-28

Line crew at work in Manzanar
Manzanar Relocation Center, California

Original neg. no.: LC-A351-T01-3-M-23-B

Mess line, noon
Manzanar Relocation Center, California

Original neg. no.: LC-A35-6-M-22

Baseball game
Manzanar Relocation Center, California

Roy Takeno, editor, and group reading paper in front of office
Manzanar Relocation Center, California

Original neg. no.: LC-A351-3-M-14

Choir, general group
Manzanar Relocation Center, California

Original neg. no.: LC-A35-5-M-19

Mr. and Mrs. Henry J. Tsurutani and baby Bruce
Manzanar Relocation Center, California

Original neg. no.: LC-A351-3-M-38

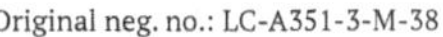

Winter storm
Manzanar Relocation Center, California

Original neg. no.: LC-A35-6-M-79

View south from Manzanar to Alabama Hills
Manzanar Relocation Center, California

Original neg. no.: LC-A351-3-M-10

Farm, farm workers, Mt. Williamson in background
Manzanar Relocation Center, California

Original neg. no.: LC-A351-3-M-14

Guayule Field
Manzanar Relocation Center, California

Original neg. no.: LC-A351-3-M-15-A

Manzanar street scene, winter
Manzanar Relocation Center, California

Original neg. no.: LC-A351-3-M-25

CHAPTER 11

Thursday, Mr. Noguchi made the rounds, delivering messages and greeting friends. People came to see him. At lunch, he stood up in the mess hall and briefly thanked the people in the block for looking after his wife and children during his detention.

Friday, he briskly set to work. He borrowed a hammer, plane,saw, and chisel. He fixed the balky windows so they would open all the way. He fixed the door so it wouldn't rattle. He smoothed over the table and chairs.

Saturday, he went to employment and secured a job as an Irrigation Specialist. In the afternoon, he went to visit friends in Camp 1, and stayed longer than expected because of the trouble. He told them about it later.

Saturday night in Camp 1, someone beat up Edwin Ikeda, strong JACL leader and special investigator for the FBI before evacuation. He accompanied the FBI in their search of Japanese homes to read documents and to interpret. He was reputed to be still working for the FBI.

The men came late at night. Posted guards. One of them entered the bachelor barrack, cap pulled low over his eyes, a club in his hand. Ikeda was having coffee with four others.

"Which one is Ikeda?"

Joe Shiba pointed. His back was turned and he didn't see the club. Ikeda did and knew what it was for. He backed away and crawled under his cot. He pulled his suitcase to him. The intruder easily upended the cot. He raised his club.

"This is for dogs!" There was the sickening crunch of wood on flesh. Ikeda groaned and stretched out unconscious.

Shiba grabbed the kettle of boiling water to throw on Ikeda's assailant. A dozen masked men advanced quickly through the barrack. They pounded into a run. Shiba put the kettle down.

In the same week, they beat up Jack Ito, self-styled FBI agent who threatened FBI action against anyone who molested him. They clubbed and hospitalized snobbishly American Larry Sasaki who "never did have much truck with Japanese outside."

They severely manhandled the parents of Masato Shibuya when they refused to divulge his whereabouts.

The young men of the block nearly caught up with them the night they tried to beat up Bob Omura but they found themselves slugging each other in the darkness while the assailants escaped.

Two persons were arrested on suspicion. Canes were discovered in their home similar to one found at the scene of the Ito beating.

Their friends and fellow Judo club members learned they were to be taken outside for trial. They surrounded the jail to prevent their removal. Sympathizers and curiosity seekers swelled the crowd.

The head man was gone. His assistant drove out to the jail and asked them to go home. Teenage girls started to boo. The booing spread. It grew ominous. The assistant head man listened to the drowning roar. He left hurriedly. He asked the evacuee council to intervene. Leaders of the demonstrators were called in. They promptly demanded a promise that the jailed men wouldn't be taken outside the camp.

The assistant contacted the FBI and the FBI acquiesed. The leaders returned to their mob triumphantly-- to discover they had been supplanted. The new leaders demanded unconditional release of the jailed men.

The FBI refused. Caught between two fires, the council resigned. The block managers resigned. All official contact was lost between the administration and the people.

New representatives were elected. One Jssei and one Nisei from each block. A heated session followed. Some talked in English, some in Japanese. Some Nisei couldn't understand the Japanese. Some Jssei couldn't understand the English. But when the vote was taken, it was unanimous. General strike, effective immediately.

The mess hall gongs rang wildly. The people against the swollen mob,--curious--half-fearful--enjoying the unexpected holiday from work.

What is it all about?

The authorities intend to take them out of camp. They'll never get a fair trial outside. We're supposed to prevent them from taking them outside.

No. That was before. Now we want their unconditional release.

They're innocent. They're scapegoats. This is purely disciplinary.

Ikeda was a known stool pigeon. He was bound to get it sooner or later. Maybe it was a nasty way but he should have cleared out of camp long ago. He doesn't belong here. All he has to do is ask the FBI and they'll let him out anytime.

The doctors found an FBI badge in his clothing when they put him to bed. They found a pistol in his suitcase when it was brought in. What would an honest man be doing with a pistol in here?

I talked to Harry Taka. He's on that new council. This is a general strike for better living conditions--to secure a more harmonious atmosphere-- to protest against that slop they feed us.

They settled down to wait. Each block gathered around its quickly improvised banner. It was too easy to tell who was there and who wasn't. Everybody was there. Whether in sympathy or not, they showed their faces under their block banner. No one wanted to be identified as an informer. Only "dog" stayed home. "Dog" meaning informers, stool pigeons.

They all left their work. The pro-American, the pro-Japanese, the fence sitter. Loyalty to country was never the issue, but some thought it was. An old gentleman in his seventies proudly paraded his Imperial flag until he was asked to put it away. They appreciated his spirit but it would only cause trouble.

When night came, they built bonfires to ward off the cold. They sent the older men and womenfolk home. The young men stood vigil through the night.

With the warming sun, they came back again, young and old, to find soldiers came during the night from Phoenix and were standing guard on the outer perimeter of camp. Communication was cut off from Camp 2 and Camp 3.

The negotiating committee slipped through on a canteen truck and addressed the councilmen of Camps 2 and 3. They asked them not to wage a sympathy strike. They wanted them to stay out and act as mediators. Otherwise, there would be no end to the strike.

The councilmen returned to block meetings. Camp 2 voted eleven blocks against striking , four blocks for striking. The situation in Camp 3 was obscure.

Dissatisfied with the results, strongly pro-Japanese elements in Camp 2 organized a bonfire rally. With fiery oratory, they worked up a frenzy. The Camp 1 negotiators didn't mean what they said. Deep down in their hearts they want us to strike, but they couldn't come right out and say so for delicate reasons. Knowing that, are we going to let our brethren down?

No. Let us strike!

Camp 2 split wide open. Several blocks held high to their earlier vote against striking and posted guards to prevent violence during the night. Prominent figures in the no-strike faction went to bed with hatchets laid conveniently to hand.

Rival factions sent emissaries to woo sympathy in Camp 3. Their council didn't know whom to believe. In exasperation, they said, you go your way and we'll go ours.

In Camp 1, the banners grew gaudier with the addition ofslogans and symbols splashed on with red ink. Soon after, they tookmon the appearance of rising sun flags. The pro-Americans thought in dismay, this is a patriotic display. You don't belong here. But they stayed. That isn't the real issue. Or is it? They looked at the bones hung below signs which read, "For dogs only."

"Dogs?" Stool pigeons for whom? For the American government, whom else? The "dogs" referred to were loyal American, doing what they thought was their patriotic duty. This demonstration is directed mainly against "dogs." Why don't we go home? Because people will think we're "dogs"? Are we afraid? They stayed and listened uneasily when the two prisoners came out and thanked the crowd for their united support.

After supper, they started their bonfires again. It was cold and the women and older men hugged the fires for warmth. The block 26 young people couldn't get near their own bonfire and built another one. Someone had the bright idea of putting up a Camp 3 banner.

The people turned to look. Delegations went to thank them for coming all the way from Camp 3 to aid their strike. They didn't ask how they got there. They took for granted that they were really from Camp 3.

"Don't mention it." the youngsters answered, grinning hugely at their deception.

They settled down to their vigil. Willing hands hammered together a stage. Lavish talent shows were organized and put on. Movies were shown. Speeches were made. The outlook was encouraging if they held out a little longer.

Volunteers 'signed up to stand guard on certain nights to go out to the slough at the west end of Camp for firewood to make coffee and rice balls for the night watch

A week passed.

The head man returned to camp. He asked the negotiators to meet with him at the administration building from 10 a.m. to 11 a.m. They said, no, we can't settle this matter in an hour. Let us meet as long as necessary to settle our differences. Meet us halfway.

The head man shrugged his shoulders and went down into the camp. The people immediately ringed the barrack. They were orderly and well behaved, but if they got out of control, they could smash to shreds the building and anyone within a matter of minutes. The entire camp must be out there.

What seems to be the trouble, gentlemen?

We want a complete review of the factors which make this strike necessary. Releasing the men alone won't settle this thing. We have to eliminate the causes. To do that, we must have the following things:

First, give us a board whose functions will be the investigation

of all persons suspected of stool pigeon activities. If the evidence is conclusive, banish such persons from the camp, since there is bound to be trouble otherwise.

Second, establish a labor board which will make certain adjustments in the labor situation. A sore point with us is the fact that the first volunteers who came to open this camp took all the desirable positions whether qualified for them or not. As a result, competent men are forced to take orders from incompetent ones.

A certain evacuee now in a key position has a record as a swindler before evacuation. A dozen people here in Poston have been cheated by this man and will corroborate this statement. For some reason, there are many other such persons with unsavory "outside" records holding important positions. Give the board authority to discharge all such persons.

Third, set up a board to act as a medium of contact between the administration and the people on all executive matters. Our present council only makes laws and has nothing to say about their execution. Trouble arises from the fact that the laws are sometimes applied without full knowledge of how the people will react.

These are the main points but there are other causes of trouble. The *Issei* will agitate as long as they are denied representation on matters which regulate their lives as well as the lives of the Nisei who now decide those matters.

When we first came in here, our new born babies died right and left from dehydration. This is in the medical records. Did the administration do anything about it? No! Coolers were ordered, but not for the hospital, for the administration building. We had to form an investigating committee and ask you to transfer the coolers from the administration building to the hospital.

When we uncovered discrepancies in certain accounts of the food commissary, we were refused access to the books when we wished to investigate further. The man in charge was dismissed but where is he now? He is working for the WRA at another relocation center. Do you wonder that we've grown to distrust the administration.

We were promised six months ago, that we would soon have ceilings for our barracks, linoleum for our floors, double walls, and stoves. It's November. The nights are cold already. Where are all these things?

Our first understanding was that we would cultivate and improve this land and that the proceeds from our labor would be pooled and distributed to us in a lump sum when the war ended so we would have something to start over with. The other day you about-faced and told us we would never be paid more than nineteen dollars a month in camp. You told us to leave camp if we wanted more.

We went through a mass evacuation. Many of us are penniless. You want us to start all over again from scratch. The heads of many families are too old for that without financial aid. Right now,many of us are admittedly dependent on the sixteen and nineteen dollars a month and the three dollars and twenty-five cents clothing allowance. Where are they? We have seen neither hide nor hair of any clothing allowance since coming here, and our pay is four months late. We need that money badly or we wouldn't ask for it. It's degrading to have to ask. Why is it that Camp 2 people have already received two months clothing allowance while we in camp 1 have received nothing? Our people tell us it is because someone in the administration is putting it into his own pockets.

In late afternoon, they came to an agreement. The prisoners would have to stand trial but they would not be taken outside. The three boards would be set up.

The chairman of the board to investigate suspected stool pigeons was asked what they intended to do with their findings.

He said, "We will submit them to the Japanese government when the time comes."

" We? You haven't even applied for repatriation!"

"Time enough for that when the war is ended."

The labor board deliberated and accomplished little of their avowed purposes.

The executive board was accused of high-handed measures and fell into disfavor.

Reports came in of the riots in Manzanar. A soldier fired a machine gun into a fleeing crowd. It had been menacing and abusive a minute before. Two were killed, a dozen wounded. The evacuee doctor who attended to the dead refused to sign a statement that the bullets entered the front of the victims. Someone else signed the statement. Boy scouts stoutly guarded an American flag from the mob which moved to tear it down.

The causes of the riots were similar to the causes of the Poston strike. Stool pigeons. That's what they say. Do you know the real story behind the riot? An evacuee investigated mismanagement and found evidence the *Hakujin* in charge was lining his pockets. The riots were a result of trying to cover up. It doesn't all add up.

I don't believe it.

It's true. I have a letter from Manzanar. I'll show you.

The uncertainty, the inaction grew rumors like a malignant cancer. An old man boasted, "I started a rumor at the north end of camp this morning and it reached the south end at three o'clock." That plot of land they' re having us clear between Camp 1 and Camp 2 is going to be an airfield. Look how level we're making it. Look at that road they're having us build all the way into Parker. They wouldn't be spending so much money to build a road just for us.

These lawns they're having us seed these trees they' re letting us bring in to plant, they're not for us. Just about the time we get things fixed up, we'll be shoved out. Do you think that million dollar canal they're building from the Colorado River is for us? Not a chance! By the time all the improvements bear fruit, the barracks will have fallen to pieces.

In Camp 2, life returned to normal more slowly. Feelings had run too high and the cleavage lay raw and ugly. Too wide to be forgotten so easily.

Thanksgiving came and went quietly. It was the first Thanksgiving Teru could remember when there was no turkey on the Noguchi table. Mr. Noguchi told them why they always had turkey.

George Motoyama's first grade teacher asked her pupils if they had turkey for Thanksgiving. Six year old George promptly raised his hand with the rest. Miss Burness singled out George.

"Did you have dark meat or white meat, George?"

"white meat."

"Don't you like dark meat? I do."

"There wasn't any dark meat. Our turkey was all white."

"Oh, no. There must have been both dark meat and white meat."

"It was all white meat." George insisted. ''It tasted good."

"It couldn't have been. Unless--" Miss Burness was suspicious.

"George, are you sure you had turkey for Thanksgiving?"

"Yes, teacher. We had turkey."

"What did it look like?"

"It was big and round like this." George held up his arms, proudly.

"Oh," Miss Burness said triumphantly, "That must have been roast pork.' '

"It was turkey." Miss Burness said, a little miffed, "I still think you had roast pork, not turkey."

"It was turkey." George said weakly.

He went straight home and asked his mother. She looked down into his tight face. She grabbed his skinny arms and huggedhim tightly, so he couldn't see the tears which fell on his shoulder ...

Ayame seemed to improve after her husband returned. She quit complaining about the pains in her stomach.

She said she would wash. Sally sorted the clothes while Ayame went ahead with the towels and sheets. Sally could find no powdered soap. She hurried to the canteen to buy some.

When she returned, Ayame was scrubbing diligently away under a mountain of suds. She pulled out a ragged towel and looked at it critically. Sally frowned. She couldn't remember any towel as tom as the one her mother held.

"Mother, I'll finish the rest of the wash. You go home and lie down for a while."

Ayame blew the sweat and the soap suds off her nose.

''This is hard work," she said. She was completely precoccupied with the one towel. The rest of the wash was untouched.

CHAPTER 12

"Who's the distinguished looking gentlemen?" Jiro asked. They were sitting on the Harada doorstep, enjoying the five o'clock sun. It was December and cold in the shade. They turned to watch the white-haired head bent to inspect the stunted rows of red beets. The spaces between every other barrack were planted with vegetables for block mess halls.

The soil wasn't worth cultivating but the plan called for Poston to grow its own vegetables. The ground was sour with alkali and they could see the white film covering the ground.

"That's Mr. Mineta, isn't it?" Gary Harada looked at Teru for confirmation. He didn't know half the people in the block. He spoke practically no Japanese and none of the older folks ventured to talk to him. When he did say a word or possibly two, his Japanese accent was revealed as being no better than that of a native of Brooklyn.

Teru nodded.

"Very pro-Japanese, isn't he?"

"Very. He wakes up at five o'clock every morning to listen to the short wave from Japan. Everyone greets him with, 'What's news today?'"

"Is that right?" Gary was surprised. " I didn't know there were any short wave radios in here."

"I didn't know either until one of my fourth graders mentioned it."

"There are two or three out our way that I know of," Jiro said.

Tom Itaya joined them. He was a pharmacist a year out of school and lived in the next block.

"Funny no one has reported them," Gary said.

"That's the only pleasure they get out of life in here and there's no harm to it that I can see."

"I think most are too bitter about evacuation yet to do anything like re-porting people for having radios," Tom said.

"I'd say disillusioned," Jiro said.

"No, bitter, "Tom insisted, "This evacuation is just a phase. We'll get over it eventually."

"You're willing to forgive and forget. Just like that?"

"Why not?" Tom asked.

''What about the stuff you were telling me the other day?

How your brother went back to Japan and liked the country so much he asked your parents if he could take out Japanese citizenship. I thought you were trying to convince me Japan was the place for us."

"Let me put it his way. If I were in Japan, I'd do the same but since I'm stuck here, I might as well act accordingly. We're all Japanese and I'm not forgetting that, but we won't get anywhere while we're in this country acting like we felt."

"This is all pretty new to me," Gary said, "There were no Japanese where I lived outside and all my friends were white people. I never thought very much about being Japanese until they discharged me from the air cadets right after Pearl Harbor. Oh, and when I found my legs were so short they didn't get in the way in the cockpit."

They laughed while Gary flexed his bandy legs, short even for Japanese.

"Hi, Teru," Dot Maeda jauntily limped by on her way to the Sakaguchi apartment to see Alice. She was sixteen and the nicest girl in the block according to Sally. She lived in 4-C right across from them.

Tom lowered his voice when she passed. "Is that the girl who was shot and abducted by Filipinos?"

"Just shot. The older sister was abducted."

"I can't go for Filipinos," Gary said, " They're too close to savages."

Teru was wishing Jiro were more like Gary. Jiro got along too well with the old folks to be as American as Gary thought he spoke as good English and seemed to have lived mostly among *Hakujin*.

At the Universtiy of California, he stayed with *Hakujin* roomates at the Barrington Hall cooperative and during his summer vacations worked on a surveying crew.

She remarked once on his fluent Japanese and he said, " It only seems so. My pronunciation is good because my mother and father are both well educated and that sort of fools the old folks. I really know very little Japa-nese. I can't read the stuff at all."

And yet, the day after Pearl Harbor, he went to his selective service board. The surprised selective service clerk said, "You've got a lot of nerve coming here. Aren't you in the wrong place?"

"I don't think so," Jiro insisted, "You can't stop me."

"Oh, I can't? We got orders from Washington to throw you guys out."

Jiro had no way of knowing whether that were true. He asked,

"Will you show me the order?"

"Not to any damn stinking Jap." The man spit the words out.

"It's guys like you who made these wars necessary," Jiro said and thought, I don't stink as much as you do. He knew it was no use and walked out.

He stayed out of camp politics completely and that made it harder to decide where he stood. He said of the strike, "It's all right to protect, but we won't get anywhere by striking. We're not holding up anything that hurts the administration and they can do as they please--when they please. Some people forget who is in the driver's seat."

He looked across the road to the barracks where the Caucasian personnel lived. "There they are, right over there. Look at that paint. Inside they have coolers, double walls, ceilings, stoves, refrigerators." He paused and no one said anything. "If they can have them, why can't we? We were told that coming here was a patriotic duty. Maybe some of THEM came to this hell-hole as a patriotic duty, too. I don't know . But how many of them volunteered to live in our barracks, share our food, work for our pay? Are they less patriotic?"

"Mr. McBain would give you a two hour lecture for saying that,' ' Kate said.

Mike Tanabe who taught the eighth grade mimicked, ''The government is doing everything possible to make amends. You must realize that. You must forget what is past and attempt to revaluate the present situation in that light."

He went on, "Yeah, kick us in the pants and say they're sorry. Or send new WRA instructions that the term Caucasian personnel is not to be used anymore. They want to be called the Appointed personnel. They don't want to hurt our feelings. They don't want us to feel any distinction, the 'Apes'."

In her class of fourth graders, Teru could almost see the changes taking place under the deteriorating influences of camp life. The clamor for an American flag to salute every morning disappeared. She even thought she could begin to tell in which families parental authority was still strong.

The children spoke more and more Japanese in their play.

She thought too that she could distinguish the other extreme in those pupils who never ate with their parent and went home only to sleep. They lived in a boys' world of their own and came less under the influence of the bitterness and disillusionment festering in their parents. When certain blocks voted to have designated family tables in the mess hall, they fell into line reluctantly or even refused to eat in their own mess halls.

She had seven boys from block 225 who became more unruly every day. They were the ringleaders in undermining the morals of the rest of the class.

They said to the others, "We're going to Japan so why should we study in an American school?"

Teru could think of no good answer to their question. She told them that coming to school developed their brains so they could more easily learn whatever they chose to learn later on but she was afraid she made no impression on them. She wished the WRA would permit separate Japanese language school for them. It would make things so much easier.

She envied Jiro who promptly told his students when they began to get out of hand, "I'm here to teach you math. I presume you signed up because you wanted to learn. If any of you have changed your mind, it's time for you to get out and sign up for some other course."

No one quit... .

It was a moonless night and only the stars shone brightly. It was dark on the ground where Teru and Sally stood in the last row of contraltos. The silhouettes of the singers in front flickered darkly in the light of the candles. They could barely make out the people seated below them.

Adeste fidelis,

Laeti triumphantes,

Alma Ohara's clear, beautiful soprano rose buoyantly above the blended voices of the mixed choir. The desert night hushed reverently while the final note hung breathless in the still air. The people bowed their heads in humility and thanked God for the faith that made this night more beautiful than any they remembered.

They lingered to watch the singers file from their places. They moved unwillingly back into their drab, barnlike barracks.

It was the brightest spot in their first Christmas behind barbed wue.

With tacit consent, they had refrained from exchanging the traditional gifts. But Christmas night was greeted with a sigh of relief by many who had worried through the day that someone might bring gifts. They had no money to buy presents even for their own children.

The games and toys sent in by churches and other organizations were more gratefully appreciated by the parents who had envisioned a giftless Christmas for their children than by the children who were accustomed to more quality and quantity ...

When she saw him coming toward her from the direction of the administration building, Teru couldn't believe her eyes. She was on her way to 216 to help Kate with the dress she intended wearing to the New Year's dance that night. They would be going together; Kate, Gary, Bill, Sally, Jiro, and herself

He stopped and stood there, grinning widely at her, a little rumpled looking and in need of a shave. He carried a black dufllebag.

"George," she gasped, "When did you get here? Why didn't you let us know?"

''I wanted to surprise you," he said.

"Where are you staying?" Teru sparred for time to think.

"Block 215 with Jim Yano. Where is it?"

"The next block on the other side of this one."

He rubbed his chin. "I need a shave and shower first. When can I see you?"

Teru hesitated. She didn't know how long she would be with Kate. She said, "We're all going to the fair this afternoon. Why don't you join us?"

"Where is this fair?" he failed to keep the disappointment out of his voice at her use of the plural we. "I heard about it in Gila."

"On the 215 school grounds. They moved out the partition and are using our classrooms. We're meeting in front of the school exhibit about one o'clock. You can't miss it and there won't be too big a crowd that early."

He turned to look at her before he disappeared behind a barrack. Teru walked slowly to the Tani apartment where Kate lived with her father and four brothers.

Kate opened the door.

"Come in, Teru. Everyone is at the fair."

She brought out the dress and slipped it on. It was white with black trimming.

"It's nice, "Teru said and concentrated on setting the pins straight in the wide, flaring skirt.

"You look so solemn." "Jiro?" Kate teased.

"George. He's here."

"George? Here? I thought that was all over."

"It's my fault," Teru said, "I wanted to tell him right off but I thought I would drop a hint first and give him a chance to come along to that way of thinking himself I thought it would be better than telling him bluntly."

"What are you going to do?"

"I don't know. I never expected him to be able to come here. It takes such a long time just to get leave clearance to go outside."

George stared curiously around at the fair grounds. A goodly crowd of early arrivals already wandered aimlessly, peering into the cages housing the rattlers, desert rats, terrapins, coyotes, or waiting for the exhibits to open. The line in front of the arts and crafts building was already several hundred people long.

Teru wasn't there. He wondered glumly what he would say to her now that he was here. He wished he hadn't come. She wasn't the kind to write that sort of letter without good reason.

He recognized Kate Tani but he didn't know the other two with her. He wondered who the girl in the red jacket was. She was strikingly pretty.

She turned and saw him.

"There he is."

She came towards him.

"Hello. George," she said.

"Hello," George said blankly. Something vaguely familiar looked at him out of the wide-spaced eyes. He stared fascinated while he racked his brains for the name that fitted the face. He knew her all right, but what was her name?

"Teru was held up and I'm substituting until she comes."

She took hold of his arm familiarly.

George obediently followed the intimate tug of her arm. She introduced him to Gary Harada. He tried to remember where he'd heard that bubbling voice before.

"The concessions are opening. Let's go," she urged.

"You two go ahead. We'll wait for Teru and --"Kate stopped awkwardly. "Let's go."

George paused indecisively, then resolutely followed. There was a challenge in the way she didn't even look back to see if the was following. He caught up with her and she grinned at him. She took hold of his arm in that intimate and possessive way.

"How's Toshiko?" she asked carelessly.

George ventured a wild guess. "I didn't know you knew Toshiko."

"What?" she stopped suddenly and searched his face. "You don't remember me." It was a gleeful statement. "Why, you don't remember me at all," she gurgled.

"I do," George protested, "I just can't remember your name." He tried to be matter of fact.

"This is rich." Her nose wrinkled. She bubbled over with laughter. He knew that laugh as well as he knew his own. He'd heard it often.

"Come on." She was off again before the obstinate cogs slipped into place. "Win me a doll."

George shrugged his shoulders and followed her to the baseball throw. He flexed his arm and she patted it familiarly.

"Good old soupbone."

George looked at her startled. It couldn't be. He knocked over the grinning cats in one, two, three order and handed her the plaster doll.

"Why didn't you bring Yoshiko with you?"

How could he have failed to recognize her? That candid look.

That small birthmark over her right eye.

"You little devil," he accused, "Testing the wits out of an old man."

Sally saw that the game was up.

"You asked for it," she said.

"You've grown up."

"It's the camouflage," she said. She was conscious of it because it was only the second time she had used lipstick and powder.

Dot Maeda was behind the counter. "Try it again," she said,

"You were lucky that time."

George grinned confidently at Sally and only missed once in his next five tries.

"Too easy,"Sally sniffed disdainfully and pulled him away.

George followed happily, unwilling to let her get even a step away. He had no time to wonder what made him so light-hearted when he'd been so glum a short time before.

"George."

They stiffened guiltily. Jiro, Gary, Kate, and Teru had come up behind them.

CHAPTER 13

Teru wondered what she should do while she waited for Jiro to call for her. Sally seemed excited about something. Her hand trembled and she smeared the lipstick.

"Darn." She wiped it off and tried a second time.

"You have too much on." Teru said.

Sally critically surveyed the red curve of her lips in the mirror propped on a side beam of the wall. She blotted off a tiny bit.

"Ready?" Jiro knocked on the door.

Teru glanced hastily over Sally's shoulder into the mirror and hurried out. She had to make Jiro understand in the fifteen minutes it took to walk to the fair grounds. She quickly told him about George.

"I couldn't tum him down," she ended, "Do you mind?"

"Of course not," Jiro said, "If you want."

"About tonight,---" Teru began hesitantly.

Jiro stopped her. They were halfway there. "Wait a minute."

He turned her around and headed away from the fair grounds

"They're waiting for us," Teru protested.

"It won't hurt them to wait."

They walked slowly. Teru waited for him to speak. Her heart began to thump vigorously.

"Are you still --- that way about him?"

I don't think so. Tero formed the words in her throat but they failed to come out.

Sally, Dot, and Alice came swinging down the road.

"I'll ask Sally to tell them we'll be late."

She did and Sally said to Dot and Alice, "I forgot a hanky. I'll catch up with you." She hurried home and wiped off a little more makeup.

They walked down towards Cottonwood Bowl where the weekly out-door movies were held. Their feet kicked up dry puffs of dust that hung languidly in the motionless air.

"I knew about George when I first met you," Jiro said, "I told myself rd be a fool to get serious. I thought I was just kidding around and could drop everything when the time came."

Tero slipped her hand in his and no more words were necessary. They headed back towards the even rows of dusty tar-papered barracks ...

"Hi, Jiro," George said when he turned and saw who had hailed him. Surprise quickly erased his guilty start. "I didn't know you knew Tero."

"Jiro is teaching, too," Tero said, "We're all teachers."

George didn't miss the quick glance she gave Jiro. It confirmed his worst guess. He'd been a fool to think any other reason had made Tero write what she did. Jiro was one swell guy. Which was a funny thing to be think-ing about a guy when the girl you loved had just made it clear she loved that guy.

George was conscious of Sally gently tugging to release her arm. He was still holding it tightly against his side.

Kate said, "Let's get in line before ifs too long." She anxiously eyed the people quickly tacking on to the end of the line in front of the art exhibit. "I want to see Yonso' s ironwood."

George tightened his hold on Sally's arm and said, " I can think of better ways to spend the afternoon. Sally and I are going to look at the exhibits tomorrow morning when there won't be so many other things to do."

He led Sally away and called over his shoulder, "See you at the dance tonight." Then under his breath to Sally, "If you'll come with me."

"I wish I could," Sally said regretfully.

Dot Maeda called to them. She had moved to the dart concession. "Bet you're not so lucky here."

She kidded him and did her best to spoil his aim. ''You throw like an old man... I distinctly heard your bones creak that time, grandpa ... No wonder you can't hit the target."

He finally put all three darts in the circle on his sixth try.

Dot handed him a corncob pipe. "Now you can go back to your old men's home."

"Remind me to buy you a rattle before I do," George said weakly.

Dot winked at Sally.

"Don't you find him a little rheumatic?"

Sally considered, "He seems to have enough rubber for another few miles."

George listened to their youthful chatter, feeling too old and thinking. She's only seventeen--or eighteen at the most.

"Let's go, young one," he tried to match their talk and failing, felt some of his exuberance leave him ...

He stared sourly at the pin-up girls adorning the room Jim Yano shared with Pete Kurasaki. George remembered Pete as one of the packing shed workers in Salinas.

"I like the one with the snaky hips," Pete said.

"Better get your mind off that kind of stuff tonight," Jim warned, "'Alice isn't the kind you play around with."

"Watch me," Pete said airily, "It took me three months to get this date."

George turned to Jim, "I don't know if l even want to go."

"Snap out of it." Jim urged, "You'll meet lots of old friends there. The crowd is a little younger than used to go to dances outside but you won't feel out of place."

The crowd WAS young and rushing Sally. George found it easier to cut in on Teru. They danced in silence, Teru wondering how to square things and George trying to recapture thc mood of that night when he'd said goodbye to her.

It was no use and they awkwardly said the easy, trite things. Both were relieved when the newly organized Camp 2 band stopped playing.

George wandered aimlessly in the stag line unable to make up his mind what to do. Alice looked at him over Pete's shoulder and he caught a worried look in her eyes. He cut in and smelled the liquor on Pete's breath.

"I was hoping you'd dance with me.' Alice said, "How is Yoshiko?"

"She's a nurse's aide."

They moved sedately around the dimly lit mess hall. He said, "You're stepping out with fast company tonight."

He wanted to tell her Pete knew too much for her and to watch her step. He didn't like the way Pete was holding her. Then he remembered how Sally had practically led him around by his nose that afternoon. He grinned ruefully and decided the younger set could take care of themselves.

He had his misgivings again when Pete cut back in and danced off, with Alice hugged tightly in his arms. He thought, Damn, no wonder the old folks frown on dancing. How many blocks did Sally say forbade their daughters from going to any dances?

He shrugged his shoulders and turned away. He didn't like the possessive way Bill was dancing with Sally either, but what could he do about it? She was his date and probably his girl too.

Dot Maeda danced by with Jim and George cut in.

" Hi, grandpop," Dot greeted him, "You haven't given up already?"

She looked meaningfully in the direction of Bill and Sally dancing in a comer. There was an urging in her voice.

"Quit calling me grandpop and I might have a chance,"

George complained. If she only knew how close to the truth that was. He looked again. Sally didn't seen too absorbed in Bill. In fact, she too seemed to be looking their way.

Sally was music in his arms. She caught the rhythm of his feet immediately and moved lightly to his every whim and fancy.

"Getting too old for much dancing?" Sally asked innocently.

George felt the unintended barb twist painfully. Why did she have to be so young?

"I was waiting until you grew out of the cradle," he said and could have kicked himself for the sudden hurt that leaped into her eyes. She floated away in the arms of a kid who still had his upper lip fuzz.

Alice stopped doubtfully for an instant at the door, then followed Pete outside.

George saw them, and silently berated himself Damn, why didn't I take her home. He half moved to follow them outside.

Bill and Sally danced by and he distinctly heard Bill say to her,

"Let's ditch this, too."

George stopped outside just in time to see Pete and Alice disappearing in the darkness of the abandoned block where the soldiers had been quartered when the camp opened.

Oh Damn, he thought, and walked in the other direction.

"This is far enough. Let's go back." Alice unsuccessfully tried to keep the worry out of her voice. She looked around at the dark empty barracks and shivered.

"What's your hurry?" Pete's hand slid around her waist and pulled her close. His heavy hand searched for and found her breast.

Alice gasped and jerked away from his hold. She ran and stumbled and he caught up with her. He grabbed her.

"I'll scream."

"Don't be such a baby." Pete said hoarsely.

"I want to go back," Alice sobbed.

"Sit down here a minute, and rest first," Pete said. "You don't want to go back all out of breath."

He was strong and he easily pulled her down on the doorstep with him. He tried to get her to look at him.

"What's the matter?" he asked. "When we were dancing, I thought you felt it like I did."

He covered her firm breasts with his hands and cupped them tightly. "It won't hurt," he whispered urgently.

"No." Alice said between sobs which grew more violent and audible.

"People will hear you here." Pete said. "Let's go inside until you get over it. "

He eagerly supported her into the darkened barrack and carefully closed the door behind him.

CHAPTER 14

George found himself walking out to the deserted exhibit buildings. He stopped by the school exhibit and sat on the front doorstep. That was where she had stood when he first saw her. Something about her had clamored for attention. Not the red jacket, for there were a dozen others of the same bright hue in sight--probably orderd from the same mail order house. He remembered the lift of her head so like Teru's and wondered why he'd been fooled so completely.

Funny how quickly he recoverd from seeing that almost wifely look in Teru's eyes when she looked at Jiro. Sally of course, had made him forget. Now Sally was gone with Bill. To look at that thin sliver of a moon, or worse.

He was startled by the sound of a foot put stealthily down behind him. She brushed his arm in sitting down beside him.

"Hello," she said cheerfully.

George tried to talk coherently above the erratic pounding of his heart. He said incredulously, "What are you doing out here?"

"I might ask you the same question."

"Where's Bill?"

"I ditched him at the dance."

"I thought you went for a walk with him."

"That's when I told him."

George looked blank.

''About you-- and me.''

George peered unbelievingly at her out of the comers of his eyes. She was staring straight ahead. The softest whisper of a desert breeze moved a few moon-touched strands of hair across her face.

He smoothed back her hair and cupped her young face in his hands. He was startled by her resemblance to Teru. He remembered again that night he said goodbye to Teru He'd been choked up with emotion then. But he hadn't felt as lighthearted and happy as he did now.

The soft desert air felt cool against his cheeks. The muted music seemed to come from far away.

He bent and kissed her tenderly ....

They all walked home together. Bill seemed in good spirits. He teased Sally, ' 'I saw that mooney look in your eyes from the time you were in pigtails. I hoped you'd forgotten but I guess you didn't."

Teru looked happily at Jiro.

" Golly, why don't girls go for me?" Bill sighed. Kate gave him a long look. ..

Teru didn't see Alice until the next day. Her eyes were rimmed with red and heavily powdered over.

"We missed you last night."

"We left early," Alice said. Her voice was heavy with a cold. She avoided looking at Teru.

George returned to Gila the next week. Pete Kurasaki left at the same time with a half dozen others on seasonal leave to work on a cattle ranch.

Three weeks later, Alice wrote a letter to the address Jim Yano gave her. She told Pete she was pregnant and was afraid to tell anyone.

Enemy alien, 4-c, classifications began to pour into camp for *Nisei*. Ito, the JACL bigshot, indignantly protested to the War Department against the new classification.

"Why doesn't he keep his big trap shut? ... He makes it sound like we all don't want to be classified 4-c ... He acts like he's our spokesman ... What right has he to speak for everybody?"

Mrs. Ito lay awake long after the last door had banged shut for the night. She was sleepy but her eyes were wide open with worry over what the night might bring. She'd gone into the latrine to wash her hands and heard Mrs. Sato's voice coming from behind the partition that separated the wash trough from the flush toilets. "Ifl were Ito-san, I'd be afraid to go to sleep."

She looked across at her husband's face relaxed in sleep but still showing the strain of the day. She wished he would quit his JACL work. It wasn't worth it. Not in camp where so many people talked ill of the JACL. Outside, some prestige had been attached to being a JACL leader and his business had been furthered.

She was instantly aware of the first slow opening of the door and the dark figures stealing into the room. She shook her husband. She started to scream. Six year old Anne woke up and added her shrill screams. Ito yelled furiously for help.

The dim figures quickly flung themselves across the room and grappled with Ito. They swung their ironwood clubs. Ito warded off their blows with his arms. "Help!"

''Hurry up.'' The warning came from outside.

Brawny, pajama-clad young men were jumping out the windows of neighboring barracks. The doors were all spiked from the outside, so they wouldn't open. Someone rushed to ring the dinner gong. It was gone.

Three dark figures ran swiftly out of the Ito apartment. One of them ran into the arms of big Johnny Oda as he rounded the comer.

Johnny knocked him to the ground.

"I got one!"

The pajama clad figures quickly ran to help. They kicked the prone figure and waved their hatchets and their baseball bats.

"Kill the bastard.''

"Who is it?''

"Okada''

"Kill the bastard. ''

Okada cowered under the menacing hatchets.

"Who was with you?''

Okada shook his head.

"Knock the 'shit' out of him. He'll tell." Johnny slammed his club down hard but Okada twisted frantically and the club glanced off his shoulder.

"Kill the bastard." Oda raised his hatchet.

"I'll tell." Okada lost his nerve pitifully. "Don't kill me."

"Who was with you?" Okada fearfully named six others, his eyes shrinking from the ugly hatchets. They prodded him to his feet and pushed him roughly away.

All except Hajime Shintani confessed under police ''persuasion.'' They were hustled out of camp overnight. Ito was hospitalized and guarded at the Camp I hospital. He left camp with his family as soon as he was well enough.

Tom ltaya said, "I wonder why they don't go after the higher ups. Those guys were only carrying out orders."

"Do you know who the higher ups are?" Jiro asked.

"Sure. I have a good idea," Tom said, "But I'm staying as far away from that mess as I can. It's that small radical bunch."

Bill said, "You can't just brand them as radicals and shrug them off They represent a larger percentage than your group of the Administration will admit. More than a few people were waiting for an excuse for a strike."

The men were sentenced to serve from two to four years in prison and still nothing happened. There was no strike.

The Army announced its decision to allow Japanese-Americans to volunteer for a special combat unit. Recruiting teams would tour the relocation centers to sign up volunteers. At the same time, everyone would be asked to fill out a selective service questionnaire.

Rumor had it that registrants would be asked to swear allegiance to the United States as a measure of loyalty.

Pete wrote back to Alice, "I'd be a sucker to go back to camp now. If I stay out, I don't have to get mixed up with that cockeyed questionnaire. If you want to get married, you better come out here."

"I'm quitting this ranch next week. The damn guy thinks we're coolies and works the ass out of us from four in the morning to after seven. I'm scramming for Denver to try and find another job. I'll let you know."

Alice read the crude writing through and crumpled the paper in her hands. She stared stonily out the window, the ball of paper clenched tightly in her hands. I'd be a sucker ... If you want to get married ... work the ass out of us ... I'm scramming for Denver ...

How could she ever have thought he was exciting and romantic?

She remembered now, he talked like that too ...

Teru said of the Army announcement, "It's a good thing."

"What do you mean?" Mike Tanabe said, "I say not so good.

It puts us on the spot."

"I don't care for the special combat idea" Jiro said, "It's too much like the segregated Negro units. Why don't they just draft us like anybody else? Give us a chance to mix with *Hakujin* and lose our identity as Japanese."

"Yeah," Jim Yano agreed, ''Ifl'm going to die for America,

I want to do it as an American not a Japanese-American."

"I think I'm going to volunteer," Kenji Hosoda said. He was the youngest of the Hosoda boys living in the next apartment from the Noguchi's. "Pack a gun for Uncle Sam."

"I don't mind being drafted, but damed if I'll volunteer," Bob Ichikawa said.

"How come you're volunteering," Jim asked Kenji. "You told me yourself, you were mighty happy when the Japanese took Bataan and Singapore."

"That was different," Kenji said, ''I felt good about it because it showed up all those guys who poked fun at the Japanese.

I'm thinking now of my brothers and sisters and my own future. It'll be easier for them when they relocate if they can say they have a brother who volunteered for the Army. I know some of you are thinking in terms of going back to Japan, but what would I do back there? I can't speak the lingo and all I have is a high school education which is lower than the high school level in Japan so I'd probably end up digging ditches or something. And you know how swell a living you can make in Japan doing that."

"I don't mind fighting in Europe, myself, but what are you going to do when you're transferred to the Pacific?" Bob Ichikawa asked.

"I just hope they aren't lying when they say we won't be used against the Japanese." Kenji said.

"What about that school you were trying to get into?"

"The bastards turned me down."

"I got a letter from South Central College that I can start this spring," Mike Tanabe said.

"I didn't know you were going out," Jim said, "I thought you were going back to Japan."

"I am. My uncle says going outside is all right as long as it's just for an education. In fact he wants me to, because there'll be a big demand for engineers to build roads from Tokyo to Singapore."

"Seems kind of two-faced to me," Gary said with ill-concealed disgust.

Both he and Jiro were there when Mike told McBain, ''I don't know ifI can finish out the year. I may be able to enter South Central in a couple of months."

"That's good news," McBain said, "I don't know where I'll find another teacher to replace you, but I'm glad you can finish your schooling."

"I figure I'm not doing much good in here, while ifI study to be an engineer, I'll be worth a lot more to this country," Mike said earnestly.

"I don't like that kind of guy." Gary said to Jiro and Teru on their way home from school."

"I know of more than a few others just like him," Jiro said,

"Mike had me fooled completely though."

"I'm going to volunteer too," Gary said, "On condition that they take me back into the air corps."

"Good for you," Jiro said, "I hope you stick to that. It's the only thing worth fighting for in the whole setup. If they're going to keep us out of the Air Force, the Navy, the Coast Guard, and the Signal Corps, it's all not good.' '

The Army recruiting team arrived in camp and addressed a mass rally at the Cottonwood Bowl. The *Nisei* and the *Kibei* listened attentively while the lieutenant droned through his prepared speech. When it was over, a *Nisei* on the platform called for the singing of "God Bless America." Some *Kibei* rose self-consciously to their feet. They looked uncertainly at the *Nisei* still squatting on the ground confident that it wasn't necessary to stand up.

"On your feet, everybody.' '

The *Nisei* looked at each other in surprise and hoisted themselves to their feet. They sang listlessly and the *Nisei* on the platform pleaded for more spirit.

Jiro stopped in to see Teru. "He didn't say much," he said to her questioning look. "The only impression I have now is that his speech was very cleverly written. There was something else." He paused to find the right words, ''They had an American flag on the platform. Looking at it, I suddenly didn't want to look at it and I knew for sure where I stood."

"It doesn't seem right to parade that flag in front of us right now. Why couldn't they knock down the barbed wire even if it does only face along the road, and tell us we were free to leave this camp whenever we pleased and then ask us to volunteer to fight for a country which believed in us?"

"Japan has already done a great deal. Look at the record.

America has given up all claims to extraterritoriality in China. England promises independence to India after the war. Holland promises a greater measure of self government for the East Indies. Call them puppet government if you will but Burma, the Philippines, and the East Indies can now call themselves independent nations. Whether they really are or aren't can be judged fairly only after the war is ended."

"Do you think that any of these things would have happened by now if Japan hadn't acted when she did? In my opinion she has hastened the day when ALL peoples will enjoy the Four Freedoms of Roosevelt and Churchill. Not just the people of Europe."

"One thing has already been accomplished whether Japan wins this war or not. Even though England once again brings Singapore, Burma, and Malay under her thumb and Holland regains the East Indies for further exploitation, the Orient has been relieved of the odium of 'white man's superiority' and future liberation has been made that much easier."

"I'm not saying that the Greater East Asia Co-prosperity sphere and the Asiatic Monroe Doctrine are all that they're cracked up to be, because I don't know. But I don't see why they can't be and I'm going back and maybe, who knows, may be able to take some small part in seeing that they are."

Teru listened uneasily. She'd heard bitter and even treasonable outpouring against the evacuation but never anything like this. She felt sad, because it made Jiro seem remote and a stranger and seemed to portend a parting of the ways in the vague future.

She felt she had to say something to tell him what was going on in her mind. She said, ''I was hoping you would volunteer."

"I would if I thought it would make any difference. But I can't picture myself after the war still wearing my service ribbons and medals or carrying them in my breast pocket to show every Tom, Dick, and Harry who thought I was just another Jap."

"Don't you think that eventually we will be accepted as Americans?"

Jiro shrugged his shoulders. "'Maybe. I don't know. Four or five generations from now, America might tum out to be all that it's supposed to be. Maybe ALL nations will live up to the sweetness and light they profess. But that's not enough for me. By that time, I'll be dead and my kids will be dead. I'm afraid I'm not idealistic enough to want to die for my great, great grandchildren."

"I don't suppose it's possible to be more optimistic when you think of the Negro record. Their equality has been on the books for a long time."

"They're practically stuck with this country. We're not," Jiro said.

That night, Teru heard Mrs. Mineta's earnest voice next door talking to Kenji Hosoda's parents. She couldn't help but hear. She was already in bed and her cot was pushed against the wall to conserve space.

Mrs. Mineta was trying to persuade Mr. and Mrs. Hosoda to prevent Kenji from volunteering. "It is a shame to the Japanese people ... Doesn't he understand the forces which put us in here? ... He'll be killed ... Don't you love your son? ... Don't you have any control over him?... Our own two eligible sons have agreed to answer no tomorrow."

Mr. Hosoda said, "I cannot tell my sons and daughters what to do. They talked it over earlier and have decided to relocate as soon as Kenji volunteers. As for ourselves, we are old and would be a handicap to them. So we intend to stay in a relocation center. It has been decided. Talk to them if you wish to pursue this further."

Mrs. Mineta left in a huff. Before the night was over, she visited most of the families in the block.

The blocks at the north end of camp registered the first day. The recruiting officer shook his head in surprise. ''The response is very discouraging,'' he said. The Army had expected no such furor over questions 27 and 28.

Fully half of the early registrants answered in the negative to question 28 asking ''Will you swear unqualified allegiance to the United States of America and faithfully defend the United States from any or all attack by foreign or domestic forces, and forswear any form of allegiance or obedience to the Japanese Emperor, or any other foreign government, power, or organization?''

Practically all answered no to question 27 asking the individual if he were willing to serve in the armed forces of the United States on combat duty wherever ordered.

"Those were 'Strike' blocks," explained Mike Tanabe when the recruiting officer asked him.

"Will YOU volunteer?"

"I want to finish school and try for the officers' candidate course,' 'Mike said.

Bill was unusually quiet walking home from work. Bob Ichikawa asked, "What are you going to do tomorrow about the 27th question?"

Bill said, "I don't know. My mind was made up until I talked to some *Nisei* who answered no to BOTH questions this morning.

Not just 27. I think it's only natural for *Kibei* to answer no, because their country is really Japan after all; but for *Nisei* to answer that way and burn all their bridges behind them when they could easily answer yes, well-- I've been thinking."

"I think they're crazy. What can they possibly gain by it?"Bob asked.

"Nothing. But I still admire their guts, "Bill said, "I know and you know that our sympathies lie with Japan. Why not be honest about it?"

"What good does it do to stick your nose out?"

"I don't know but I'm going to try to find out."

CHAPTER 15

Bill told his father after supper. Mr. Yamada's tobacco stained molars showed plainly in a wide, approbative grin.

Mr. Kai came in and left right away. ''I want my son to hear this too,'' he said and walked out.

He returned with Yoshitaka, and almost immediately after, Mr. Itaya and Sammy came. Sammy was three years younger than Tom.

"I want this son to listen, too," Mr. Itaya said, "He might understand. The older one is too pigheaded."

Bill said, "This is something you're going to have to decide for yourselves. I want you to listen in while I thrash this matter out with my father. It's up to you."

There weren't enough chairs so they squatted on the floor and leaned against the walls . They warmed up by roundly cursing the "son of a bitch" responsible for their detention in camps.

Mr. Yamada told how he'd been hustled into internment without a chance to say more than two words of goodbye to his wife or make any arrangements. "I was sure, then, this country was not for us. If there should happen to be another war in the near future, the same thing might happen again. And even the bare possibility makes it unworthy of another try. I don't want this to happen again to anyone I love."

Mr. Itaya thrust his face out and pointed a finger at it. ''Look at that," he said vehemently, "As long as we have that, we're all Japanese. There's no use trying to delude ourselves that we're American. If our skins were white, it would be another matter. Look at the Indians around here. They say they're discriminated against even yet. Then look at the white-skinned immigrants. They don't even have to be born here to be considered full-fledged Americans.''

Mr. Kai said, ''If you want to be Americans, it would be smart to forget our Japanese sweethearts. Find yourself a *Hakujin* wife and start diluting your blood.''

The talk turned to Japan and Mr. Kai and Mr. Itaya described it in glowing terms.

Bill said, "I'm going after a Nisei who's lived in Japan for a while.''

He came back with Mas Maeda, a cousin of Dot's.

Mas said, "I'm not sure you can appreciate exactly what I mean when I say you haven't really lived until you've lived as a Japanese in Japan, Englishman in England, or a Swede in Sweden because it's something I can't hold up and show you.''

He waved his arms vaguely.

"I'll try to explain it this way. Any one of you can walk into the Imperial Hotel in Japan and feel perfectly at home. You can expect obsequious service in the best restaurants and barber shops you can find in Tokyo. You can go to movies and project yourselves in the hero's role or wait at the stage door for your favorite actress to come out.

''If a sudden bolt of lightening tells you that the beautiful girl sitting across the streetcar from you is the only girl for you, you can follow her home and lay siege with telephone calls and flowers and candy--with fond expectations.

"Most important of all, you might be held back in life by inefficiency, or not having influential friends, or plain laziness, but never because you're Japanese.''

"What about the poor living conditions you hear so much about ?" Bill asked.

"*Nisei* who've lived there longer than I tell me they sometimes wish for this country's luxuries but I never saw anyone unhappy about it. If a man needed a high standard of living to be happy, he certainly would have been an unhappy man if he'd been born as little as fifty years ago.''

"Eighty million people are living over there and very happily, too, I thought. Perhaps I'm prejudiced because of that one-day stopover in Honolulu where everyone seemed to be smiling all the time, but it seemed to me when I landed in San Francisco that there weren't quite as many happy faces over here.''

"What about restrictions on personal freedom, censored press, indoctrination and the like?' '

"I didn't notice anything that affected the life of the people I lived and worked with," Mas said, "Those things don't seem to bother the average person. He never notices them, unless he wakes up some day with a fever that tells him the whole system of organized society in which he lives needs a radical change. You seem to think they're non-existent in this country. You should read an English history book and compare it with the history we studied in school. Slanted stories are little different from censored stories."

"Some *Nisei* say they' re followed every minute they're in Japan. What about that?"

"My personal opinion is that *Nisei* are to blame for the reputation they've earned. Shall I tell you what they do? Not all of them of course.

They continually proclaim that they are under the protection of the United States government. They try to photograph everything in sight including places where signs plainly state that photographs are forbidden. They sneak into the slums and the poorer sections of the country trying to take the seamiest pictures they can find -- to show the folks back home. They clump into restaurants and prop their dirty shoes on top of the tables. They go into theaters and poke their feet into the backs of girls unfortunate enough to be sitting in front of them. I heard one fellow brag how he squeezed behind a girl in a crowded movie house, slipped his hands through her kimono sleeves, and squeezed her breasts. He thought it quite funny that she was too embarrassed to make a commotion.

''I never heard one *Nisei* with a job complain. It's the visitors who flash their money around and act American instead of Japanese as they're expected who find themselves 'followed and persecuted'.''

"So many *Nisei* say that anyone brought up in America can't stand the life in Japan. ' '

"That's easy,"Mas said, "Those who can stand it stay there. Those who can't, come back here. You only hear the latter. While I was there, I was told that the Nisei population of Tokyo alone was over three thousand. If you could hear them, you'd get a different picture."

"Before Pearl Harbor, I got a letter from a girl who came back to America on the same ship as I did. She came back because she hated the country and couldn't stand having to be always so careful how she acted. She wrote later that she made a mistake in coming back to America and wished she were in Tokyo. That was before evacuation. Now she writes that her only hope is that someday she can go back."

"I don't understand any of what you're talking about," Mr. ltaya said, "But my second boy is going to Waseda University and he doesn't want to come back to this country. I had such a hard time persuading him to go in the first place, too."

"To get down to brass tacks, what can we do for a living once we're back there?" Bill asked.

"Manchuria and North China are wide open if you have any kind of technical training at all." Mas said.

"I don't have any," Bill said.

"There'll be plenty of jobs. You don't have to worry at all,"

Mr. Kai said, reassuringly. "And you' II be alive at the end of the war to work at these."

"The East Indies will offer thousands of opportunities," Mr. ltaya added enthusiastically, "I have my eyes on a foreman job." ...

The thirty-odd 18 to 37 year olds from block 213 boarded the truck, some grim, some grinning. Charlie Omoto bragged, "I'm going to sign no--no."

Tom Itaya was waiting for them in front of the registration barrack. He said to Sammy, "Everybody is signing no-yes this morning and getting away with it. You do that, too."

He said to Bill, "Most fellows are signing no-yes. Looks like the smart thing to do."

Bill's interview was shorter than he'd expected after hearing the stories of browbeating and long persuasion when anyone tried to answer no to the loyalty question. One Kibei said the soldier tore up his questionnaire and threatened him with a jail sentence.

Itchy held up the line for a half hour. His scratchy, indignant voice could be heard all through the barrack. "The Navy turned me down when I wanted to volunteer just because I'm a Jap. How do you explain that?"

The sergeant's answer couldn't be heard.

"You still haven't answered my question." Itchy's voice could be heard plainly. They strained in vain to hear the sergeant's answer.

"If I'm not good enough for your Navy, I'm not going to take crumbs from your Army ... What do you expect me to do? Say no and get slapped in the jug. I'm not going to give you the satisfaction."

Gary was closeted with the interviewing officer even longer.

He told Jiro about it after lunch.

"He couldn't tell me any of the things I wanted to know and he's arranging a trip to regional headquarters in Utah so I can talk to some higher-ups about my case. He was pretty frank about everything and really seemed to appreciate my stand. He said he hoped the Air Corps would be opened at a later date so I could be reinstated.

At the end, he told me, off the record, that I was doing the right thing and shook my hand before I left."

The older ones went straight home with the decisions. The younger ones gathered uncertainly by the block manager's office to compare notes and take comfort in having done what the others had done.

Four others besides Kenji had volunteered outright.

"I offered to volunteer if they would guarantee me my citizenship rights. They couldn't do it, so I walked out without answering," Jack Y anaga said defiantly but he looked worried. In the afternoon he and Satoru Kono went back and volunteered.

The next morning, three more volunteered; and before the day was over six more had changed their minds and volunteered.

"I don't want to be the only one left in the block," Itsumi Wake said over and over again while his father and mother pleaded with him and begged him to go back and cancel his volunteering.

Jiro registered the last day. he said his answer was no to both questions. The corporal was surprised.

"Why?" he asked.

Jiro had the answer on the tip of his tongue. "I don't want to be a part-time American. Give me the full rights of a citizen, exactly the same as those YOU enjoy. Then ask me those questions again.' ' The corporal looked down at Jiro's questionnaire. "I see, you're a University of California graduate. Don't you feel that you owe something to the United States for the education you have received at State expense?"

Jiro thought a moment. "Any debt of gratitude I may have acknowledged was wiped out at evacuation. I think we' re even now.

What good is that education doing me in here? Where I'm going, I probably won't be able to use any of it."

"I take it you' re going to Japan."

"Yes."

The corporal wrote it down on the back of the questionnaire.

Tom Itaya said to Gary, "Those guys signing no-no make it ~ harder for the rest of us." He didn't know Jiro was a no-no.

Gary answered, "By the same reasoning, the volunteers make it easier for you. ' '

"I suppose so if you put it that way."

"Where do you stand, answering no-yes?" Gary asked pointedly.

"Most people answered no-yes." Tom said evasively andquickly changed the subject.

Tero was home when Mrs. Yanaga came to see her father.

"He's all we have," Mrs. Yanaga said, her face dead with worry. "We can never start over again if he leaves us. Our whole life had been built around him."

Mr. Noguchi twisted his nose sharply. "There is nothing we can do," he said sympathetically. ''Their decisions seem foolish after what we've ·gone through but we can never make them understand. If we did dissuade them, they would begin to doubt as soon as things started to go wrong and eventually come to hate us."

"We have property in California but his life is infinitely more precious to us," Mrs. Yanaga said.

Mr. Noguchi said, "It is a brave decision for them. It is not easy to forsake one's parents and strike out alone. I envy their confidence that war can mean only glory for them. Do you remember when we came to this country? How our folks tried to dissuade us, too?"

Mrs. Yanaga stared dully at the cracks in the floor. She roused herself and went back into her apartment

Satoru Kono slept with Bill for one night. The next night he went back to sleeping at home. Mr. Kono stopped going to the bonfire to warm himself and talk.

After that, Mr. Imada helped Mr. Mineta and Mr. Noguchi build the early morning bonfire which served as a gathering place for *Isseis*. They talked and warmed themselves and carried home the live charcoal to warm their apartments.

The new oil heaters failed to heat the drafty barracks even when turned full on in defiance of the administration request to keep them turned down to the medium position.

Mr. Mineta said, ''I had quite a time convincing my oldest son to sign no-no. He held out for some time because of the property we have back in Salinas. I told him to forget about the property and consider it already lost. He seemed a little doubtful but he finally came around to my way of thinking."

"Having been a soldier of the Japanese Army it's only natural that your sons should show the true Japanese spirit," Mr. Imada beamed approval. Mr. Mineta had been a sergeant during the Russo Japanese War.

"Mine surprised me when he answered no-no," Mr. Yamada said, "I'm especially proud that he reached his own decision."

Mr. Mineta said, ''My second one seemed to have his mind made up himself He made no fuss."

"I wonder what's the matter with my Jack?" Mr. Yanaga hung his head. "I explained to him so carefully, too. Maybe he couldn't understand because he speaks so little Japanese."

They looked at him sympathetically.

No one knew that Sam Ogawa had volunteered until the list was published.

"He should volunteer," Charlie Omoto said, "They say he was a stool pigeon outside like Kajitani.' '

''Who told you that?" Bill said quickly. He didn't like Charlie who was the block's one-man rumor factory and whose stories were usually exaggerated or fabricated from thin air. He had his radio rigged up for short wave, too, but his accounts were so garbled that everyone took his "news" with a grain of salt. He spoke both Japanese and English poorly.

"A friend of mine who used to know him outside told me,' ' Charlie said.

"Who is it?" Bill insisted.

Charlie said vaguely, "I forget his name."

"Well, I used to know Sam outside myself and he wasn't a stool pigeon," Bill said heatedly. "He volunteered because he's one guy who really thinks he's an American."

"*Hakujin* say if we were loyal we would report how close Pearl Harbor was and help catch all the spies. If he's American he must have been a stool pigeon."

"Hell," Bill exploded, ''Did YOU know Pearl Harbor was to be attacked? Can YOU name me one spy?"

Charlie shook his head. "Maybe some of them fishermen in Monterey."

"Jim used to work in those sardine boats and he says no. I'm not saying Sam would or wouldn't have reported any supposed spies if he knew of any because I don't know, but I think a fellow can be a loyal American and still not go around telling the FBI about every suspicious move he sees. Seems to me most of the people were turned in because they'd expressed pro-Japanese sentiment at one time or another or were simply community leaders. I can't see

Sam doing that."

Jiro said, "right after Pearl harbor, I told my boss that I didn't go for the 'dastardly treacherous' business because I was Japanese and had some sympathies for Japan even though I volunteered and would fight as well if not better than the next guy if I'd been accepted. He said, 'What did Roosevelt expect, a calling card?' and told me he felt the same way about

England. He's an EnglishAmerican.

He didn't fire me even after several people asked him to."

Bill said, "Taka says right after Pearl Harbor, an officer stopped by a group of them at Fort Ord and asked them if they would shoot their own fathers if they discovered they were Japanese spies and were escaping. When some refused to answer and others said no, the officer got mad and said that in the Civil War, father killed son and brother killed brother. "Then, Taka said, Japs were more civilized; and the officer, I think he was captain, got really mad. A week later, Taka got his discharge.'

"Is it true about the submarine coming up in Monterey Bay and stopping a sardine boat?" Jiro asked.

"Jim swears by it. He says the sub commander asked what boat it was and the sardine boat skipper said, Santa Lucia, and then the sub commander asked if he was Italian and the guy said he was and the sub commander said, 'Go on home. We're looking for Americans." ...

Mrs. Sakaguchi called anxiously , ''Alice, aren't you getting up this morning again?"

There was no answer from the cot in the comer.

"It will get to be a habit, so get up," she said and pulled back the blankets.

Her daughter's scared, wide-awake face peered up at her.

"I don't feel like eating," Alice protested.

"Don't you feel well?" Mrs. Sakaguchi asked, her mind frozen with the worry that had been in her ever since Alice had come home with her dress tom and immediately gone to bed without stopping to tell her about the dance.

"I just don't feel hungry," Alice said. Her face was pale and blotchy.

"Alice," Her voice was tight. "Something hasn't happened, has it?"

Alice stared pleadingly at her mother. She didn't say anything.

The door banged. Emily was back from brushing her teeth.

"Emily, I don't want any breakfast so you go ahead," Mrs. Sakaguchi said. Paul and Mr. Sakaguchi had already gone to breakfast.

"Shall I bring some home? Maybe they'll have something besides toast and coffee this morning."

"If there's an egg, bring it home for Alice."

"Not a chance," Emily said, "We had an egg two weeks ago. There might be some cereal though."

When the door had banged shut again behind Emily, Alice began to sob uncontrollably. Mrs. Sakaguchi sat on the edge of the cot looking down at her daughter. Her eyes were wet.

"Tell mother what happened."

"You were right," Alice said between racking sobs, "On New Years."

Mrs. Sakaguchi stared at her daughter, unable to believe what she knew was true. She'd begun to suspect the worst after Alice stopped getting up for breakfast. "I tried to tell you." She gripped her daughter's shoulders. "What can we tell father?"

She had to repeat it.

"Alice is pregnant."

"What? Who?" Mr. Sakaguchi said at last.

"The Kurasaki boy."

"The Kurasaki in 215?"

Mrs. Sakaguchi nodded.

"Do you know what you're saying? Don't you know he is *"Etta"*?"

Etta was a whispered word. No longer safe in Japan where it had been outlawed by government edict. Nisei gave it little thought until they reached marriageable age, when their parents took in hand those who hadn't heard enough.

Alice stopped just inside the door, her cheeks flushed from the exertion of her walk home. She had stopped at the block manager's office and found a letter from Pete. She was burning to know what was inside.

Her father was waiting for her . She could tell from the way he looked at her. Her mother was nervously darning socks.

"Sit down," he said, "I should have kept a closer watch on your comings and goings. Until your mother told me, I didn't know your relations with the Kurasaki boy had gone so far. It cannot be undone so I will not say anything further. It is the future I am concerned with. I don't want you to do anything foolish like the Kato girl did. Do you have any idea of marrying him?"

"Yes," Her answer was more a sob than a word.

"Is it settled?"

Alice shook her head. She wished there were some other way out than marrying Pete. She was afraid to go outside to him.

"I want you to give up that idea. You must think of the family. Your mother and I are old and won't live much longer but Emily and Paul will have to find a husband and wife someday. If you go through with this, it will be impossible to find suitable persons for them."

"But if l go away, won't it be all right?"

"You cannot run away from this. It is the same wherever Japanese are. Have you ever stopped to think why go-between are always necessary for marriage even in this country? They are to eliminate the possibility of *Etta* antecedents in the family."

Alice stared down at the envelope. There was no return ad· dress on the outside but it was postmarked Denver. She could see clearly Doris Kato running off with Ray Minami. Mrs. Kato confid· ing to Mrs. Sakaguchi, ''There was no other way out. Things had gone too far and Doris wanted it that way."

Kate was seen everywhere with Jimmy Kawakita. Kate suddenly was seen everywhere with everyone but Jimmy. People whispering that Jimmy's family were *Etta*. *Etta* indicated quickly by four uplifted fingers meaning fourth class following the nobility, middle class, and low class. She and Sally curiously asking Mrs. Noguchi what it was all about and listening with complete absorption while Mrs. Noguchi explained carefully, "We shouldn't talk about such things anymore and I shouldn't tell you only our society is too narrow and nosey."

"The origin of the *Etta* is rather obscure but I was told that they came from Korea a long, long time ago. The rich ones were immediately absorbed into Japanese society but the poor ones were economically forced to accept the most menial position, especially the butchering of animals and of condemned people. That, together with their habit of eating meat, which was taboo, set them apart.

"Nothing as bad as the slaves in this country but they were treated as a class apart. Personally, I have nothing against *Etta*. When I was a little girl in Japan, I visited an *Etta* home several times and was surprised that their homes seemed cleaner than other homes I visited. They seemed healthier, too, perhaps because of the meat they ate.

"However, our society being the narrow thing it is, you should be careful whom you marry. In the big cities like Los Angeles, I have heard that many of the socially prominent and powerful Japanese are *Etta* and the question isn't raised so strongly, but here in a small place like this people are still careful."

After her father left her with the admonition to think over very carefully what he had told her, Alice opened Pete's letter. It was written in pencil.

"I landed a job as pearl diver in a slop house at eighteen a week plus meals. You' ll have to stay with me in a hotel room.

"If you can make a go of it, hop the next train and ask for me at the Tonkin Restaurant if you get here during the day; Traveler's Hotel at night.

"Some guys are talking about a shipping shed here so maybe I can get on when it opens."

A postscript said, ''Have you told your parents? They might say something but I can't help that."

Alice tore up the letter and walked blindly out of the barrack. She walked past the site for the proposed school buildings where the adobe bricks lay baking in the sun and headed west into the thick mesquite bordering the camp.

CHAPTER 16

Teru was already in bed when the dinner gongs began to ring wildly. Ever since the strike, two strokes meant a block meeting, three strokes meal time, and a continuous ringing such as now, a riot or a senous emergency.

She heard subdued voices outside. Excited voices.

"Something's happened," Tad said. He pulled on his clothes and hurried out.

Mr. Noguchi herded him back. "'Tadao, you stay home.' '

"What's happened?" Sally asked.

"Alice hasn't come home. No one has seen her since four o'clock."

"I thought Mrs. Sakaguchi looked worried when she came after supper and asked if Alice was here." Sally said.

"Are you going to search?" Teru asked.

"Yes," Mr. Noguchi said, "Tonight, we will ask for a few volunteers from among the young men only, but we are letting the people know so they will be ready to start out early tomorrow morning. Do we have a flashlight?"

"No," Teru said "Remember, we gave them both to Mr. Johnson after it was announced that flashlights over two cells were contraband. We were afraid to keep the small one we had."

"Those were terrible times." Ayame sat up in her cot. Her eyes were fearfully wild and her hair spilled in disorder down her shoulder. "We were so afraid you would be arrested."

Mr. Noguchi looked at her sorrowfully. "'You women better go back to sleep. Teru, fix your mother's hair for her."

"Is Paul going to search, too?" Tad asked anxiously. "Can I go?"

"No," Mr. Noguchi said. "No boys are going tonight. You can help tomorrow morning."

He joined the men outside. They could hear his precise voice raised in command. ''This group will cross the slough and search due west.''

Their footsteps tramped quickly away. Silence followed briefly.

The voices went indoors. Teru and Sally crawled into their cots and looked at each other in the light streaming fitfully from the Maeda apartment. The burlap sacking hung outside the windows to keep out the summer sun was tom and needed patching. It flapped idly in the drafty air.

"I hope they find her," Teru whispered.

"I hope they do it before she--" Sally added quickly, ''I hope she's all right.''

"She is."

"They say that man from 226 was dead six hours when they found him the next day. That was summer though."

"Sally, stop it," Teru said, her voice rising sharply. They had found Mr. Nishijima curled up under a mesquite tree less than a hundred yards from the trail leading to camp.

"I'm sorry." Sally said.

"I'm sorry too," Teru said, "I don't feel so good."

"Me either," Sally said.

The young men called to each other as they beat their way though the dark mesquite. They held their feebly flickering torches as high as they could and poked their flashlights here and there through the underbrush.

They gathered the full power of their young lungs to send their calls echoing into the darkness.

"A--lice!"

But none could match the agonized cry which pierced and upbraided the night for concealing his daughter.

"Ma-sa-ko!"

They heard it once and suppressed the involuntary shivers that chilled their spines. They heard it twice and opened their mouths to drown out that agonized call.

They moved their lights slowly along the reed covered bank of the slough, fearful of what they might find. They eyed the dark waters with dread and passed it by in favor of a more thorough search in the morning.

One plunged into the hip deep water and started to wade to the other side.

"Wait," another called futilely and followed quickly through the oozing mud bottom. The others searched for and found the crossing and picked their way across the crude bridge of logs and planks.

The moon came up and hid its face behind a cloud as though in protest against the rescue of what nature had already claimed for its own ....

Alice didn't know how long she walked. She followed the slough for a while, then crossed on some logs. The last ones she saw were Bill and Kate sitting on a blanket spread on the bank. They were too absorbed in each other to notice her as she circled around them.

She let the tears run unchecked down her cheeks as soon as she was alone and stumbling numbly forward, trying to get as far away from camp as she could. She didn't know when she left the trail leading to the river.

She nearly stepped on a rattlesnake and heard its warning rattle after she'd passed. She was unnerved and ran until her breath came in dry rasping gasps. She slowed to an exhausted walk.

Once she thought she saw the skulking form of a coyote through the mesquite and shivered. When she finally tripped over a protruding root to sprawl full length on the ground, she lay where she'd fallen, sobbing quietly, her face resting against the cooling sand.

She cried until she fell asleep.

She awoke and it was dark. She thought she could hear the faint clanging of a bell. She listened hard but she couldn't be sure. It was too dark to have been the dinner bell.

She sat up quickly and looked around and could see only the vague gnarled shapes of the mesquite trees. She stood up on unsteady feet.

Her mother must be worried. She had to go back. She gently rubbed her arms where they were bruised and tom by the mesquite thorns. She looked at the caked blood with surprise.

She looked around again and couldn't even tell which way she had come. She fought down a rising surge of panic. She wanted to run but couldn't make up her mind which way .. what was it Gary had said when Mr. Nishijima had gotten lost?

"All he had to do was keep walking until he hit either the road connecting the camps or the river. It's only an hour's walk from the road to the river. If he happened to head north or south, he would have hit one of the trails leading from the camps to the river."

She remembered Bill had been there, too, saying, ''Easy for you with your navigation training, but it's hard to go in a straight line through that mesquite. The first time we went to the river, we took almost three hours and we had a compass. There was no trail then. ' '

"When we went, we missed the trail and spent over an hour looking for it."

Sammy Itaya said, "We didn't bring much water and we were scared."

Alice looked up. There weren't many stars. The North Star had some connection with the Big Dipper, but she couldn't even find the Big Dipper. She started to pick her way through the dense mesquite. The thorns and the protruding branches tore at her clothes and skin. She hit a clear spot and half ran across it. She stumbled ahead for what seemed hours.

The moon disappeared behind a cloud and she could barely see the sprawling roots and gnarled tree trunks underfoot. She finally stopped indecisively. What if she missed the trail in the darkness? She'd better wait until morning.

She sat down and felt the blood tearing wildly through her heart. The noise was deafening in her ears. The sweat stood out on her body and it was cold and clammy under her clothes. Her throat was parched and burning. She could taste the salt on her tongue.

She must have been going in the wrong direction, she thought. She should have reached either the river or the road by now. She got up again. If she found the river, she would have water anyway. She could wait at the river until they found her. You could live a long time without food as long as you had water. Mr. Nishijima had died of thirst. Finding the road would still mean a long walk to camp before she could drink water. She'd better find the river first.

She started off again at right angles to the direction she had been following. There she thought the river was. She was tired physically and mentally. Her mind wandered from the grim struggle to keep her feet going in as straight a line as possible.

How would she explain the impulse that made her walk so far away from camp? Her poor mother would be frantic by now. It would do her father good to suffer a little. The tears dropped off her cheeks leaving smudgy streaks behind.

What would she do when she got back to camp? She couldn't stay there. People would wonder why she'd run away. Why couldn't they mind their own business? You couldn't even have diarrhea without people knowing.

Every pregnancy was a block affair. She knew the routine herself First the husband began to take home his wife's coffee and toast in the morning. Then he more and more frequently turned up at the laundry to do the washing.

Back home where their nearest neighbors had been two miles away, she'd wished there were more people around. Until assembly center. She changed her mind after that.

She shuddered at the memory of the terrible man who at first always managed to sit at the same table with them. She would still feel the impact of his ugly sensual eyes. His nostrils thinly flared like a pig's. His repulsive table manners. His plate held greedily to his thick slobbering lips. The food slurping up into his mouth. His tiny beady eyes never leaving her. The food curling in her stomach.

She remembered how they'd tried in vain to move when they discovered themselves assigned to the apartment directly facing the men's latrine. She remembered the men coming out of the latrine still buttoning their pants or hitching them to a more comfortable position.

She remembered how few people came to visit them and she had to suggest immediately visiting someone else whenever they did. How she lay half suffocating at night, her nose buried in the scratchy blankets. Her friends never lingering on the doorstep to talk and cut up the way they did at the Noguchis' or the Katais'. She and Paul and Emily and even seven-year-old Joan almost never staying home after the first few weeks and gradually taking to eating with whomever mealtime found them with.

The bitter night when she and Paul left their apartment before breakfast and stayed out until eleven that night. Their father flying into one of his rare rages and savagely lecturing them for two solid hours on behavior fitting to a Japanese. On family, filial piety, and conducting themselves at all times with pride and honor and an example to this rotten country...its racial discrimination, its eternal bragging, its self-righteousness. On Japanese being Japanese wherever they went and their solemn duty to spread Japanese wherever they went and the so solemn duty to spread Japanese culture to the "eight" comers of the universe.

Are you proud to be an American now? After this so-called "humane" evacuation? This assembly center? This pigsty of a home?

Her own tearful flareup of emotion. Trying to make him understand. They HA VE to evacuate us. They had to do it in a hurry because Japan was all ready to invade California. These barracks are only temporary. This is an assembly center. Relocation center will be better.

Better? Where will we go from there? I had to sell our tractors and equipment to pay back the money I borrowed on this year's crop. The company took over the crop for the balance and it's like a weed patch now.

I'm a farmer. I can't farm without equipment or capital. I brought up you children somehow, because I was a farmer. How can I possibly support you working for day wages?

You don't think of those things when you talk so glibly of relocation and starting life all over again. As though I were still twenty-five and single instead of fifty-five with five dependents.

Assembly center had been like a bad dream.

She remembered the disillusionments. About acquaintances and even close friends. Discovering things that would never have come to light if they hadn't been thrown so closely together in camp.

Only angels could stand the close scrutiny of barrack life.

Molly who had always seemed so sweet and good. Molly bawling out her mother for not leaving the apartment when her boy friend came to visit.

Hearing things, ugly things, about people living right next to you. May was half-American, born while her mother had been working as a maid in San Francisco. Helen was half-Chinese, foisted, some said, on an unsuspecting husband who had enticed her away from home with a Cadillac and a thick roll of banknotes which she later learned were the joint property of fourteen other Filipinos. Pete was *Etta*. That's why he was so bitter and cynical about life. He was hard--hard like his body. Like his fingers digging into her flesh. Like the pains and shock that followed her limp surrender to his body.

She stopped and sat down to await the dawn ...

Teru was awakened by her father's suppressed sneeze. It was still dark but she could hear people getting up next door. She heard her father saying to Tadao, ''You help this morning, too.''
They hadn't found Alice.
Teru threw off her blankets and swung her feet on the floor. It was cold and she dressed quickly.
"You girls don't have to get up yet." Mr. Noguchi said, but
Sally was dressing, too. He asked Teru for a dry pair of trousers.
"You aren't going out again, are you?" Teru asked.
"I have to," he said, and he and Tadao left as soon as he had changed from his mud-caked trousers.
After breakfast, Teru and Sally stayed in the mess hall to help make sandwiches for the search parties. They searched all day and dragged the slough immediately below the camp.
They finally found her bruised and blood soaked body on the second day near the river opposite Camp I.. ..
George wrote from Gila that he hadn't volunteered but that he had

signed yes-yes and would take his chances on the draft. He was surprised that Bill and Jiro had both answered no-no.

Bill got a letter from Otis Terakawa who'd been moved to Tule Lake instead of Poston from the Salinas Assembly Center.

"What's the matter with you guys in Poston and Manzanar? We thought you fellows would lead the way in resisting this damned registration. We're not registering here. Why should we have to?

The Japanese outside the center aren't being asked to. Neither are the rest of the American people.

In March, the WRA announced plans for the registration of all aliens and all women over eighteen years of age, "to set up a mass leave clearance procedure." Instead of having individual interviews with Army representatives as in the January registration, the interviews were to be conducted within the blocks by evacuees.

Teru gave the coming registration little thought until Sally announced that she intended to answer no-no.

"Why?" Teru asked, taken by surprise and unable to say more because Jiro was there.

"Look what they did to Mother," Sally said bitterly.

Teru could only stare pleadingly while Jiro quickly changed the subject.

Sally was the only girl in the block who answered no-no.

However, Jiro told them that more than a few girls in other blocks were answering no-no, though the overwhelming majority were being "sensible" even where their husband and brothers had answered no-no.

"Women don't count so they may as well answer yes-yes." Bill said.

Jiro disagreed. "I should think they would answer the same way as their men folk," he said, "There's the possibility they may separate us according to our answers."

"They would never break families up." Teru said.

"I wouldn't be too sure." Jiro said, "We didn't think evacuation was possible either. Why take the chance?"

"Maybe we girls really don't feel disloyal to this country," Teru said. Her eyes were on Sally while she said it.

Jiro looked at her thoughtfully, "I guess not," he said, "I suppose there's no reason for you girls to feel disloyal or especially bitter about anything outside of evacuation. You lead your, shall we say, sheltered lives and never run into some of the things we do," he paused and grinned, "when we go out into this cruel world to make a living."

"We take some hard knocks for you gals," Bill said. He was grinning too.

Jiro came to their block to help register but Teru was interviewed by someone else. She answered yes to the two questions that took the places of #27 and #28 in the selective service questionnaire.

She was willing to serve as a WAAC if *Niseis* were allowed to join, and she was unreservedly loyal to the United States.

Mr. Noguchi snorted when he learned of the sudden decision to cross out the loyalty question for *Issei* and substitute a question asking if they would abide by the laws of the United States. "What an asinine question. Who is going to put down in writing that he intends to break laws?" he asked.

"They must have been in such a hurry to cancel that loyalty question they didn't have time to think up a good substitute." Mr. Kai said.

"They should have asked us the original question," Mr. Mineta said. "Then we could make our stand clear. I don't want to be separated from my sons who answered no, but on the other hand I can't answer no to the question they're asking us."

"They are afraid to ask us that loyalty question." Mr. Kai said, "No *Issei* would answer no."

"I wouldn't be so sure," Mr. Noguchi said.

"No," Mr. Mineta agreed, "Even in this block, there must be a half dozen *Issei* who would swear loyalty to the United States.' '

"I suppose so," Mr. Kai admitted.

Ayame insisted on registering with the rest. Teru was surprised because she had shown little interest during the January registration. Teru and Sally happily escorted her to the mess hall. It was the first time she'd shown any interest in anything beyond the affairs of the moment and it seemed a real sign that she was finally returning to normal.

There was no question in their minds how she would answer. Practically all *Issei* were answering that they would not obstruct the war program or break laws ....

CHAPTER 17

After registration, the rumors of an impending segregation quickly died down and life settled into an almost pleasant routine. The older folks went back to their ironwood sculpture and their "go" and "shogi" and dress making and crafting and flower arrangement, the younger set to their project work, their basketball, block parties and dances.

The bitter taste of evacuation, the open strife of the November strike, and the furor of registration had come to a head and burst like a long festering boil, and the people who'd been emotionally keyed up for so long relaxed gratefully to lick their wounds and enjoy quiet living once more.

They knew now where most people stood. The earlier suspicion and distrust were gone. The Japanophiles made no bones about their sympathies. They basked in the approbation of their elders. They'd made their stand clear and were no longer worried about "dogs."

Opposite stands cemented friendships rather than ruptured them. The army volunteer and the no-no found admiration in the unequivocal stand of the other. Each despised the fence sitter who gave lip service to loyalty.

The peace loving majority settled back with a sigh of relief that no more trouble seemed brewing. Even the opening of the camouflage factory brought only a flurry of excitement.

Some blocks voted to boycott the net factory because it produced materials of war. Most blocks paid no special attention to it and adopted a hands-off policy.

Only *Nisei* were concerned because *Issei* as enemy aliens, weren't allowed to work in the factory, eliminating possible friction from that source.

A few workers immediately and blatantly announced they were working at the factory as patriotic duty. They received only pained attention. The majority of workers told all who would listen, Why not? There's good money in it. Somebody's going to get it so why not us? We might as well get paid decent wages for a change."

The community councils set up a plan where twenty-five percent of the wages earned at the factory would be turned into a community fund to be divided among the project workers. Army volunteers, however, would be allowed to keep their full pay.

Some of the workers protested loud and long against having part of their pay taken away. The group who refused to have anything to do with the camouflage factory quickly noticed and made much of the fact that the complainers came from the loudly patriotic group. Mr. Kai sneered, " They make ten and fifteen times what we make and still they complain about having to put some of their money into a community fund. We ought to kick them out of the blocks and let them shift for themselves. Cook their own food. Take away their own garbage. Clean the latrines. Do all those other things we have to do to keep this camp running."

They sniffed at the dollar and eighty cents monthly allocation to project workers which could be directly traced to the camouflage factory. Some refused to accept it and much of it was channeled into block funds to buy curtains for mess halls and mirrors for the latrines.

Reactions to the outbreak of skin rashes among the net factory workers ranged from pity to back handed satisfaction.

Bill said, "That's probably why they brought the factory here in the first place. They most likely can't find anybody to do that kind of work outside."

The skin rash and the adverse sentiment were too much for some of the workers and they quit. Others left the center, emboldened and incited by the sudden feel of heavy cash in their pockets.

Two months after it opened, the net factory closed. There weren't enough workers to run it efficiently. The money that had flowed freely from the camouflage factory had its effect. More and more people began to talk about the futility of camp life and the money to be had outside.

The Hosodas relocated to Chicago and their empty apartment next door was a constant reminder to Teru that relocation centers could only be temporary. Before leaving, Ralph, Kenji's older brother, told Teru, "I'll say goodbye but we'll meet again. Japanese always manage to stick together somehow."

Teru thought, that's not the right way. We should go out as individuals and make our way as individuals. Not as members of a racial group. As

Americans. Not Japanese-Americans. But Ralph was so much older than she so she was silent.

Kenji stayed to wait for induction but moved into a bachelor apartment.

Soon after, the Kanadas in the next barrack relocated to Denver. Both sons had volunteered and immediately gone outside to work. They needed the money to help their parents get settled somewhere. Evacuation had taken their last penny.

Satoru Kono went out on seasonal leave to wait for army induction and enjoy himself while waiting.

Sammy Itaya said, "He told me he wants to have some fun with dames. He says you can't do it in here."

Jack Y anaga and Sam Ogawa were the first ones to be called for induction from the block. Gary went on the same train with them.

He came back right away.

"They won't take me back into the Air Corps," he told Teru,

"I guess I'll have to sit tight for a while."

The next day he went on a hike to the river and stayed overnight. He came back the next afternoon and was so enthusiastic, he persuaded their group to go with him the next Sunday.

Sunday, ten of them with shoulder packs headed for the river. Teru, Sally, Dot, Lena, Kate, Bill, Jiro, and Jim, with Kenji and Gary leading the way through the mesquite and the arrow weed.

They spent the day swimming, playing cards, fishing, or just talking lazily about inconsequential things.

It was the first time Teru had been outside the confines of the camp and she reveled in the luxurious sense of freedom that came with looking at the hills in the distance and the clean, cool water slipping by. No dusty, tar-papered barrack, no hot sun beating back up from the sand.

Jiro and Kenji came back from their fishing , proudly holding up a wildly flapping duck in addition to a half dozen black bass and several carp and catfish.

Despite the immediate and vociferous chorus of disbelief, they held to their gleefully pantomined story that they'd chased and caught it with their bare hands.

No one actually believed them but no one could suggest a better story; and since the two couldn't be shaken one iota from their original story, they listened to Bill tell Gary it was a female mallard and Gary tell Bill it was a canvasback.

It remained for Teru and Kate who cooked it into a slightly smelly but delicious stew to discover the shotgun pellet lodged in the upper part of the duck's leg crippling it and rendering it unable to fly.

Teru helped gather together their belongings with reluctant hands when it was time to go back. She wanted desperately to stay out there away from the ugly barracks and the drabness of camp.

Everyone was in high spirits until they crossed the slough. Immediately, they felt the hot, oppressively humid air which was so different from the air they'd been breathing until then. Their canteens were empty and their throats were parched but their feet dragged unwillingly the rest of the way into camp.

They went to the river for three more unforgettable Sundays.

The last time was a farewell for Dot who was going to Chicago to work in a doll factory and for Kenji whose induction call had finally come

On the way home, they stopped at the gully where the mesquite began and looked back at the line of tall cottonwoods which marked the river.

"Last time for us," Dot said, and looked past Kenji at Jim.

"We had good times back there."

"Maybe for us too," Jiro said quickly, and Teru wondered if he felt as she did, that it wouldn't be the same again with Dot and Kenji gone. That they, too, were looking at the trees lining the river bank for the last time.

It was a depressing thought so tied in with the distressing pattern of their existence. First, there had been Janet and those other friends. Then evacuation to break those ties. Then assembly center and new friends, all Japanese. Then removal to Poston and separation again. Then Camp 2 and Dot, Gary, Lena, Kenji, Jiro. And now relocation. Dot and Kenji would be gone next week. Jim was sure to leave before long. Gary and Lena would be leaving one of these days. Bill was talking lately of several good farming opportunities in

Colorado. Jiro would never leave camp but he would probably be segregated some day.

Teru suddenly wanted to leave camp, too. She determined to talk to her father the first chance she got.

She was silent with that thought while they trudged along the dusty trail back to camp. She wondered how her father would take it. She had a feeling he would put his foot down at first but might consent if she persisted enough.

She'd gathered lately that he himself had no intention of relocating to the middle west. Sometimes she even doubted if he planned to return to their farm in California.

When Mr. Otis had written that the present tenant wanted to make some improvements in the house at Mr. Noguchi's expense, Mr. Noguchi said, "It is no use throwing good money after a bad investment. I have written the farm off as lost already."

"But we're going back there, aren't we?" Teru asked alarmed.

"The army does not permit it," Mr. Noguchi said, "And it doesn't look like it will as long as the commanding general of theWestern Defense Command maintains that a Jap's a Jap."

Her opportunity came sooner than she expected when Mr. McBain called her to his office after class the following Friday.

He was smiling broadly as he pulled a letter from his pocket. He held the envelope in his hand, tapping it lightly on the desk while he said, ''Teru, I have a letter here from a former roommate at State University. He owns a small factory in Cleveland that makes roofing materials. Until recently, he handled all the paper work himself, but with increased orders and priorities and such, he needs a secretary.' '

He paused and looked at Teru a moment. "Let me read what he wrote."

He started to read from the second page, "send me the one you think will best prove your point. You tell me that they are no different inside from your sons or my daughters but never remembering having seen any Japanese, I can't completely digest everything you say though I am pretty well convinced."

"To make it easier for you, the girl doesn't need much working experience. I wouldn't be surprised if one of your June graduates could handle the w9rk. I've been thinking of asking Molly to take over, but she apparently has her heart set on going right into college this May."

"I'll start her at one hundred and twenty five a month. And she can stay with me if she can't find suitable lodging."

Teru was sitting straight in her chair, her attendance book held tightly in her hands. She could feel the excitement send the blood surging through her veins. It sounded too good to be true. Far removed from the usual job offers that came through the placement office. Domestics, farm couples, factory worker, technicians.

Few *Nisei* had found secretarial work. Even Nora, who'd gone to Chicago just before Christmas on a hundred dollar a month clerical job, had written Teru that she'd laid aside her first rosy dream of having her competence quickly recognized and being promoted to secretarial work.

"There are better positions opening now and then," she wrote, "but being *Nihonjin*, I'm not even considered for them. Within the last month, two *Hakujin* just out of secretarial school who started after I did, were chosen from the clerical pool to take dictation with a ten dollar raise in salary. My Woodbury diploma and experience don't seem to count very much.

"I'm not the only one who's griping either. Other *Nisei* out here agree with me that there are lots of good jobs but the desirable ones aren't for *Nihonjin*. However, I'm not griping about being *Nihonjin*. I'm still glad to be one."

"P.S. I could certainly use ten extra dollars a month. Some girls manage to have quite a good time by scrimping on their food, but I just gotta eat my three squares a day. Though I'll never go back to that awful heat and dust of Poston, I wish I had my old job back again. I hear Helen Taylor is there now. Remember her?"

Mr. McBain was beaming happily. "What do you think, Teru?"

"It's the best offer I've heard of," Teru said.

"Will you take it?"

"Me?" Teru said, confused by the suddenness of it all.

"Yes. I've watched you very carefully this past year and you'll make the best ambassador I know. Perhaps I should ask one of my office staff first but I'm convinced that you should go. What do you say?"

"I'd like to," Teru said earnestly, "I'll have to ask my father first though. I'll ask him as soon as I get home."

Mr. Noguchi came home from work looking rather grumpy and Teru decided to let him settle down before asking him.

She listened only half attentively while she busily searched for the best way to broach the subject.

Mr. Noguchi was saying, "I still wonder how the government chose the Caucasian personnel to head the agriculture program. The people in charge here don't know anything about farming. I suppose that is too strong but they certainly don't know much."

"This afternoon, Mr. Sakaguchi and I spent almost an hour explaining to the Hakujin why you can't transplant young eggplants during the heat of day. Even then, he couldn't understand and wanted the work done between eight o'clock and five o'clock. He told us we had a heat phobia and insisted on transplanting so we did set out a few plants but they withered and dried out by the time we came home.

"Then he blamed it on the plants not being vigorous enough and our not giving them enough water when we transplanted."

"It's fortunate we didn't plant them all. He wouldn't have any for our messhalls otherwise. We' re going back after supper to transplant the rest of the eggplants.''

It all went in one ear and out the other. Teru knew it was a bad time but she immediately told him about her talk with Mr. McBain.

She watched his face eagerly for some sign of approval, but there was none. Mr. Noguchi stared almost fixedly at his daughter.

"Do you want to go?" he said quietly.

"There aren't many opportunities like this," Tern said.

Mr. Noguchi studied her face a moment longer, then said, "We will talk about this tonight after I come back from work, together with Tadao and Sally."

CHAPTER 18

"What's he going to say?" Sally kept asking, "Didn't he give you any kind of hint?"

Teru couldn't answer and she finally lapsed into a silence which, however, continued to probe into Teru's thoughts.

"Are you going?" she asked after a moment.

"I don't know," Teru said, "he might say no."

"Why don't you go anyway," Sally urged. "Why not? There's nothing to do here."

Teru followed Sally's scornful, smoldering eyes around the cramped room. It still looked dingy and dilapidated despite all their efforts. The clean, starched-white curtains looked out of place against the bare, unevenly spaced wall boards. The hastily nailed together stools and benches were already battered and dirt marked beyond repair. The floor boards had shrunk and curled away from each other, making the cracks even wider than they had been. The drapes which separated the "bedroom" from the "living room" reached dismally and unwillingly up to the rafters and in protest were uncooperatively drab.

She could hear her mother getting ready for bed on the other side of the drapes. She could feel Sally's eyes on her. Tad had come back and was outside talking to Paul. She could hear them plainly.

"Waste time," Paul was saying, "'I gotta take general science from Henry Ikeda next year. He was only a junior outside. He should be only two years ahead of me if I didn't quit school right after curfew. I should be a sophomore this year instead of a freshman."

"I think one of the seniors is going to teach algebra and geometry next year, too," Tad said.

"Waste time," Paul said with even more disgust. "Is Mr. Nishikawa going to quit next year, too?"

Teru was still unaccustomed to hearing Jiro referred to as Mr. Nishikawa. She only halfheard Tad's answer.

"Yeah, he's a no-no so they won't let him teach next year. They ought to let him. There won't be anybody left next year."

Teru was occupied with her own thoughts again. Sad thoughts this time which suddenly made the opportunity seem less wonderful. She would be leaving the good with the bad. If only she could take her family and friends with her.

Mr. Noguchi appeared tired when he came home from settling out the eggplants. He seemed uncertain how to begin. He looked gravely at Teru, Sally, and Tad sitting on the cots pushed against the wall of the vacated Hosoda apartment. They'd started to sit on the bench pushed against the wall separating them from the Yanaga apartment when Sally quickly said, "Let's sit on the beds. I don't want everyone asking tomorrow if we're really planning to relocate."

Mr. Noguchi cleared his throat carefully and began, "I want you to weigh carefully what I tell you tonight. Teru wishes to relocate. That is good. It is good to become dissatisfied with this miserable barrack life and wish to leave for something better. There is no future here.

"Teru is also a girl and I regard relocation and marriage in the same light. Your mother and I have known, as all parents know, that we must steel ourselves against an eventual way of parting while at the same time we daily tighten the bonds. It is difficult. In a Japanese family it is considered a disgrace for a married daughter to return home. Her decision is an important one."

He paused uncomfortably to look at Ayame, sitting quietly on her cot next to the window. "Your mother is ill now or she would take this burden off my shoulders." Ayame looked up, a puzzled expression on her face. She came over and sat beside Teru.

Mr. Noguchi continued more firmly, ''It is not unreasonable to wish to relocate. I know that many of your friends are talking of leaving and that some have already left camp. I am the unreasonable one."

''I will not stop you. However, it is my duty to have this talk with you before you decide. It is an obligation I took on myself when I undertook to raise a family in this country."

"You are at an age when you seem to have time enough to reach any goal you set for yourself. Your future is as bright as your imagination set by standards you have learned in school. I am a failure. In that light, my experience and what I say tonight may not be worth much to you."

He ignored their quick protest and went on. "'I am a failure by your standards; however, I have done well by the standards of my farm youth, though I may have faltered considerably from the goals I set for myself and the goals I might have reached. This is partly because, as I grew older, I found myself satiated with sense of well being that comes with a well-ordered, middle-of-the-road life. It is good to strive but it is also good to enjoy.

"There are many things I have never told you. I remember the time Sally asked me if your mother was a picture bride. The idea of choosing a mate by means of a picture seems 'awful' according to your standards, does it not? Such outlandish procedure is fit only for 'heathen' is the way you have been taught. They don't teach you that the same thing happened even in this country all through its history.

"However, the facts are, I first saw your mother's picture in a schoolmate's room and our marriage was carried out by proxy while I was in America and your mother was in Japan; however, I had known her quite well in between. In truth, she was my reason for coming to America."

"'I have sometimes felt that we did not tell you enough of our early life and our backgrounds; however, on the other hand, I wondered if it weren't better to cut completely the ties with Japan since we were embarked on a new life here in America, and I also didn't think it fair to burden you with so many cultural conflicts while you were still young.' '

"I will tell you as much as time permits tonight."

"Immediately after I finished college, I broke both legs while mountain climbing and spent several weeks in the hospital where I did considerable thinking and came into considerable debt which I could not afford. I was able to watch objectively while my classmates scrambled feverishly for positions which suddenly seemed to me quite low for persons who had graduated from college. It would take years to pay my hospital bills."

"A cousin from Hiroshima visited me at the hospital. He was on his way to America; and although he had barely finished grammar school he described America as a place where he would make more money in a few months than I would make in a year. His plans were to work hard for five years and return to Japan with enough savings to buy a house and farm."

"After he left, I suddenly saw what I thought was my big opportunity. Until then, I had spent sleepless nights knowing I had little chance of marrying until I was thirty, by which time, your mother's parents would have found her a suitable husband."

"I came to America as soon as my legs healed and my first job was cutting wood. It was back-breaking work but I was making money. It was not as much as I had expected, and I was discouraged terribly at first. I could not speak the language and I was completely cut off from the cultural side of life that my college training had equipped me for. I had no books to read. No discussion with thinking people. No one to talk to of things other than the bare necessities of physical life and the task of cutting so many cords of wood a day."

He smiled. "My first opportunity came when the foreman of the ranch asked if one of us woodchoppers knew how to handle a team of horses. We all looked at each other blankly and no one volunteered."

"Of course, I did not even know how to harness a horse.

However, I knew that Deguchi, the regular driver, was earning almost two dollars a day more than I. I stepped forward, thinking that I should be able easily to learn with a little instruction from Deguchi for whom I had written several letters to relatives in Japan."

"The foreman said gratefully, 'Good, Deguchi is sick and the fields have to be marked for planting tomorrow. Bring the team out by the north gate in the morning and I'll tell how I want it marked."

"I could not confess then, and there was nobody else anyway; and so that night, I went to see Deguchi who gave me a general idea how to harness and steer the team. After which, I slipped out to the barn and harnessed the horses by lantern light and led them to the north pasture. Then for three or four hours I experimented with the reins and the harness and giddyupped and whoa'd the horses until we were all nervous wrecks. I crawled wearily into bed, fairly certain I could handle them adequately.

"The next morning, I was right on time though the foreman looked at me very strangely because I had the belly strips hooking the horses to each other. However, he simply rehooked the straps under the bellies without comment and left after giving me instructions."

"He came back in midmorning and seemed on the verge of reprimanding me on the slow progress I was making when he noticed how strangely tired and lathery the horses were. He watched me go slowly and steadily up and back another row. Then he apparently changed his mind and told me I was a good man to be so careful of the welfare of the horses. Next he wondered aloud what made them so tired while I wondered ifhe suspected. He made me a regular driver when Deguchi decided he had saved enough money to go into farming for himself' '

"I remember this well because it was also the turning point of my stay in America. I decided then and there that America was really a land of opportunity with a limitless future for anyone with ability.,,

"I was able to follow Deguchi's example soon after, and I immediately wrote to your mother and she joined me here."

"Those early days were happy ones if you can leave out the incessant toil. Especially hard for your mother who was not accustomed to manual labor."

"We laid wonderful plans in those days. By then, I had improved my English to the point where I could read newspapers and books, though my conversation was still very poor and I seized avidly on the idealism that had laid the groundwork for America.

Your mother was also taking lessons from a private tutor even though the expense cut quite heavily into our slender income."

"However, we thought it necessary after the day we discovered that we intended to make America our permanent home. When I first wrote of that decision to my parents and brothers, they scolded me and told me to come back immediately. I stayed because I firmly believed I was opening a bright new chapter in the saga of the Noguchi clan. The American Noguchi, I thought of myself"

''When you children came, we did our best to give you every advantage in fitting yourselves into the American stream of life. It was not easy. I am not a moneymaker. A few times I did not have the money to buy bread and your mother would bake a loaf with flour scraped from the bottom of the flour bin so you could have sandwiches for your school lunch instead of rice balls as other Japanese children did. Sometimes, your mother pretended she wasn't hungry so you would have enough energy for your play at school. Helpless, I used to watch her grow thinner and call on the Lord for help."

He paused. Teru looked quickly at Ayame listening attentively as though all this were about some other person only remotely connected with herself She was remembering the time Ayame said to her, "It hurts too much to talk about those things now. Someday when we have lots of money and have no worries and we can look back and laugh about it, I'll tell you all the trying experiences we went through. That time isn't yet."

Mr. Noguchi began again. Luck smiled on them a little following the Depression. The future looked brighter and all their earlier sacrifices seemed vindicated. They themselves were shut out but their children were being admitted to a bright new world of opportunity. However, it was hard, knowing that they themselves would never be accepted as Americans. To their neighbors and even to their children, they were irrevocably Japanese.

Out of the blue sky, Mr. Noguchi was offered a position in a large commercial firm in Japan to serve as a liaison man in the South.

Pacific. It was a position of importance and prestige. He turned it down for it would mean talcing his family back to Japan. America still seemed a wonderful land of opportunity and though he himself would have unexpectedly made a success of himself, he thought his children would have a better chance in America.

He seriously doubted his decision in the following year when he and Ayarne sought in vain to find a reasonable answer why their oldest daughter hadn't been awarded one of the three school scholarships when she was the standout scholar of her class. The Latin teacher had said as much to Mr. Motoyarna when he told him that the Noguchi family had come up for discussion at a faculty meeting because Tadao, Sally, and Teru, all stood at the heads of their classes and he had been delegated to make inquiries into the background of the Noguchi family.

He had a doubtful moment, too, the night they gathered their tearful second daughter into their consoling arms while she sobbed out her story of having been disdainfully snubbed by a *Hakujin* classmate whom she greeted on the street. The worst was hearing the classmate say to her out of-town companions in passing, "Oh, she's a Jap girl in my class but I don't- know why she speaks to me. I never do to her."

Other doubts shook his belief from time to time. George Motoyarna graduating from engineering school and unable to find a position. He learned from Mr. Motoyarna the contents of the letter Teru had also seen.

The Yarmadas' son Bill, giving up the idea of going to college and declaring to his father, "There's no use your sacrificing your health to put me through college when that college training will give me no help in making a living. Outside of doctors, dentists, and druggists, there aren't any occupations where the run-of-the-mill university-trained *Nisei* can find any kind of work in his chosen field. There are too many commerce, foreign trade, economics, chemistry, engineering, and what-have-you majors working on the farms, in the vegetable markets, and in the sheds. I better stay home and help on the farm."

A worried Mr. Yamada coming to see Mr. Noguchi, who could only sympathize, "I don't know what to say. He is looking at the practical, concrete side and he sees his point proven on all sides. He raised questions in my own mind. Your son is too practical to be swayed by such things as the value of college background and hope in the future."

Mr. Yamada saying, "I wouldn't think of it if my health were good. During the summer, I've come to lean on him quite heavily."

There had been minor irritations. Having to bring Tadao all the way across town to get their haircuts when there were so many other barbershops much closer. Refusing Tadao permission to go on a picnic to Gilroy Hot Springs because he knew that the swimming pool was closed to Japanese. Explaining to Sally why she couldn't go to the same Sunday School as Betty Hanford.

However, they were overlooked in the overall good intentions of a bountiful America, which still held the promise of golden opportunities.

Then came the evacuation and the singling out of those of Japanese ancestry for persecution.

To Mr. Noguchi, the clamor for evacuation and the debasing of Japanese ancestry reached the proportions of a popular movement. Even his friends advised him it would be for the good to be in the safety of a concentration camp. They were afraid some "hoodlums" would get out of hand and cause them harm. No one suggested that the overwhelming majority of the people believed in them and would protect them against such hoodlums. Apparently they either cowed themselves into inaction by the imaginary threat of those few hoodlums, or they believed that the hoodlums were in the majority. Being interned himself without trial or evidence, he more forcibly realized that innocence or good intentions meant nothing. Japanese ancestry was the stumbling block. Having Japanese ancestry singled them out for discriminatory treatment.

He faced the facts. His ancestry would always be Japanese. He could do nothing about it. If being Japanese were such a handicap, it would be better ifhe gave up his illusion about America.

"Because," he continued, "this war and this racial propaganda directed against Japanese blood will leave scars that will take two generations to erase. The psychological difference between fanatic and courageous will set Japan apart from America for a long time after the war. As will such name calling as - bestial, treacherous, inhuman, yellow monkey.

"It is inescapable now. Japanese ancestry is tainted for the present American taste. Any progress that we make in the future will be made in spite of our Japanese ancestry."

"A German-American or Canadian-American is acceptable anywhere in Congress in Cabinet offices, as President. However, can you imagine even a Japanese-American Henry Kaiser or for that matter, a Chinese, a Negro, or Mexican, Cordell Hull? No, the skin is not the right color. There is still a strong color line. It hasn't been breached yet despite the earnest efforts of a hard working minority."

"A little after I came to this country, I received a letter from a former college friend asking me why America of all nations should have voted against and had been instrumental in defeating a racial and religious equality clause in the Covenant of the League of

Nations. At the time, I paid little attention and wasn't particularly disturbed by the fact which excited my friend very much. After evacuation, I remembered ...

"If we stay in this country, we shall have to make excuses for our ancestry. I could not stand that. I am proud of my ancestry. I am proud of being Japanese. I am not treacherous. I am not bestial. My friends and relatives in Japan are not treacherous and bestial. I cannot sit quietly and listen to ignorant and intolerant fools slander my ancestry and people. I cannot listen to distorted propaganda whose sole purpose is to engender a murderous fighting spirit in a people. I will not shrink into a shell and cringe each time someone slanders my ancestry. As for those Japanese who mouth those same lying phrases simply to curry favor and further their own standing..."

Mr. Noguchi stopped suddenly, ashamed of his outburst of temper. He continued more quietly. ''I know that some *Issei* are planning to relocate, although most of the relocatees are *Nisei* so far. They have apparently come to different decisions than myself However, I know also that many Issei who think as I do are also planning to relocate because of more practical considerations such as schooling for their children and the necessity for building a reserve fund for their old age."

"Mr. Motoyama is concerned about the futility of camp life. I realize that I may be wrong in my decision to stay in camp and return to Japan at the earliest opportunity. I feel that it is not too late to pick up the threads of life once more. You, however, have been brought up as Americans. It is too much to expect you to desire expatriation to Japan, of which you know practically nothing. That is why I will not stop you from relocating.

"If you go, it will be with my full blessing. It would be unreasonable otherwise. After all, we have tried for twenty years to make you a good American. We have never tried to hold you to Japan, either by sending you to language schools or to Buddhist churches. Tadao, however, is young, and it is easier for him to start all over. It is my desire that he return with me to Japan and build together with me on a firm foundation .... "

Teru tossed restlessly all through the night, her mind tom and distressed by tearful parting scenes, firm resolves, and bright-eyed glimpses of herself setting up a fresh new life of her own in America.

Maybe later calling Sally after she'd established herself and found an apartment. She pictured her father and Tadao struggling to take care of their invalid mother. She pictured them struggling and half starving while they battled to establish themselves in Japan.

She tried to leaven the firm picture with Sally. Sally usually cheerful, sometimes martyr-like. She wondered what there would be for her in the future. There would be no Jiro. No Jiro saying, " I definitely want Japan to win this war. Not just because I'm Japanese but because there is only one nation in this world that can prove in our lifetime that the degree of pigmentation is not a measure of superiority. China is too weak and is not united. She' ll probably be tom by civil wars as soon as the war is ended. She can't even get back Hong Kong from the British and she's supposed to be one of the Big Four. Russia will never give up Outer Mongolia. This equality business is rotten with hypocrisy. If Japan fails, we're sunk. That's why I can never go out for the duration of the war. Even to my old job in San Francisco. Not even as a janitor, because manpower is going to win this war."

"Do you think, I want to stay in this comer of hell? Don't you think I hate this hand-to-mouth existence just as much as the next fellow?"

Would there be someone like Jiro out there? What would she do when it came time to marry? She would want to marry in a few years. To whom? Some *Hakujin*? Someone like Fred Johnson? Fred had said some strange things that time coming home from that movie in Monterey, about the half-caste heroine. They'd switched seats for the drive home and Janet was in the front seat with Bill.

Fred had talked mostly about hybrid virility-Japanese-Caucasians.... good looking, smart... how different she was from other girls he knew.

Teru had felt an undercurrent of groping uneasiness beneath his word.

Afterwards, he squeezed her hands tightly when he said goodnight and from the look in his eyes, Teru knew that he would be in love with her if he let himself On the surface it never got beyond eager glances and a predilection on his part to seek her out on all occasions, but the relationship had raised the question strongly in her mind. She'd decided then that she could never marry a *Hakujin*.

There was something distasteful about the thought. She couldn't put her finger on the cause or explain. Her parents never mentioned the question. Possibly it was because of the disrepute attached to the very words half-caste and halfbreed. She shut it from her mind. She rolled over on her sagging cot and readjusted the lumpy pillow made of remnants stuffed into a cotton bag. She knew that she couldn't marry a *Hakujin* until her outlook changed still more. And yet, there would be few Nisei out in Cleveland. She couldn't seek them out. What had she thought when Kenji's brother had told her Japanese always got together wherever they went? That there was only one way to solve the problem. Go out and lose their identity as Japanese. That meant inter-marrying. Not looking for someone like Jiro.

Marrying a *Hakujin* would make it definitely "signed and sealed" with delivery waiting to complete the cycle of assimilation. Jiro agreed on that. "If I go out, I'd marry a *Hakujin*. It means setting the clock back another generation if you marry a Japanese."

However, throughout the exhausting sleepless night, Teru's thoughts kept returning to the family. When all was said and done, it was the only family she would ever have. The family she raised herself wouldn't be the same. The friends she'd made in Salinas--in Assembly Center — in Camp 1. They were gone from her life already. Those she was making now would be gone with relocation. Friendships were so fine and heartwarming but they didn't always last. You had to be there to tend them like a fire. They were broken, they languished, they cooled, they met with intolerance, they met with forced evacuations. Families were more permanent. They meant more. You went back to them after quarrels that would have ruptured the finest friendships. You were part of them. They were part of you.

CHAPTER 19

Teru had scarcely resigned herself to staying in camp when a letter came from George saying that he was relocating to Detroit. After some hesitation, he had accepted a routine drafting job paying one hundred and twenty dollars a month; however, there was some hope of working to a better position. The next day, segregation was announced for September. All no-no's and all Issei who had applied for repatriation before July would be segregated at the Tule Lake center in northern California. Families would be allowed to accompany segregees on a voluntary basis. Rehearings would be held and no-no's would be given a chance to change their answers. No-yes answers would be treated the same as yes-yes answers. In the middle of it all, George proposed to Sally by letter. He hadn't time to make arrangements to get to Poston before the rehearings and he wanted desperately to have Sally change her answer. Sally showed Teru the letter which was heavily laden with postage stamps. "You have to change your answer now," Teru said, "Mr. McBain says Tule Lake will be war durational."

However, she didn't know whether to be happy or sad when Sally finally agreed.

Previously, all her persuasion had met with a stubborn silence that was as like Sally for the stubbornness as it was unlike her for the uncommunicative silence, and Teru had taken for granted that the family would go to Tule Lake with Sally. Mr. Noguchi made no attempt to influence Sally's stand and evinced no interest in the rehearings other than to say with resignation that he couldn't understand the workings of the WRA which seemed so often to him to be based on a hit or miss method that failed to take into consideration the human factors involved.

" I wonder what they intend to gain by this segregation," he said," everything is based on the answers to the army questionnaire and they mean nothing."

Teru said quickly, "Then you mean it's true what so many people are saying? That the Japanese way is to judge everyone by what is in his 'stomach' and not by what he says? That even when a Japanese puts something down in writing, it means nothing because of what he may have him 'stomach'?"

Mr. Noguchi frowned, ''That is not what I meant. Who has been saying such a thing?"

"Oh, the Kuwahara boy, the Sato boy, the Harada boy ---"

"They are mistaken. They probably misinterpret what they may have heard about the 'stomach' being the core of action and seize on that misinterpretation to cover their present shortcomings. Some Japanese may possibly hold to that postulate; however, it cannot by any stretch of the imagination be set up as a national characteristic. They make the same mistake that Occidentals do when they throw up their hand and say they cannot understand the Oriental mind. They are trying to fit the Oriental mind into a simple pattern which can then be applied to all things Oriental like a pass key. It cannot be done. Each of us is different and acts accordingly."

"What I meant was, the dishonest and the untrustworthy would be the last persons to reveal their nature. A potential saboteur is not going to answer no-no."

Jiro had said much the same thing when they'd discussed the questionnaire.

"We were all forced to answer one way or the other but that doesn't mean that those of us who answered the same way did so for even approximately the same reasons. Lots of us had somewhat the same basic restrictions but there must have been hundreds of other influencing factors like family ties, money, fear of public opinion, brother already in the army, and one's contacts which were the real deciding factors."

"Even the volunteers signed up for all sorts of different reasons. Take the fellows from your block. They're pretty representative. Kenji says he is no more loyal to this country than I am and ye~ he's willing to take the chance of being mutilated or even killed because he thinks it would be better in the long run for himself and his family. He doesn't fit my interpretation of loyalty and yet can anyone say that he isn't loyal, besides Kenji himself?"

''Look at Gary. He refused to volunteer because he doesn't believe in segregated units; however, he's willing to go back into the Air Corps any time. He thinks he's entitled to the same privileges as any American. Is he less loyal? I would say he is more true to his country's principles than those who volunteered for the segregated unit. They're making a concession to their different status. He wants no compromise between what is said to be his birthright and what certain elements believe should be allowed him."

"Henry Kitano answered no-no because he doesn't believe it's constitutional to pick on citizens of Japanese ancestry. He thinks that the very fact that the questionnaire is discriminatory and that question Number 28 implies a previous loyalty to Japan makes a yes-yes answer both an admission and acceptance of his treatment and formerly divided loyalty. He used to be a strong JACL leader outside and I'd say he was as loyal as most. Still, on the records, he's listed as disloyal."

"And what about the fellows who are loyal to America but can't face why they should disclaim any loyalty to Japan? That may be splitting hairs and unjustifiable in time of war but I've heard that statement several times. Under other circumstances, they'd be in the front lines fighting wholeheartedly for America. Even myself, if the army had accepted my applicaton, I'd be in the army now, and if evacuation hadn't happened, I'd be doing my part in the war effort even though I might have felt some sympathy for Japan."

"Evacuation, though, seemed to sour me on everything," he said hastily when Teru seemed about to say something.

"Some people remained loyal in spite of evacuation," Teru pointed out

"Sure," Jiro agreed, "lots of people decided their only possible future is in America and their only recourse is to endure and hope or fight and hope. Still, there aren't many like Harry Moneda and Sam Ogawa. They're what I call real Americans. No doubt. No holding back. Proud of their ancestry. Their country right or wrong. Sam once told me he thought the big boys made a mistake in getting into this war."

"Joe Shimada volunteering is a laugh. I wonder what the army examiners think when all those people like him turn up with their glass eyes and their stiff arms and legs?" Teru agreed that Satoru Kono and Itsumi Wake volunteered because "the other fellow did," and that Jack Yanaga probably hadn't made his own decision. They weren't sure about the others but guessed that Shiro Oda was telling the truth when he said that he was just tired of camp and wanted to get out. Just before registration, he'd been trying without success to get leave clearance to Denver and now figured that volunteering was the quickest way out since there was a good chance that the army would tum him down because of his hernia

Bill joined them and talk turned to the no-yes group. He was pretty bitter because the no-yes group would be treated the same as the yes-yes group.

"Why should they be free to relocate when they come right out and say they refuse to fight for their country?" he wanted to know. He had his own ideas about why they answered that way. "Fence sitters," he called them, ready to tum to which ever side the fortunes or war favored. Jiro and Teru didn't agree. They thought the no-yes group was the most difficult to understand. Included were probably those like Kuwahara and Sato who claimed that their answers meant nothing. That what they felt in their 'stomachs' was the only thing that counted. They didn't want to come right out and show disloyalty to America by default and yet they didn't want to be caught up in any future draft.

Others like Tom Itaya were no-yes because the grapevine had said the interviewers weren't making an issue of such a mixed answer and were concentrating on the yes-yes and no-no groups. It was the smart thing to do because they were committing themselves the least. If they could get away with a no to 'willingness to serve in the armed forces,' they were that much ahead and would be foolish to do so.

Some felt that they shouldn't have to serve in the army because of the experience of evacuation. "We've done our share," they claimed. Some felt kind of loyal to America but not enough to fight and die for it.

Many of the no-yes group seemed to be people who preferred to have themselves considered with the no-no group because whenever they were asked by Issei what their answers had been, they usually hedged by simply saying they had answered no.

The yes-yes group seemed to be easiest to understand if you left out the "stomach" answers and those like Kuronami who "refused to be tricked by the army" and lay himself open for prosecution.

A large number seemed to have been like George Motoyama who would take his chances on the draft and was perfectly willing to go into the army if he were called. He felt nothing about renouncing any allegiance to Japan, because he didn't have any that he knew of. He hadn't volunteered because he wanted to be treated the same as the rest of the American people. He wanted no part of segregated units.

A great many, however, had simply taken the path of least resistance, hiding behind a passive show of loyalty that would continue to give them protection against persecution and untoward treatment. They were doing what they were expected to do.

Others were apprehensive of the draft but were more afraid of possible prosecution. They belonged to the no-yes group in reality.

There were also those who didn't know what to do and yes-yes seemed the majority answer so they sought security in numbers.

The no-no group was easier.

A few were like Henry Kitano who still clung fast to his constitutional rights and a few were simply draft dodgers.

A few were bitter about evacuation and a few were disillusioned like Jiro.

A larger group included those whose parents had a stake in Japan and to whom filial piety came first.

The overwhelming majority were those who had decided they were Japanese. They didn't care who knew it and had made up their minds to endure whatever treatment might be meted out to them. With Buna and Attu fresh in their minds, their lot could be nothing but easy by comparison.

When the slips were finally passed out for rehearings, there was one for Ayame but there were none for Charlie Omoto and the Mineta brothers.

Charlie immediately proclaimed that the army interviewer had misunderstood him but that he had applied for repatriation and would join the segregees at a later date.

Mr. Mineta was grim when his sons admitted that they had answered yes-yes. Mas, the older son, defended himself lamely. "I didn't want to lose our property. You'll be grateful later on."

"The property is yours," Mr. Mineta said, ''never refer to it as mine again."

Mas was silent, waiting for the storm to pass. He'd already made up his mind it would be no use arguing. "Do you by any chance intend to serve in the United States Army and fight against your mother country?" Mr. Mineta asked.

"No," Mas said, "I don't expect to."

"Didn't the army man say that you will eventually be drafted?'

Mas nodded, his jaws set under his father's contemptuous tone. "I can still refuse induction," he said placatingly. It was his one hope of remaining in the good graces of his father.

The grim lines around Mr. Mineta's set lips relaxed a little. "Why couldn't you have answered like a real Japanese?" he asked. "What can I say to people now? I have lost their respect."

As soon as she recovered from the rude shock of having her own sons showing disloyalty to Japan, Mrs. Mineta started a whispering campaign. "The no-no are baka. They're fools to be tricked into going to Tule Lake. They'll find out when they get there what the government has in store for them."

Only Mrs. Y anaga told her to her face, ''Then why did you make the rounds pleading with us to have our sons answer no-no?"

"I was misled,"Mrs. Mineta protested, "I didn't know that there would be any segregation. The fact to consider now is that all Japanese should stick together at a time like this. We should watch the trend and do as the majority does. My son is smart that way. He knows everything that is going on in camp."

The younger Mineta announced under his father's tongue lashing that he was going to relocate to Denver and proceeded to pack his clothes.

Mr. Mineta looked on silently; then said, with icy calm, ''No longer consider yourself my son. I look on that crate you are nailing together as your coffin. Do not come near me again. I am not your father."

Sam sullenly went on with his packing and left camp the next day. He stayed with friends in Camp I until his leave clearance was properly channeled.

Teru brought home the slip for Ayame and handed it to her father without comment. Mr. Noguchi smiled. "This is good," he said, ''Mother is smarter than I. After Sally decided to change her answer, I feared that I would not be segregated and that I would be thrown together with the loyal American group when I am not sympathetic to their stand. I intend to apply for repatriation to Japan as soon as forms are available again. They told me the other day that they did not have any at the present time."

Teru could say nothing. Sally announced that she wouldn't change her mind either and would go with the family to Tule Lake. That night, Mr. Yamada came, ostensibly to play 'go' with Mr. Noguchi. Teru paid little attention while they carefully placed their black and white rocks in strategic and then fighting positions back and forth across the go board.

Around eleven, both she and Sally were lifting their books to hide their yawns. They couldn't, however, overcome the inertia of reticence about getting ready for bed while a visitor was present. Ayame and Tad, though, quietly went to bed and pretty soon they could hear Ayame's gentle snoring.

"She never did snore before," Mr. Noguchi apologized as he picked up a white rock. Teru knew that much.

She thought, the Orient does so many things differently. Their saws and planes cut on the pull stroke; they build their roofs first and then build the walls under it; they belittle themselves; they venerate age; they write from the opposite side.

Mr. Yamada yawned widely, ''I'm getting sleepy, too," he said. Still, he stayed, while Sally and Teru debated going to sleep themselves, their minds only partly occupied with their books and more and more aware of their heavy eyelids and the desultory conversation across the go board. Ayame's quiet snoring deterred them from any action.

Suddenly they noticed how quiet it was outside. The Maeda apartment was dark and the Maedas were usually the last family in the block to put out their lights. They exchanged glances and Sally followed Teru's lead in getting towels and soap from the rack placed next to the door.

Only the lights from the latrines and the poles at the comers of the block cast their yellowish glow towards the ground and faintly illumined the now darkened barracks. Seeing them without lights and without life, it was hard to believe that anyone could possibly be living in them. They looked deserted and unlived in like rows of empty hulks built around a mirage that had faded after building and left the desert harsh and forbidding to bum and bleach the life that the mirage had promised. The broken and unreplaced window panes, the tar paper tom in ragged patches from the walls, the crude porches erected from logs hand-hauled from the slough were robbed of their everyday familiarity by the darkness and loomed ugly and forbidding.

It's not right. If they could only see this. If they could only feel this shrinking I feel, they wouldn't allow this to keep on. Not the people I went to school with. Not the people I know. Where are they? Why can't they put a stop to this? We're people.

She pulled shut the latrine door which always seemed to be half open as a concession to the heat and the smell. She began thinking again of her first visits to the latrine. The bashful little girls who time and again scurried out to wait until the latrine was empty or they forgot their bodies' promptings. The not-so-bashful little girls who came to stand and stare at you. The not-so-little boys who came with their mothers and stared at you until you felt uneasy and uncomfortable. Yoshitaka's brother, especially, who was almost eight. The very little ones perched precariously on the oversize toilet seats, wide-eyed and reluctant and childishly unaware of any filth that may have been splashed on the seats.

She was glad that as far as she knew there were no syphilitic women in the block. Alice had told her that one of the bachelors was under treatment at the clinic and that a doctor friend guessed that some blocks had as many as three and four who should be talcing treatments.

When Dr. Katayama had visited her just before he left camp, he told her he broke out in a cold sweat whenever he thought of the consequences of a serious epidemic getting a foothold in camp. It had been a rather odd visit. She'd been surprised when Sally told her Dr. Katayama had come to see her, since she'd met him only infrequently after that first week in Camp 1.

He seemed ill at ease and very undoctorlike. He'd made no mention of his coming relocation, and when he later unexpectedly left camp, Teru had been disappointed. He had seemed so sincere about his efforts to help 'his people' and about his resolve to stay in camp as long as he could be of service, not only because of that angle but because he had benefitted, too, since he was performing operations which he couldn't have dared attempt outside without several more years of assisting.

In fact, he had talked as though he were still bent on setting up a complete laboratory system in Poston, so they wouldn't have to send specimens outside for special examinations since that took too much time. He even outlined a program for teaching more hygiene and sanitation in the schools.

When Sally and Ayame were gone for a minute, he said abruptly, "Have your ever considered marrying a doctor?" Teru looked up, startled at the sudden change in his voice and manner. A moment before, he had been telling her about the incidence of infantile paralysis in Camp 1 and how well publicity and preventive measures had worked in stopping a more serious outbreak.

His face was flushed and intent. There was no mistaking what he meant. "Ifs not a very peaceful life," he groped on awkwardly, "you'll have prestige."

Teru looked steadily into his anxious face. She couldn't help but feel disturbed by the intensity of his look. She slowly shook her head. She couldn't think of anything to say.

"George wrote me that you two had broken up so I ..."

"I'm sorry," Teru said, finding her voice.

"I want you to be my wife."

''I hardly know you."

"That's all right."

'Tm sorry," Teru said again, "I couldn't."

"Think it over," he pleaded, "and let me know."

His voice broke and he stopped when Teru shook her head. He left almost immediately. Sally came back in time to see him go and she wanted to know what made him look so flustered. Teru told her and she said, "Just like a Kibei. They're all alike. You barely know them, and boom, they ask you to marry them or something. I sure don't understand the guys."

Teru didn't agree that all *Kibei* were like that but she knew that there was a wide gulf between *Nisei* and *Kibei*, a gulf that was bridged only by a minority. Dr. Katayama was a poor example to make generalizations on, anyway, because even his friends thought he was Nisei until he told them he was really *Kibei*. He was far removed from the average pre-evacuation Kibei, who, because of language and cultural difficulties, had been forced to play a secondary role in all activities while Nisei took the lead. They worked for day wages and at whatever jobs they could find and were taking the same course *Issei* had taken when they first came to the country. *Nisei* tended to look down on them for that reason. However, in camp, *Kibei* found themselves no longer semi-outcasts and often felt an upsurge of superiority over *Nisei* who couldn't even speak Japanese. They began to assert themselves and earned the resentment of *Nisei* who could see nothing to get excited about in *Kibei* who could point only to a knowledge of Japanese and had nothing else to commend them.

What had been passive awareness before often turned to active dislike.

Teru learned the purpose of Mr. Yamada's visit the next day. He had been asked by the Motoyama family to sound Mr. Noguchi out in regard to marriage between George and Sally.

"Marrying her off to someone like George will ease my mind considerably," her father told her, "ordinarily, we would ask them to wait until you were married; however, with the situation what it is, we will tell them to go ahead with the arrangements since both parties are willing and delay will only complicate matters."

George's parents were strongly Buddhist and insisted on a Buddhist wedding. They also took for granted that the wedding would take place in accordance with Japanese custom at the groom's home. George came two days before the second contingent of Tule Lake-bound segregees was scheduled to leave Poston. Two-hundred thirteen were included in the second group.

"I couldn't make it any sooner," he explained. "First, they promised me I could come last week, then they told me I couldn't leave until the section head came back from a conference in Denver. He got in yesterday and I took the next train which was a half day late to top it off."

He immediately pitched in and helped them with the packing. Jiro was there, too. He was leaving with the first group the very next day.

"Where's Bill?" George said. He looked up from measuring the sewing machine for re-crating. Mr. Otis had sent it into camp only three months ago but Mr. Noguchi had immediately broken up the original shipping container to make shelves. Fortunately, they had left the sewing machine with Mr. Otis, and Mr. Johnson had no chance to take it away with the other things. "That's strange," Teru said, "I haven't seen him lately either. He should be packing too."

"I didn't ask but the Yamadas didn't look like they were getting ready to pack when I dropped in before coming here," George said.

"I don't think they're going," Jiro said, vigorously sawing away. "I hear he's changed his answer."

"He might have," Sally said. "He was the first one to go in for his rehearing and he took the longest. The rest of us didn't take very long."

"Did they ask you much?" George asked.

"No," Sally shook her head. "I just told them I made a mistake the first time and wanted to change my answer. They asked me why and I told them I was getting married and that was all."

So that's why I haven't seen Bill lately, Teru thought, he's probably ashamed of having done an about-face after having talked so strongly.

"I wonder if many of the requests would be granted?" Sally said.

"Why do they allow it?" Jiro wanted to know.

"What is segregation for then? It can't be a question of wanting to get all the disloyal together. Otherwise they would allow yes-yes people to change their answers at this time too. In my opinion, there are more people wanting to change from yes to no instead of from no to yes. I've heard several people say that they intend to go to jail if they are drafted."

They were all through with the crating when the *Hakujin* inspector came. A *Nisei* was with him. The *Hakujin* poked aimlessly here and there. He stopped by a crate and asked importantly, "What's this?"

Teru went to see. It was the crate with the table, stools, and ironing board. They were plainly visible through the slate. She thought he meant the ironing board because project regulations forbade all ironing in apartments and they were supposed to use the ironing room at the far end of the block. She'd tried to iron there once on the badly warped and uncovered boards and half way through, a dust whirl had swirled through the broken windows and made a mess of both the wet and the pressed clothes so she'd never gone there again. Others stayed away, too, as soon as they'd persuaded their husbands and brothers to hammer together private ironing boards, because of the inconvenience of bringing irons, ironing pads, covers, baskets of unpressed clothes, and hangers and baskets for pressed clothes and then carrying them all back again. Most kitchens had gradually appropriated the rooms as storage places for pickling vegetables; and during the heat of day, the smell took over and the few who lived fairly close to the ironing room and didn't mind the other inconvenience or passerbys looking in on them waited for the cool oflate evening to press their clothes. A few more started to use the ironing rooms after project regulations made it mandatory for all persons to turn in their irons and electric stoves to the block manger's office and check them out each time they used them. However, the majority continued to iron in the comparative privacy of their apartments.

"That's our ironing board," Teru answered, wondering what was going to happen.

"I mean these," the *Hakujin* inspector said, pointing.

Jiro said, ''Look like stools to me." The inspector failed to catch the sarcasm.

"You know you can't bring those," he said.

"We were told to bring all our chairs and tables because no lumber was available at Tule Lake," Jiro said.

"I don't know who told you that, but my job is to see that these things aren't sent," the inspector said, "it costs too much money to freight those things. They're not worth the cost of the freight."

"Maybe not," Jiro said, "but they're all we have to sit on."

"Do you realize what it would cost the government to send this stuff?" the *Hakujin* asked.

''How about it?' ' Jiro turned to the Nisei who had come with the *Hakujin*.

"Didn't you tell me yesterday when we were packing that we should bring our stools and tables. Didn't the Administration say so, too?"

The *Nisei* shrugged his shoulders uneasily.

"He's in charge at this end," he said.

George came out of the barrack and wanted to know what the argument was about. They told him, and he said explosively, ''Heck, in Gila, they're packing even worse things. Even beds made from sawed legs. They gave them better crating lumber, too."

The *Hakujin* inspector grinned crookedly, "Well, if you want to take the chance, go ahead. Maybe they'll pass this stuff at the other end, but if they don't, you're going to be out the freight bill."

"You mean we'll have to pay the freight if they don't accept it?" Teru-asked

"That's right," the inspector said, "if you send this stuff, you're taking that chance." He looked around triumphantly and moved on to the Maedas' in the next barrack. Mas and Joe, three years his junior, were both no-no and their parents were going to Tule Lake with them.

Helping pack was Maeda's father who wanted to go with his older brother to Tule Lake but was deterred by Dot's relocation and the fact that they were considered separate families by the WRA. Mr. Noguchi said, "We will need the ironing board so we better transfer that to another crate."

"Aren't you going to bring the others?" George asked.

"No, it would be foolish if we had to pay the freight."

CHAPTER 20

Teru could feel the tension growing taut inside her. The driver of the truck kept nervously lifting his arm to look at the watch on his wrist. They were all there except Bill and a few who wanted nothing to do with the segregees. Mrs. Sakaguchi and Mrs. Yanaga were weeping copiously. Mrs. Yamada was soberly formal until she reached Ayame to say goodbye and then she broke down completely. Ayame moved about looking vaguely distressed. Teru wasn't sure she knew what everything meant. Even the younger girls like Emily were wet-eyed and ill at ease. Teru's former fourth graders were there with a going-away present. Nancy Ota was the only one from her class whose family were segregees. The surprising thing was that not one of her problem children was going. Apparently there were no boys of questionnaire age in their families and their very pro-Japanese parents had neglected to apply for repatriation.

Sally was smiling brightly through it all. "I'm not going to cry," she announced.

"That's the spirit," George said. Tad was standing to one side with Paul. Both were paying close attention to their feet. Slowly smoothing the sand; making little ridges; obliterating them. Mr. Noguchi was waiting by the truck, shaking hands with last minute well wishers from neighboring blocks. Ayame climbed into the familiar army truck which was piled high with their hand luggage and bags of fruit and food to eat on the trip.

There was no knowing what kind of meals they would get and Mrs. Maeda, especially, had been careful to pack enough canned milk and soft food to last her husband the whole trip. His stomach ulcers had incapacitated him during and just after the trip into Poston and she was taking no chances on his being invalided again when he was needed most.

"Time to go," the driver of the truck announced.

Mrs. Kuratani was urged into the front seat because of her baby. She had refused to take the third and last train which would have provided pullman cars because, despite assurances that Poston people would be allowed to remain more or less together after they arrived in Tule Lake, she was afraid she would be separated from her friends.

Everyone wanted to shake hands once more and Teru was busy with promises to write and take care of herself. Until suddenly there was no one left in front of her but Sally. The others subconsciously moved back a little.

Teru was conscious of the surrounding babble of farewells and Godspeeds only as a dull roaring in her ears. Her eyes were on Sally. Sally smiling hard through tears that were just beginning to gleam wetly in her eyes. Sally stripped bare of all pretense. Looking too young without makeup and with her lower lip clenched white between her teeth. Too young to be getting married. It shouldn't have been time for her to marry. It shouldn't have been time to say goodbye. Not for as long as this farewell seemed to portend. Parting comes but once forever. The way I feel, this must be forever, Teru thought, while she heard herself say, "Sally, I guess it's time to say goodby for awhile."

Sally stood stock still. Her eyes widened and she raised her hands as though to take Teru's hands in hers. She opened her mouth but no voice came out. Only a low agonized cry and she stepped numbly into Teru's arms. She buried her head in Teru's shoulder and her silent sobs tore achingly at Teru's heart.

"We'll see each other again," Teru said. Her voice lacked conviction and she knew it. A tear dropped onto her shoulder and rolled wetly down her back. Sally looked up with anguished eyes. "This war can't last forever," Teru pointed out, but she was thinking, I'm going to Japan. You're staying here. This is our last moment together. Ayame was getting off the truck.

"Here comes Mother," Teru gave Sally a quick squeeze and the two of them moved to meet her. Ayame was looking at Sally with stunned and sorrowed eyes. She knows, Teru thought, she realizes now that Sally isn't going with us. Ayame held out her arms and Sally went directly to them.

"We'll meet again, so keep your health good until then,"

Ayame said. She gently smoothed Sally's hair.

"Yes," Sally choked over the words. "We'll meet again."

Is that all we can say at parting? Is that all that is in our minds? The wish to be together? Is that all? There seems so much that should be said. There is so much that's in our hearts.

"Bye."

Teru looked back until a turn hid the figures of Sally and George following out of the road. Their truck fell in line behind other trucks coming from adjacent blocks. The procession passed throngs of people still clustered around trucks that were just getting started. The women all waved handkerchiefs that hung limp with tears. A larger group lined the road by the gate to the camp. There was no crying there.

Tom Hamada was leading the choruses of banzais that greeted and sent each truck rolling on its way. "See you in Japan," he shouted at Mas Maeda but Mas merely waved perfunctorily.

"Then why aren't you going with us?" he said in a conversational tone of voice which wasn't meant to and didn't carry farther than the inside of the truck.

Joe Maeda laughed. "Maybe, he wants to start over again too."

Teru caught on immediately. The talk about Tom Hamada's older brother was too recent in their minds. Ben Hamada had suddenly left camp with the announced intention of continuing his studies which had been interrupted ten years before when he'd married dumb and dumpy Chieko Tanda who'd then borne him two children now aged nine and five. It would have been all right if people hadn't written back that he was working instead of studying and that he was running around with another woman.

People in camp needed no more than that to believe the rumor that he'd told a friend in a confidential moment, "I'll never get any place with Chieko and those two kids tied around my neck, so I'm going to get out and start all over again. With the contacts I've made here, I can't miss. Evacuation should have happened ten years ago. Damn it. I can't afford to pass up this opportunity. If things go right, maybe I can take care of Chieko and the kids, but I'm afraid they'd anchor me down again. Take my advice. Never marry a woman who can't keep up with you no matter how far you advance."

Unlike Tom, Ben had gotten along well with the *Hakujin* personnel and people immediately blamed it on the *Hakujin*. "They fill the minds of our young people with all sorts of tempting offers and persuade them to leave us," they said. "Sure, those young people will make a go of it outside. What about us though? They don't make enough to take care of us, and we're left all alone. It boils down to a breaking up of our families. What's the matter? Don't Hakujin know anything about filial loyalty and family cohesiveness?"

Teru was depressed all the way into Parker where they would board the train that would take them to Tule Lake.

She looked out the back of the truck curiously. The dust had obscured everything that first time. Now the road was oiled and lined with macadam for part of the way.

The whole countryside appeared broken down and abandoned looking compared to the fertile Salinas valley. It didn't seem possible that Indians could still be living in the dilapidated shacks she saw over the fields of stunted maize. For some reason she'd always pictured Indian reservations as well kept because they were under government protection.

The oiled road ended and the dust enveloped them again almost as it had done over a year ago. The stinging particles of dust reached through the truck as though in a last reminder of a phase of life they were leaving forever behind them. They buried their heads and eyes in handkerchiefs and towels and it wasn't half bad. The October sun was at its zenith but the air felt only warm against their cheeks.

The army was in charge and the train jerked out of the station as soon as the last segregee had climbed aboard. Teru was surprised because they weren't scheduled to leave for another hour. Tad wanted to sit next to the window so she peered over his shoulder. She waved back at the Indian road gangs waving from the stations. She sat still and uneasy under the stony stares of the Hakujin they passed. She cringed at their occasional obscene gestures and turned her attention back into the car. To her father and mother sitting across from them. To the odds and ends of getting settled in their corner for the trip ahead.

When she settled back to relax, she immediately began worrying about Sally. She would be all alone that night. Tomorrow, she would be on her way to Gila, then Detroit with George. Detroit was as far away as the moon.

She felt a twinge of sadness that Bill would be leaving for Colorado in the near future to try his hand at growing sugar beets. She wondered if Jiro would be able to reserve apartments for them in the same block at Tule Lake. She'd talked to his older brother for the first time when she'd gone to see him off. Like his parents, she'd met Ichiro before but only for a moment. He took after their father, solid looking and dependable. He was five or six years older than Jiro and looked even older, especially when busy rounding up his three children, Patricia, aged two, Constance, aged four, and Donald, aged six. Teru suspected that he'd chosen their names because of the commonness of his own name, Ichiro, which meant first-born son.

Jiro meant second-born son.

She'd seen his name listed among the honor graduates in his University of California yearbook, and she sometimes wondered what quirk of fate had turned him into a vegetable-market manager when his B.S. was in electrical engineering. Somehow in the bustle of departure, she found him saying to her, "Maybe this will lead me back to what I studied for. I'm pretty rusty but I should be able to brush up enough to get by."

Before he could say more their attention was attracted by an altercation taking place at the edge of the group.

"You've got a lot of nerve," Bob Santo was yelling at a man whom Teru knew by sight and reputation as leader of the pro-Japanese element. "Get the hell out of here. You and me are washed up. Go on. Scram!"

Teru was surprised at the utter lack of respect in Bob's manner. She knew him to be outspoken but not so crude.

"What's the matter?" she asked Jiro's brother.

"It's pretty mixed up," Ichiro explained. "You see, Bob was one of Kurisu's '*kobun*', followers, you might say, Kurisu advised Bob and the rest of his group to answer no-no, too. Bob had a lot of faith in his judgement; and so, he did as he was advised, satisfied that they were all in the same boat together. However, at the last moment, Kurisu's son changed his answer and now Kurisu isn't coming to Tule lake with us. Bob feels that he's been double crossed and is quite upset as you can see."

Bob was hitching up his pants truculently.

Mr. Kurisu retreated a step. "Don't be hasty," he said, "until you hear my side."

"How many sides have you got?" Bob ground out fiercely, "all I have to know is that you pulled a dirty, sneaking double cross. You with your fine talk about Japanese spirit. Well, I'll show you who's the true Japanese."

"We're all Japanese," Mr. Kurisu said. "We must all work together despite what may appear on the surface to be a cleavage. Those of us who stay here will continue to work for the aims which we rallied around during our life together in Poston. In Tule Lake you must do the same."

He held out his hand. Bob looked at his proffered hand and hesitated. He turned away without taking it and he was visibly shaking, his face contorted.

Teru wondered how many others there were like Bob. Not too many for there weren't too many Nisei in the first place, at least from Camp 2. She remembered how disturbed she'd been the day the family had gone to Social Welfare to make final arrangements for moving to Tule Lake.

The people being interviewed were mostly strangers. Mostly Kibei and what her group referred to as Japansy. Outside of Mas and Joe Maeda and Yoshitaka Kai, there hadn't been one person who was more than a mere acquaintance. Jiro, however, said that there were a surprising number of Nisei making the trip and Teru wondered where they were. The young people in her car were Nisei but outside of the Katai family, they had that Japansy look about them. Jane was sitting with her family near the front of the car but she kept her eyes glued out the window. Teru thought she'd wait a bit before going to talk to her. Sally had told her of the tearful fuss Jane had raised when Mr. Katai announced that they were going to Tule Lake.

Yoshitaka was sitting with the Maedas. At the last moment, his family had decided not to go with him to Tule Lake on the promise of the Administration that he would be given another hearing at Tule Lake and be allowed to change his answer.

"Geez," Joe had said when he learned Mr. Kai had asked Mr. Maeda to let Yoshitaka stay with them while at Tule Lake. "What a setup. I never did like the guy and now I have to live with him. How are we supposed to treat him? He'll probably rat on us the first chance he gets, and think of the smell that other guys will connect with us when they learn up there that he's a loyal American."

Mas quieted him. "There's nothing we can do about it. He's afraid to stay alone up there. Besides, he's always shooting his mouth off about 'son-of-a-bitch Americans,' so people will never dream that he's coming back to Poston. If anybody's anti-American, he's it."

Joe said, "Just like his old man. Did you hear him this morning? Blaming it on his wife and saying that he's positively going back to Japan after the war and that if she balks again, he'll leave her behind. He sure talks big. I bet he won't, not with his ten thousand bucks worth of war bonds like he said he had in assembly center. I wonder if he really has all that?"

"Probably. He's pretty tight with his money so he most likely has it someplace where he can't touch it."

"Say, what'll we do with ours?"

"I guess we better get rid of them."

"Yeah. Good idea."

The segregees from the car ahead began filing through on their way to the mess car near the middle of the train.

Sanae Goto was the last one through the door. She stopped happily by Teru's seat. Teru hadn't seen her since assembly center though she'd been living in Camp 2 from the beginning.

"Teru, I heard you were on this train, but I couldn't believe it, not your family," she said, shoving her two boys ahead. "Go ahead with

Papa. Mama is staying here."

"That soldier is looking at you kind of funny," Teru said.

"Oh. They counted us before we left, too," Sanae debated with herself. Soldiers were stationed between each car to prevent people from leaving their assigned cars. "I don't suppose it matters, but maybe I better go. I'll eat fast and come back."

She hurried after the others. She was back immediately. "I'd have been back earlier only they had some real butter and I couldn't resist eating a little," she said, "it was real honest to goodness butter."

Teru laughed, "It must have been good."

"Gosh, they're coming back already," Sanae said. Then abruptly. "I suppose your father repatriated."

Teru shook her head.

"Then it's true. I heard about it, but I wasn't sure," Sanae said.

"You know it's a funny thing. I suppose people told me because of what happened to us. My husband, he's Issei, so we went on the same day to register and I went and answered no-no. Then I came home and find he's answered yes. It was funny because I'd expected him to answer no from the way he's been talking and he thought I'd answer yes because I always used to fight with him about it. But he was certainly glad I answered no-no after they decided to segregate us."

The stragglers began coming back through the car. Mr. Goto appeared, herding the two boys ahead of him.

"I suppose I better go," Sanae said. "I hope we're closer together up there. Poston was so hot I almost never left the Blocks."

She followed her family through the door and Teru settled back to wait until it was their time to eat. They'd have four or five more such mealtimes before they reached Tule Lake.

CHAPTER 21

The train pulled into Tule Lake after dark so they waited one more uncomfortable night curled restlessly in their cramped car seats. Jane again determinedly erected a barricade of suitcase so she could have a little privacy.

They were all up early hoping to get up and stretch their cramped legs and bodies; however, they weren't allowed to leave their cars for another hour. Meanwhile, they peered through the window to catch a glimpse of their next home.

All they could see was a dark pall of smoke blanketing the camp. They shivered, their spirits dampened considerably by the unhealthy looking smoke.

"Let's go back to Poston," Joe Maeda said, "that place don't look so hot to me."

"Too late now," Mas said gloomily.

It is too late, Teru thought, even though Mr. McBain did say that he would help us anytime we wanted to get out.

"They say this place is five thousand feet above sea level," Joe observed, "and the nearest city is Klamath Falls across the border in Oregon. The army sure went to town finding places to put us."

The hypochondriacs immediately became conscious of a laborious thudding in their breasts and an increased difficulty in breathing.

With the sun, people began to appear between the barracks and pretty soon trucks were rumbling through the gates and backing up to the train.

The truck ride was short. The first things they noticed were the green-painted barracks and the flowers growing alongside some of the apartments.

"Not bad," Joe said, brightening considerably. "This is lots better than Poston. They look like the barracks they have in Jerome."

Teru smiled, "Still want to go back?" The smile grew stiff on her lips when the rows of green-painted barracks ended and were replaced by tar-papered ones.

"I thought so," Joe said bitterly, "those others looked too good for us."

"Those must be warehouses," Tad said. "It doesn't look like anybody is living in them."

"They must be," Teru agreed, accustomed to the homemade porches, the sun shelters, and the gardens of Poston. These also had single roofs like the warehouses and mess halls of Poston.

The truck pulled up in front of a large group of buildings while they were still pathetically twisting their necks trying to make up their minds whether the tar-papered barracks were their future living quarters or warehouses.

"What's this?" Mas asked the driver.

"The new high school," the driver answered.

"Looks big enough to have a basketball gym," Tad said hopefully.

"There is one. In that big building."

"Pretty snazzy," Joe said, and looked at Tad. Both had sweltered on the dirt courts of Poston playing for the champion block 213 basketball team.

It took the whole morning to work their way slowly through identification pictures, fingerprinting, temporary passes to enter the center, assignment to barracks, issuing of blankets.

Jiro was nowhere to be seen though Tad thought he had seen him in the crowd lining the road by the high school. No one was allowed inside the registration area.

It was almost noon when they finally climbed up on the truck that took them to their assigned quarters. There was no mistaking their future homes this time. The long squat barracks stretched monotonously in all directions. People were moving between the barracks, and curtains could be seen in many of the windows.

Teru watched the uniformly drab barracks roll by with a sinking heart. She was tired and sleepy and she was all the more depressed. There were no trees, no flowers, nothing green at all. The few porches that could be seen here and there were mostly built of misfit slates and shabbily detracted from the already ugly barracks. The doors were all closed and few people were outside. The wind blew and it was cold on the truck.

There was a deserted look about everything and yet she knew that there must have been four or five thousand new arrivals besides the original six thousand who hadn't left. What had the people been doing in the year they had occupied the center?

It was obvious that 3515-c was occupied. Suitcases were stacked outside the door and they could hear people talking inside. Teru thought in panic, was housing so short that they would have to share their apartment with another family? She remembered how so many people had thought in assembly center that mistakes had been made when their assigned quarters turned out to be already occupied by small families who weren't entitled to full apartments.

"You're not supposed to be here," the driver told the stocky middle-aged man who came the door.

"The apartment they gave us was too dirty and half the wall boards were taken away so we moved here," the man said.

"You'll have to go back to the apartment they assigned you to," the driver said. "These people are moving in here."

The man looked resentfully at them. He mumbled something which Teru failed to catch.

"It's noon already so I guess we'll have to go back," the driver said and climbed into the truck.

They went back the way they had come and ate at a mess hall near the high school.

"Where do we go now?" Teru asked when they were on the truck once more. She wanted desperately to get settled anywhere so she could lie down and relax even for a minute.

"Same place," the driver said.

"We don't want to force those people to move," Teru protested.

"We can go somewhere else."

"We can't allow that," the driver said, "if we allow them to get away with things like that, we'd never get anywhere."

Teru was too depressed to say any more but she dreaded having to face the original occupants again. However, the apartment was empty when they went back.

Teru couldn't see how any apartment could have been dirtier and less desirable than the one they stepped into.

Trash was scattered over the soiled flooring and the soot was black on the ceiling while the sheet rock walls were profusely inscribed and illustrated with obscenity apparently scribbled on by the persons who had occupied the apartment before segregation.

Damn Japs, lettered hugely on one wall, was the most innocuous phrases depicted. One of the occupants seemed to have had a flair for caricature.

A part of another wall was kicked through and the occupants of the next apartment had placed a trunk against the wall to cover the hole.

Teru wanted to scrub the walls first but getting cots and mattresses from the block manager's office was more important. One could never tell. There might be a shortage.

No mops or brooms were available and they debated whether they should try borrowing them from their neighbors.

"They don't even show their faces so I wonder," Mr. Noguchi said.

"Hello," someone said cheerfully from the door.

"Hello," Teru turned, startled by the familiar voice. It was Sanae Goto, carrying mop, broom and bucket.

"I saw you come in," Sanae explained, "and I knew you'd need these. We're in that apartment over there." She pointed to a barrack in the same block directly across from 15-c.

"I got those from a friend of my husband's who lived in this block. He knows a fellow in the housing department."

She looked around. "Dirty, isn't it. I suppose ours was the same only our friends cleaned it up for us before we came."

She insisted on staying to help mop and sweep, and Teru was grateful because she was dead tired from the strain of standing in line all morning and the two restless nights on the train.

She was glad, too, because Sanae cheered her somehow, even though she knew Sanae was putting on a front after she said, "When you write to Poston don't tell them how bad it is. They'll get to laugh at us if they hear it's so terrible up here."

Jiro came in time to help Tad with the cots. He had run into Mas near the high school and Mas had told them where Teru had gone.

"Where did the Maedas go?" Sanae asked.

"Block six," Jiro said, "that's why I met him. It's next to the high school."

"Where are you?" Teru asked fearfully. It was a big camp and the high school had seemed such a long distance away.

"Block 24," Jiro said, "it's only two blocks away from this one. Same quad, I think. Only they call them wards up here and there are nine blocks to the ward instead of four to the quad like in Poston."

"I asked them to reserve an apartment for you and the Maedas in our block when I registered and they said they'd leave a memo but I guess it didn't do any good."

"You have to know somebody in Housing," Sanae said. "Our friend might have arranged it if we'd known earlier. I don't like this place," Sanae protested. "There's something cold and unfriendly about everything. Outside of our friends, nobody showed his face when we came. Remember in Poston how we pitched in and helped the late comers?"

"The people are pretty stand-offish," Jiro agreed. "We thought nobody lived in our barrack until we saw people come out for lunch. We ate at the same table in the mess hall and they didn't even say hello. We were upset and didn't say anything either."

"Maybe it's because everybody is new here and is waiting for the other person to make the first move," Teru said.

"Could be, but that doesn't account for it all. Half the people in our block are stayovers. I should think they would be more friendly. I hear this center has always been that way. There was quite a lot of friction to start with between the California Japanese and the Northwest Japanese."

"I think it's because they're city people here," Sanae ventured, "Poston 2 was mostly *'inaka'* [rural] people. Besides, the block managers here aren't elected by block people like Poston so they're good for nothing. They just do what the administration tells them to do and that's all. That's why they don't even welcome us. They call them messenger boys here."

That night, Teru tried to write to Sally.

"Desolate is the only word I can use to describe this place," she began. She was sprawled on her cot and using a magazine to write on. Mr. Noguchi thought he could hammer together a table and chairs from the crating material when the freight came but that wouldn't be for another three weeks or three months. Meanwhile, they would have to get along with what they'd packed into their hand luggage.

They were back to living out of suitcases once more. Tule Lake Segregation Center was starting out in the same way as Salinas Assembly Center and Poston Relocation Center.

Teru hated it all with a despairing hate. She hated the war above all for its shackling and hounding of the good in man.

"I talked in the shower with girls from Topaz and Jerome and they say they wanted to cry and did when they saw this camp. Remember how we thought Jerome and Rowher with their heat and humidity were the only centers which might just possibly be as bad as Poston? Well, the only people who think Tule Lake is any good apparently are the stayovers who came here from Walerga Assembly Center which seems to have been much more primitive than Salinas Assembly Center. Can you imagine?

"Our block is at the edge of camp, like 213 was in Poston. The one different thing which we noticed when the wind changes is that the sewage-disposal plant is just across the double row of fences which completely surrounds the camp. I saw a jacket today with Sewer Heights lettered on the back. I think that's what they call this district.

"This center is going to be different from Poston. For one thing, there seem to be so many young bachelors, mostly *Kibei*. They don't look or act like the *Kibei* we're accustomed to. I can't explain how different but they leave me with an uneasy feeling.

"Jiro tells me there's some trouble brewing in the center already. Not about *Kibei* though. There's lots of dissatisfaction with conditions here. The newcomers think the Tule Lake people have been victimized by a corrupt administration. They feel that they have been denied too many things that other centers have, like water, brooms, mops, linoleum floors, screens.

"There is also a great deal of comparison with the internment center at Santa Fe. Since this is a segregation center, people feel that they should be treated like internees instead of evacuees. The food is said to be so much better at Santa Fe.

"Isn't it funny that evacuees who are under the protection of the United States government should receive poorer fare than internees under the protection of the Japanese government? I don't understand.

"He told me my first rumor today. It seems to be on the tongue of every newcomer. It comes from the people evacuated from Hawaii. The way they tell it, flyers strafed and killed all the Japanese-Hawaiian fisherman unfortunate enough to have been at sea during and after the attack on Pearl Harbor. They say many of the Japanese-Hawaiians here are the sons and brothers of the fishermen who were killed. I suppose that's the kind of thing we'll be exposed to up here from now on."

Teru stopped to reread what she'd written. It was too depressing so she tore it up and put her pen away. She went outside intending to walk a bit and get some fresh air.

She reached the road and saw the lighted sentry towers and rows of lights that illuminated the tall outer barbed wire fence. Beyond the barbed wire she could see the lights of farmhouses twinkling in the distance.

A faint glow on the horizon marked the city of Tule Lake. Over there and beyond was the life she'd known. Inside the fence waited the unknown.

The barbed wire separating her from the lights made wishful thinking impossible. The reality lay cold within her breast. Goodbye, America, she thought, don't do it again. Follow your heart and no few people can dictate a facade of greed, intolerance, or bigotry. I love you still even though you failed me when you said I could be different because of my ancestry. I only wish there might have been the slightest justification for mass evacuation. If, fearing invasion, you could have taken just our men, leaving our women and children to carry on, we could have kept the lights still burning.

You didn't. You snuffed out fires which would have burned with steady flames as long as you let us have faith in your justice. You could have written bright pages untouched by bitterness and cynicism. You need never have left history that will look better glossed over in your records.

It is done now and I am here. I do not want to leave the life I used to know and yet I must. If pride and honor are to be served, these people with whom my lot is cast have no choice but to presevere in their stand.

These are good people. They came, fearing the worst kind of treatment. They delivered themselves into "enemy" hands when they need not have. That integrity is my hope in the future.

They are enemies through the fortunes of war. Don't make them monsters in the interests of war.... The peace-loving have been led to the slaughter again...why don't we let the seekers of power and glory fight their own battles and know themselves the utter futility of dying and killing?

The hope of this century is a shining example that all people can live together in harmony and tolerance -- a nation that can show it need not economically enslave others in order to live in comfort and happiness.....

Teru began to feel the sharp bite in the night air. She turned around and went back into their apartment. Tad was getting undressed. Ayame was already in her cot, staring at the faint outlines which remained on the wall despite the soap and water scrubbing. Mr. Noguchi sat smoking on his cot, gazing contemplatively about the room, wondering where he could build the closet when the freight came and if there would be enough wood left after the tables and chairs were made.

Suddenly there seemed to be too much room in the twenty by twenty five feet of space allotted them. The space next to Teru's cot loomed bare and empty.

In the quietness of the room, she seemed to hear from far away, the faint echo of high pealing laughter -- the whispering, trusting words of a confidence no one but she would ever be told.

CHAPTER 22

Dear Sally,

The strike is probably old news to you, now, but to us the stringent curfew keeps us painfully aware of it at all times. We have to be in our apartments from seven p.m. to six a.m. and can only go to the latrine. We're not even allowed to visit our next-door neighbors. During the day, we can't be seen together with more than three other people.

Jiro was here the other night until nine o'clock and was caught by an army patrol while going back to Block twenty-four. One of the soldiers threatened to shoot him but when Jiro managed a rather strained smile, the other soldier smiled back, so Jiro refused to scare as much as the mean soldier probably hoped.

Then when they put him in the patrol car, the soldier said to the driver's escort, "This guy is a tough egg. If he makes a false move, shoot to kill."

Quite melodramatic, no?

Jiro talked his way out of having to stay in the stockade, but an old man they picked up the same night is still there.

The "stockade" is a kind of jail that started out as a place of confinement for the so-called strike leaders. Anyone who speaks up for maintaining the strike is liable to be confined at any time.

It's quite confusing. No one knows on what grounds these men are held. They don't have trials or anything. Maybe they can do that to aliens but I didn't think they could do it to citizens. Not that I think anyone is justified in hiding behind his citizenship in here.

I'm looking at it from the standpoint of our being people. Those imprisoned have wives and children they should be looking after. And yet, they are held in confinement without having done any wrong or even being suspected of having done any wrong. Who says it can't happen here?

We're not even allowed the right to live. When a man was shot and killed by the sentry they had a trial all right but the sentry got off free. That kind of trial is worse than having none at all.

Mr. Maeda has been in the stockade over two months now because he was so outspoken during a recent block meeting about whether volunteers should help the army distribute certain foods to the mess halls. Fresh vegetables and *shoyu* to be exact.

I don't know why on the fresh vegetables but they say the army won't deliver the *shoyu* because it "stinks." Right now some mess halls get fresh vegetables and *shoyu* but some mess halls don't, so there's a lot of name calling and mutual distrust in the center. Dad is disgusted.

We thought there would be a greater cooperative spirit here at Tule Lake because of mutual pro-Japanese leanings, but it hasn't been noticeably different from a relocation center in that regard. People still arrive at different interpretations and squabble quite as frequently.

There are already those who have turned from their earlier passive acceptance of the stockade leadership and are now engaged in gaining that leadership for themselves. It is said that much of the desire to lead arises from a feeling that the Japanese government will later take cognizance of such activity.

About three hundred people are in the stockade now. It's across the fence in the administrative area but you can make out faces: so every day, cold or windy, women and children line the fence and wave to their husbands and fathers. That is, they did until a few days ago when they put up wall boards so you can't see anymore. Man, isn't it something?

This strike of ours really started as a lockout, because the morning after the trouble at the warehouse where several people were said to have been machine gunned while attempting to prevent food from being taken outside to the volunteer strike breakers from relocation centers, we tried to go to work but were stopped by soldiers firing tear gas bombs at us.

Somehow, the scene made me think back to the Salinas strike when we saw the police shooting extra tear gas bombs at the strikers so the news photographers could take more pictures. I guess it's fun to fire those things. I don't know when the lockout ended and the strike started. The first thing I knew, the newspapers were calling it a strike.

Yesterday, we were subjected to another humiliating experience. We were confined to our apartments all day and soldiers came and searched our homes. Luckily, our block was one of the last ones to be searched, so we were better prepared than the others.

They say some of the soldiers were pretty bad. They took everything they could. Sometimes they took things openly, saying things like, "This is too good for Japs to have."

For one thing, we all wore our newest shoes because we heard the soldiers were confiscating all new shoes. Mr. Inada, our neighbor, says they found and kept his expensive leather boots which he hid in the garbage can.

The two soldiers who searched our apartment were about average. They searched quite thoroughly and pawed through all the suitcases and they weren't rude, but they weren't nice though. We watched them closely every minute as we were warned to do.

They say some of them just dropped in and had a cup of tea instead of searching. Being veterans of that FBI search, we weren't bothered too much because this time they didn't take dad away.

Otherwise we felt pretty much the same. Pretty HELPLESS. I hear that the only real contraband they seized was home brewed sake which seems to be plentiful in here. Everyone pokes fun at Mr. Goto who was watching over his fermenting sake like a favorite grandchild in anticipation of a party on New Years.

We don't know the real purpose of the search but some think it was to apprehend Mr. Tamaki who was hiding out with records which showed discrepancies in the mess accounts. He doesn't trust the Administration and wants to hand his report directly to the Spanish consul. I hear he gave himself up voluntarily. No one knows anything for sure.

Isn't it strange how so much trouble seems to arise from mess problems? They say the man in charge here was trying to feed the people as cheaply as possible to save the government money and thus enhance his record. He had brought the cost of one meal down to less than ten cents. We didn't get much to eat is all I can say.

I'm certainly glad you're in Detroit where you don't come in contact with these things anymore.

I'm worried though when you say that George is to take his induction physical next month. What are you going to do when he's accepted as he most likely will be?

You're always welcome here, but they won't let anyone even visit here.

Not even husbands and parents separated at the time of segregation. However, George will most likely want you to go to his parents in Gila. I have a feeling Mr. Motoyama will disapprove of your continuing to work and staying in Detroit.

I seem to be crossing bridges before we get to them. I'm sorry, but continued camp life narrows one's outlook so. You got out just in time. The radio and infrequent reading of the newspapers weren't enough to keep one abreast of the pace. I guess our brains deteriorate when we don't have work and healthy recreation. This minimal subsistence level is getting me down.

The young people are getting very lazy. They seem afraid to use their muscles. The old folks worry how they will react when they are confronted with the necessity of earning a living. Myself, I think they will adjust themselves very readily though I'm a little doubtful about those who entered camps too young to have known what real work is.

I'm not worrying about Tad because he did his share of work at home. Dad is, however, worried and asked me to talk to him. You know how exasperatingly uncommunicative Tad can be. Lately, he's retired into himself even more than usual.

It turned out he's satisfied with Dad's decision to return to Japan but can't help feel confined and helpless because of the lack of anything definite to look forward to. You know how badly he wanted to learn radio. He's taking a correspondence course but it's really hard to study on your own.

It's a very sorry state of affairs for boys his age. Don't worry about us, though. We're getting along as well as can be expected. It's you I'm worried about. I have my fingers crossed and hope that things come out all right.

Love,
Teru

Dear Sally,

The strike was finally settled last week. Soldiers still patrol the camp but we don't have to stay inside our apartment anymore.

The voting procedure though didn't seem quite fair. To me, it was a mockery of the democratic procedure which the word 'vote' seems to connote.

Before the actual voting, the strike leaders were picked up and put into the stockade, and before that, anti-strike propaganda was allowed distribution to the exclusion of all else. Then the army stationed armed guards at each of the block votings and no one was allowed to say anything. I felt funny having to vote like this. The whole atmosphere seemed charged with threat of intimidation and arrest.

Our block, incidentally, voted to continue that strike and the vote was very close. Enough to make one sure of results under other conditions.

Still, it's just as well the strike is ended. A considerable number of people were said to be suffering because of the lack of income. It's pitiful how dependent people are on the sixteen dollars monthly wages and the three dollars and seventy five cents clothing allowance.

Tomorrow, I'm going to Placement about a job. They won't give dad one.

I'm rather dubious about my own chances because of what happened to Sanae Goto. She went to the Placement office and asked for a clerical or typist job when her husband couldn't get work. She told the interviewer she was a little rusty but could still type about fifty words a minute and the interviewer told her, "Not good enough. You have to be able to type at least one hundred words a minute to be considered for a job here."

Can you imagine? I know I can't do it anymore.

Jiro had an argument with the same man the other day, too. The supervisor of the Recreation Department offered him a job so he accepted and went to placement for his assignment slip. The man told him that all jobs had to be applied for and okayed through Placement and that he had no business trying to get a job through other channels. Jiro didn't like his attitude and told him off and left.

You can see what kind of person I have to apply to for a job. He may be mostly bluff because Jiro starts work tomorrow and he didn't go near the Placement Office after that one time.

I was offered a job earlier with the civic organization which corresponds to the block mangers in Poston but I didn't accept because of the bad reputation of the office. One trouble here is that so many people who are scheduled to leave camp hold important positions and thus give their departments bad names with the people.

Dad was quite upset when you sent that money in your last letter. He was visibly moved, but he asked me to tell you never to do that again. Everyone is appreciative but I wouldn't if I were you. Dad was very strong on that.

I'm getting tired trying to learn those Japanese ideographs but I guess I better do some studying right now.

Love,
Teru

Dear Sally,

I'm working as stenographer for Community Analysis. The office has a bad *inu* reputation like Sociological Research had in Poston but I've ceased paying much attention to such name calling.

You can't get any kind of office work without some of it, probably because of the contact with *Hakujin*. The stay-at-homes have too much time on their hands to review with suspicion anyone seen even talking with a *Hakujin*.

I don't have to do too much work until some staff member gets a bright notion to do too much writing. Whereupon I have to get busy and type. It's lots easier than teaching though and I have time to go to language school at night.

I'm catching on to the language a little and it gets a bit easier after you've mastered the fundamentals. Remember how Dad and Mom used always to encourage us to speak English at home. Here, Dad reminded us once to use more Japanese but he hasn't persisted and isn't very strict because he realizes how hard it is for us.

I'd be very discouraged if I didn't stop to think sometimes that if a hundred million people can get along with the language I should be able to do the same.

I must admit I do get discouraged at times. I wish something would happen and quick. It would be terrible if the war should drag on for another ten years like they say.

Dad is so worried he'll be too old by the time he gets back. Jiro is worried too. Like everyone else, he kind of expected repatriation to Japan before too long. Every year in here makes it that much harder.

You get desperate when thinking of a future held too long in abeyance. However, there isn't much of a rush to leave the center. You know this place is now a relocation center as well as a segregation center and people can leave as soon as they get clearance.

I guess they've made up their minds to take whatever fortunes or misfortunes are in store for Japanese whose sympathies lie with their ancestral country.

They're standing by their convictions and to me it's a good sign that the people who came here are really people of high integrity. Of course there are a few who have reversed their stand now that the war is going badly for Japan. Sometimes it's quite a surprise when you hear who has left. They're so very pro-Japanese up to the moment of departure. I should think they would keep their mouths shut. They must tell the Hakujin all sorts of lies to get out.

I don't suppose you out there give the matter such thought anymore. Must be something like before the war started when we paid no attention to things like loyalty and such. Who would have dreamed then, that we'd be like this now.

I'm glad you and George convinced Mr. Motoyama that it would be better for you to stay in Detroit rather than go back to Gila. It's senseless staying in camp when you have a future to build. In a relocation camp, there is no future. In here, there is no future except waiting for exchange to Japan.

You're lucky George is slated for a desk job and is stationed so close he can come home weekends. No matter how dark things look, we always seem to have some little things to be thankful for, don't we?

I find myself glad that we haven't been touched by the blood and horror of war. I'm praying the war's end will come before we are.

Love,
Teru

Dear Sally,

It's not bad once you've made up your mind to it. Here, you see everything interpreted in a different light and you begin to feel that the other side is not so bad after all.

I've ever gotten used to the Kibei. At first, they seemed so uncouth and scary but now that I know some of them better, I believe that much of their seeming boorishness comes from a feeling of long suffered inferiority.

Of course, there are a few who are really unbearable. They're so arrogant and crude. I dislike especially the rabid few who can see no good at all in America. I always want to ask them why they came and stayed long enough to be caught here by the war.

For the most part, however, they are people whose ties with Japan are stronger than those with the United States. Many have their brothers, sisters and parents over there.

Among *Issei,* too, many have a bigger stake in Japan than in America where they lost everything they had during evacuation. People like us who have everything in America and nothing in Japan are in the minority.

Dad was called up for questioning the other day and they asked him why he wanted to return to Japan when in all probability his ancestral home would soon be burned down and his relatives killed off. His answer was that such things weren't the issue -- that he was a Japanese and was conducting himself according to the realities of the situation -- that he hadn't asked for confinement into assembly and relocation centers or at Tule Lake -- that he had been forced into the present situation through no fault of his own except that he had been born Japanese -- and that would continue as such, since there was nothing he could do about being Japanese.

He in turn asked why he was ineligible for U.S. citizenship when white immigrants were eligible and he was told, "That's out of our hands."

There is no shaking him from his determination that we are doing the right thing. The problem is rather with us.

I'm afraid we're a little disappointing to the old folks, though they accept it all with more or less resignation. A few of us have made the adjustment from being American to being Japanese but most of us have not, at least on the surface. We're still not noticeably different from what we were in the relocation center and before. We can't help but talk English most of the time, and our speech of course is the most in evidence.

This whole thing is still one big mess for us. It's very discouraging sometimes. Especially with things getting so desperate now that Japan is standing alone.

We all comfort ourselves with the vision of starting a new life away from these ugly barracks and all that they stand for. Racism, intolerance, stupidity.

There's something refreshing about the idea of starting all over again, even though I can't begin to picture the actuality of that process as it will affect me -- how I'll be dressing -- what I'll be eating -- what I'll be doing.

Can you picture me in a kimono with parasol and sandals going to look at cherry blossoms? The dreary side, I'll skip, because that's something I know nothing about either.

Love,
Teru

Dear Sally,

The war is over. What is going to happen to us now? I'm so thankful that we've all come out alive.

Jiro says, at least I haven't killed anybody in the name of democracy or anything else, and waits gloomily for whatever the government has in store for him.

No one here dreamed that the war would end so soon and in unconditional surrender. Everyone is bewildered and groping for reasons and a way of thinking to face the situation.

A third of the *Issei* population is from Hiroshima and had relatives or homes in the area which was devastated by the atomic bomb. Dad says our uncles lived within the blast area so must be presumed dead.

Everywhere you go you see people clustered around maps of the bombed area of Hiroshima trying to search out the last bit of information that might show their homes or relatives who might have escaped the effects of the bomb.

The talk always turned to the probability of deportation or exchange and forced relocation. With an air of helplessness now. The future they'd hoped for is gone. Many are saying that starting all over again in a beaten and crushed Japan is an impossibility -- that it was hard enough just to make a living in a normal Japan and now they would be forced to bear heavier taxes to pay for war damages and an army of occupation.

Dad was hard hit but he says let's wait and see what the government intends to do with us before hurrying to the relocation office and trying to get outside. He may have no choice again.

Jiro, like the seven thousand others who renounced their citizenship, can't leave camp even if he wants to. There are those who regret their renunciations and are trying get their citizenship back but Jiro doesn't seem too concerned.

He says that his renunciation was a natural outcome which was inevitable, at least for him, after evacuation and segregation. Feeling as he did and confined in a segregation center as he was, he had no choice when the government offered the renunciation procedure.

He felt it was a challenge and he accepted. It was simply one more racially discriminatory step -- this time sanctioned by an act of Congress. He said at the time, "When Congress legislates against you on a racial basis, you haven't got a chance."

Those who want to cancel their renunciations are pleading that they were pressured into renouncing by their associates. They don't have much pride in their ego do they? Too bad their egos thought Japan would never surrender at the time they renounced.

When I asked Jiro what he planned, he said he wouldn't know until he got to Japan, which makes it definite where he's going and which is all anyone going there can say. Even those who had money invested in Japanese stocks, bonds, and banks no longer depend on their being of any value.

Despite all this, the defeat has only hardened the determination of some to return, although the majority seem just resigned to gleaning whatever they can from the ashes of Japan.

Many, however, have changed their minds and have decided to remain in America. They see no future in a denuded Japan without land to develop. So many had envisioned work in places like the East Indies.

A note of optimism is only just beginning to appear which pictures the new Japan as a more livable place with more emphasis on the rights of the common people and less demands from the government and moneyed interests. There is talk that taxes will be less with no and navy and less expenditure on developing regions like Manchuria. There is a growing belief that under the new setup, culture will flourish and the arts will come into their own in a manner surpassing the world. The idea of race is such a hard thing to break down, isn't it?

The women seem a little more worried than the men. Many know how hard life can be in the old country and they will be the ones who will have to make ends meet with whatever their men manage to make in an inflation and shortage ridden Japan.

Today, another note of worry crept into the talk with the announcement that anywhere from five hundred thousand to one million American soldiers will occupy and police Japan for an indefinite period of time.

Mrs. Omura voiced that worry first when she said, "What will we do if, when our husbands are at work, some soldiers force their way into our homes?"

We've all heard from sisters or parents of Nisei veterans of the Italian campaign how the soldiers conducted themselves with the Italian women and I could notice no illusions about the gallantry of conquering men even though they be American. I gathered that the fear was a real one. Which will no doubt be a surprise to you who read every day newspaper stories of chivalrous and courteous behavior.

"Even if we're killed, we won't be able to do anything," was Mrs. Ikeda's very uncheerful comment.

I wonder if life under a force of occupation is going to be a continuation of our life in relocation and segregation centers. If I were sure it would be, I'd start screaming now. I've had enough of this miserable life.

I wonder what the real situation will be. As I've said before, I can't picture it at all. Lately with the more gloomy descriptions by people who are relocating, I have less enthusiasm about my future. I'm even afraid I may not be able to make a go of it. They tell me I won't know how to go about even simple things like shopping for meals or clothes. A fine time to be telling me that. Just because they're the very same people who only a month ago were still telling me how nice it was to live in Japan.

I console myself with the thought that I will be going somewhere where eventually I will be one integral part of a people. I will not be set apart because of my ancestry. I will not be looked down upon. I will not be pitied. I will not be feared. I will not exist through mere tolerance and broadmindedness. It may take a year or more, but at the end of that time, I will be among people I can call my own and who will protect me as their own.

Sally, I'll be praying you'll be looking into the same kind of future someday. This war has broken down a few of the barriers and others will be overcome with time. I wish sometimes that I were staying to help fight that battle with you but it's a comforting thought to know we'll both be working for the same thing though we'll be separated by an ocean.

Beyond this treadmill that saps our will to do good, there must be some common meeting ground where all peoples can mingle with liking and with trust. There must be within our lifetimes, a day when all people will be humble enough to know that whether we are born in a palace or a hovel, from a black, white, brown or yellow womb, we share the common bond of being human, with sensibilities that can be hurt, pride that can be injured, honor that can be admired.

We've got to come to realize that the atom bomb in Hiroshima didn't just wipe out a city, remote and far removed from our own existence. We've got to feel the horror of knowing as we would know it if it happened to loved ones of our own, the grief of a mother looking at her new born babe smashed to a bloody pulp in her arms, the dying gasp of a child with his eyes searching in vain for someone to comfort him.

We can't continue to pass it off as twenty thousand killed and one hundred thousand wounded; if only because someday we will find our own lives and loved ones lost in the anonymity of round numbers killed and wounded.

We who have passed through evacuation have learned a lot. We mustn't forget.

God willing, we'll meet again. Where or when is uncertain but let's pray it's soon.

Love,
Teru

NOTES

1. WCCA: Wartime Civil Control Administration. On March 14, 1942, the Western Defense Command established the WCCA to administer the evacuation and the temporary camps, the assembly centers, of which there were sixteen. Most of them were in or near large urban areas on the West Coast. There was one in Arizona. One, Manzanar, CA, became a relocation camp. Several days after the WCCA was established, the War Relocation Authority (WRA) came into being. This agency was formed to administer the ten relocation camps.

2. On December 11, 1941, the Western Defence Cammand was established. The Command's jurisdiction covered the western portions of Washington, Oregon, and California, and the southern portion of Arizona. Its commander was Lt. General John L. DeWitt. From January 29, 1942, to February 7, Attorney General Francis Biddle announced a number of prohibited areas from which persons of Japanese ancestry could voluntarily leave under the voluntary relocation program. Nine thousand took this course of action. This program was then rescinded on March 29. An 8 p.m. to 6 a.m. curfew was in force for Japanese in Zone 1 of the Western Defense Command.

3. Isseis were inelgibile to become U.S. citizens and only in 1952 was this restriction changed, under the new McCarran Act. Niseis, on the other hand, because they were born in the U.S., automatically were U.S. citizens. The term Kibei is used to refer to American citizens of Japanese descent who had received part or all of their education in Japan prior to the war.

4. This rumor turned out to have had a factual basis. See, for example, R.J.C. Butow et al. , "The FDR Tapes: Secret Recordings Made in the Oval Office of the President in the Autumn of 1940," *American Heritage*, 1982, vol. 33 (No. 2), pp. 9-24; "FDR Ordered Internment of Hawwaii Nikkei [persons of Japanese descent] in 1936," *Pacific Citizen*, February 11, 1983, p. 1; New York Times News Service, "Official says Japanese Internment Possibly not Justified by Cables," *Omaha World-Herald*, May 22, 1983, p. 11 (evening edition).

5. For "vigilantism" against the Japanese on the West Coast prior to evacuation, see Morton Grodzins, *Americans Betrayed: Politics and the Japanese Evacuation,* 1949; Chicago: University of Chicago Press. "Assaults [against persons of Japnese ancestry] took various forms, including beatings, clubbings, shootings, stabbings, and rape or attempted rape" *ibid.*, p. 139). "Identifications [of the assailants] were vague in the largest number of cases, and Filipinos were probably blamed for a larger number of crimes than they committed. Neverthelss, the largest number of cases at one place (five, including two murders) occurred at Stockton, California, where one of the state's largest Filipino colonies was close to a sizeable Japanese community," ibid, fn34, pp. 139-140). On January 1, 1942, unknown persons fired shots at a house in Gilroy, CA, a community not far from Salinas, whose residents were Japanese: Carey McWilliams, *Prejudice: Japanese- Ameicans: Symbol of Racial Intelerance;* Boston: Little, Brown & Co, 1944, p. 113.

6. Shortly after the attack on Pearl Harbor, in some cases that very day, the FBI rounded up members of the Japanese community along the West Coast. The vast majority of them were Isseis and heads of households. More than 4,700 were rounded up and detained for long periods of time, some of them until well after the end of the war. "...[The 4,700] comprised a disproportionate large number of family heads. The significance of the figure 4,700 becomes clear upon noting that there were over 23,000 family heads among the Japanese-Americans in the Western states (Arizona, California, Oregon, and Washington). The capacity to adjust for any family would be damaged by the loss of its responsible head; the effect on the Japanese-American family with ts heritage of patriarhcal responsibility was often shattering. The statistical support for the statement lies in the fact that 45.6 percent of all *issei* (sic) in the four Western States were listed as family heads by the 1940 census, whereas 6.0 percent of *nisei* (sic) were

so listed. It is important to note that the condition was not merely a temporary one. By January 1943 about 1,400 detained persons had been placed in relocation centers with their families. 2,000 had been sent to internment camps [Bismark, ND; Crystal City, TX; Missoula, MT; and Santa Fe, NM] where aliens defined as disloyal are incarcerated, and the remainder are still in detention camps awaiting hearing," Leonard Bloom, "Familial Adjustment of Japanese-Americans in Relocation: First Phase," *American Sociological Review, 1943, vol. 8, p. 558.* In addition to the camps noted, there were also the citizenisolation camps, in Moab, UT and Leupp, AZ.

7. The *M.S. Gripsholm*, a ship of the neutral nation Sweden, was an exchange ship used to transport Japanese officials and those of Japanese ancestry in the U.S. not in an official capascity wishing to repatriate to Japan during WWII, while Americans caught in Japan were returned to the U.S. For a darker side of how the U.S. Government used the *Gripsholm*, see Michi Weglyn, Y*ears of Infamy: The Untold Story of America's Concentration Camps*; New York: William Morrow, 1976, p. 62.

8. On the lobbying efforts of the Western Growers Protective Association, the Grower Shipper Vegetable Associaiton of Central California, the Salinas Chamber of Commerce, and the Salinas Citizens Association to mass intern Japanese Americans, see Grodzins, *op. cit.*, pp. 22-28. On the various West Coast chambers of commerce behind this same kind of effort, see *ibid.*, pp. 34-36. In 1954, Jacobus ten Broek, Edward N. Barnhart, and Floyd W. Matson's *Prejudice, War, and the Constitution* was published as part of the series of the University of California's Japanese American Evacuation and Resettlement Study. Among other objectives, the book tried to dispel the notion that agricultural interests in California had been a significant lobbying entity for the mass evacuation. The University of California and the decision makers of the Japanese American Evacuation and Resettlement Study attempted to suppress publicaiton of Grodzins' book, about which, see, Peter Suzuki, "For the Sake of Inter-University Comity: The Attempted Suppression by the Unviversity of California of Morton Grodzins' *Americans Betrayed*," in *Views from Within*, Y. Ichioka, ed. Los Angeles: Asian American Studies Center, UCLA, pp. 95-112.

9. The concept of the core class was part of the progressive-education philosophy practiced kn the camp schools. On this philosophy at work in the camp schools, see Thomas James' outstanding study *Exile Within:*

The Schooling of Japanese Americans 1942-1945; Cambridge, MA: Harvard University Press, 1987. "There was constant criticism of the school program by the parents [of Poston] who watched, disturbed by the downgrading of education brought on by the whole stupid evacuation program," Paul Bailey, *City in the Sun: The Japanese Concentration Camp at Poston, Arizona,* 1971; Los Angeles: Westernlore Press, p. 95.

10. On the beating of "Ikeda" and his real name, see Bill Hosokawa, *Nisei: The Quiet Americans, The Story of a People, 1969*; New York: William Morrow, p. 351. Also, on the beatings of "Ito" and "Sasaki," and the "manhandling" of "the parents of Masato Shibuya," see Bailey, *op cit.*, pp. 119-121.

11. On the strike, see, Bailey, *op. cit.,* pp. 114-140, *et passim*, among other sources.

12. On the registration (loyalty-oath) and the drive for volunteers to form an all-Nisei regimental combat team among Postonites, see Bailey, *op. cit.*, pp. 141-148, 150-165 *et passim.*

13. "Despair and incarceration had bred more than its logical share of drunkenness, abetted by the whiskey bootlegged into camp by the liquor entrepeneurs at Parker and Yuma. Gambling, always endemic (sic) with Japanese, had become a way of life to many an internee. "But worst was the discernible breakdown in morals of the most moralistic people on earth. Close confinement of the thousands of young people had brought its inevitable results. Marriages were not quite catching up with the births. And, among one's people, it was neither mete nor proper to take public notice of the unwed mothers and their babies, of which the hospital was an important ministry." Bailey, *op. cit.*, p. 172.

14. See, Alexander H. Leighton, *The Governing of Men: General Principles and Reocmmendations Based on Experience at a Japanese Relocation Camp,* 1945; Princeton: Princeton University Press (paperback) pp. 142-143; and Bailey, *op. cit.*, p. 137, on the short-lived camouflage-net factory.

15. General DeWitt made the statement that, "A Jap's a Jap," on April 13, 1943, while testifying in San Francisco before the House Naval Affairs

Subcommittee. He continued, "They are a dangerous element, whether loyal or not or not. There is no way to determine their loyalty.... It makes no difference whether he is an American, theoretically he is stall a Japansese and you can't change him.... You can't change him by giving him a piece of paper." Quoted in McWilliams, *op. cit.*, p. 115.

16. "Cycle of assimilation" refers to the famous sociologist Robert E. Park's theory of race relations. "He developed the thesis that all interethnic relations go thorugh an invariable and irreversible four-stage succession of contact, competition, accommodation, and assimilation," William Petersen, *Japanese Americans: Oppression and Success, 1971*; New York: Random House (paperback), p. 219. Park first posited this thesis -- often termed the cycle of assimilation -- in "Our Racial Frontier on the Pacific," *Survey Graphic*, 1926, vol. 9 (May), pp. 192-196; see, also, his "Race Prejudice and Japanse-American Relations" (a retitle of his "Introduction" to: The Japanese Invasion, ed. by Jesse F. Steiner, 1917; Chicago: A.C. McClung, pp. vii-xvii); and "The Race Relations Cycle in Hawaii," (a retitle of his "Introduction" to: *Interracial Marriage in Hawaii*, ed. by Romanzo Adams. New York: The Macmillan Co., 1937, pp. vii-xiv).

17. "In terms of illness, the greatest attention by far is given [by Japanese] to the abdomen, including the stomach and intestines. The importance given to this part of the body, called hara or icho in Japanese, has often been pointed out by those studying Japanese culture." Emiko Ohnuki-Tierney, *Illness and Culture in Contempoary Japan: An Anthropoloigcal View, 1984,*. Cambridge: Cambridge University Press, p. 57. "The Japanese give extra attention to the stomach and use various means to protect it. [Remainder of paragraph omitted.] Scholars of Japanese culture often point out the symbolic significance of *hara*, or abodomen, in the past. The *hara* used to be considered the seat of the soul; it was the *hara* that the samurai cut open with his sword to commit suicide in defense of his honor.... In contemporary Japan, the term *hara* may be used to mean either the entire area between the thorax and the pelvis...or the lower abdomen, excluding the stomach." Some contempoary expressions which include the term *hara*:

    "Personality or other characteristics:
    hara guroi: the abd men being black (not trustworthy, crafty)
    hara no ookii: the abdomen being big (generous)

hara gitanai: the abdomen being dirty (base, evil)
hara gei: stomach performance (an extraordinary ability)
Thoughts and emotions:
Hara ga tatsu: the abdomen stands up (get mad) hara o iyasu: to heal the abdomen (to wreak one's anger on someone)
hara no mushi ga osamaranu: the worm in the abdomen is not satisfied (I am not yet satisfied; I am still angry)
hara o watte hanasu: to cut open the abdomen and talk (to talk frankly without holding anything back)
hara o shimeru: to tighten the abdomen (to be prepared, determined)
hara ni ichimotsu ga aru: there is a thing in the abdomen (to have an ulterior motive)
hara o sueru: to set one's abdomen in position (to be prepared for doing something)
hara o yomu: to read the abdomen (to read someone's thoughts)
hara o miseru: to show hone's abdomen (to be frank with; to show one's cards)." *Op. cit.,* pp. 58-59.

18. "Dysentry [in Poston]... was epidemic. Measles, influenza, and the mysterious lung congestion of the desert [i.e., valley fever], already endemic in the Army's desert camps, had set their claws upon the internees. Tuberculosis was on the rise. The crude, inadequate hospital was stuffed to overflowing." Bailey, *op. cit.,* p. 93.

19. For an important analysis of conditions in Tule Lake and the circumstances which led to the strike and the strike itself, see Weglyn, op. cit., pp.156-173 *et passim;* while the stockade is covered in her book on pp. 202-215.

20. Each camp had a Community Analysis Section, in most cases headed by an anthropologist or sociologist. The kinds of activities many of them undertook were of a questionable nature, for which, see, Peter Suzuki, "A Retrospective Analysis of a Wartime 'National Character' Study," *Dialectical Anthropology,* 1980, vol. 5, pp. 33-46; "Anthropologists in the Wartime Camps for Japanese Americans: A Documentary Study," Ibid., 1981, vol. 6: 23-60; "When Black was White: Misapplied Anthropology in Wartime America," *Man and Life,* 1986, vol. 12, pp. 1-13. Nakamu-

ra's mention of Sociological Research is in reference to the Bureau of Sociological Research, a multi-disciplinary (but primarily anthropologically oriented) research project in Poston, directed by the psychiatrist/anthropologist Alexander H. Leighton (see o*p. cit.*) For Bailey's interesting observations on the social scientists of the Bureau, see *op. cit.,passim*; see, also, Suzuki, 1981, *op. cit.*, and 1986, cited above. Nakamura, an otherwise astute observer, fails to mention another major research project which was undertaken in both Poston and Tule Lake at the same time. This is understandable in light of the following fact: the University of California's Japanese Evacuation and Resettlement Study was a *covert project* (see, Suzuki, "The University of California Japanese Evacuation and Resettlement Study: A Prolegomenon," *Dialectical Anthropology* 1986, vol. 10, pp. 189-213; on the research project as a clandestine operation, see, Suzuki, 1989, p. 111. For reports on the dire effects of this research project on a camp inmate (Jerome Relocation Camp, AR, and Tule Lake, CA), see, Violet Kazue de Cristoforo's, *A Victim of the Japanese Evacuation and Resettlement Study* (JERS), 1987, Salinas, CA.; and "J'Accuse," *Rikka: Cross-Cultural Journal*, 1992, vol. 13 (No. 1), pp. 16-37, 70- 71.